PENGUIN BOOKS

TAIPING TALES OF TERROR

Julya Oui is an author, a screenwriter, and a playwright. She has published four short horror story collections, written numerous feature films and TV movie scripts, and a few stage plays. Her second book *Here be Nightmares* was longlisted in the Frank O'Connor International Short Story Award 2015 and won the third prize for Popular-The Star Readers' Choice 2016.

Taiping Tales of Terror

JULYA OUI

PENGUIN BOOKS

An imprint of Penguin Random House

PENGUIN BOOKS

USA | Canada | UK | Ireland | Australia
New Zealand | India | South Africa | China | Southeast Asia

Penguin Books is part of the Penguin Random House group of companies
whose addresses can be found at global.penguinrandomhouse.com

Published by Penguin Random House SEA Pte Ltd
9, Changi South Street 3, Level 08-01,
Singapore 486361

First published in Penguin Books by Penguin Random House SEA 2020
Copyright © Julya Oui 2020

All rights reserved

10 9 8 7 6 5 4 3 2 1

This is a work of fiction. Names, characters, places and incidents are either the
product of the author's imagination or are used fictitiously and any resemblance
to any actual person, living or dead, events or locales is entirely coincidental.

ISBN 9789814882170

Typeset in Adobe Garamond Pro by Manipal Technologies Limited, Manipal
Printed at Markono Print Media Pte Ltd, Singapore

This book is sold subject to the condition that it shall not, by way of trade
or otherwise, be lent, resold, hired out, or otherwise circulated without the
publisher's prior consent in any form of binding or cover other than that in
which it is published and without a similar condition including this condition
being imposed on the subsequent purchaser.

www.penguin.sg

For the greatest storytellers I know:
My dad, Brother Matthew Bay and my relatives
who used to live in Assam Kumbang

Nothing in life is to be feared, it is only to be understood.
Now is the time to understand more, so that we may fear less.

—Marie Curie

Contents

Introduction

I grew up in a time when Taiping was steeped in ghost stories, terrifying myths and legends, back in the '60s and the '70s. Whether I liked it or not they shaped my psyche during my formative years. The street lights were dim back then. Black magic and spells were considered real. The demons and the devil were out to get you, and the sheer numbers of vengeful spirits loitering around were astounding.

We trusted everything we read in books and newspapers. We believed everything we watched in the cinemas and on TV. Who would dare deny the existence of P. Ramlee's *Sumpah Orang Minyak*, or William Peter Blatty's *The Exorcist*, or Tea Lim Kuon's *Puos Keng Kang* aka *The Snake Man*? They were the staple diet of our conversation pieces everywhere we went especially when there was no other forms of entertainment. It was the pre-internet, pre-computer, pre-digital days when all we had were board games, sports, school activities, bicycles, and the wonderful art of storytelling. Everyone in Taiping was a storyteller as far as I can remember. We were blessed with the gift so greatly that we could make a fashion statement with the yarns we spun.

The stories you are about to read, frightened me as a kid and were very briefly recounted to me without any beginning or ending. They were more like anecdotes, narratives, or reiterations that had changed one too many hands before they found me. With so little to go on, I took the liberty to extend and exaggerate them while twisting the story within a story into full-fledged tales.

Now that I am older, Taiping, with its naturalized Lake Gardens and exquisite backdrop of forests in the surrounding hills, is nothing short of magnificent to me. Even if you were to live your whole life in this town, its unpredictable weather, with its incessant rains and the scorching heat of the sun, can still make you restless, and its consummate beauty can still mesmerize you every single day. If you were to let your imagination run wild, you may glimpse the dark underbelly of the town—just as any darkness we encounter in life, it can be exquisitely romantic or utterly terrifying; that's for us to decide.

To this day I still love storytelling, be it in the form of a book, a movie, or in good company. And what better place to tell them than in a town as illustrious and timeless as this.

This book is an homage to my favourite authors, my hometown and anyone who has a strong affinity to this quaint little paradise.

Prologue

It was always dark in Burmese Pool.

The only way to get there was through a dirt road with uneven mounds, rocks, and potholes; accessible only on foot, or by bicycle or motorcycle. One could also drive a car up to a certain point although parking was at one's own risk.

Since there was no proper path for a safe and comfortable journey, punctured tyres, cuts and bruises were commonplace. Anyone attempting to ride the irregular surface would have to be extremely good at manoeuvring or would have to pay a painful price.

The route in was long, quiet and deserted except for the wildlife teeming in the trees and shrubs on either side. On rainy days, Burmese Pool's infamous flash floods made the road extremely dangerous.

It was darker still when the cold seeped under the skin and penetrated the bone despite several layers of clothing, cardigans and jackets, and blankets. It was hard to tell if the darkness was simply elongated shadows, distorted silhouettes, or supernatural beings borne out of superstitions.

Other than the moon and stars, there were no other light sources except for the flashlights, hurricane lamps and the bonfires.

The twelve figures who sat around the camp-fire were calm and unperturbed by the sound of water gushing over the boulders and tumbling into the pristine pools. Not even the hooting of owls or the chirruping of insects stirred them from a distrust that came with the darkness. They were lost to the enticement of the shape-shifting fire, each pondering on something that took them far away from the present moment.

Minutes passed without so much as a peep from anyone as they were lulled into the beguiling quietness. Billycans and cutlery lay scattered around, stained with baked beans and other unidentifiable morsels of food. Each of the campers held metal mugs of thick black coffee, some half empty and others, half full.

Ser Ling retrieved the stick from the fire and took a bite into the charred dough twist. He felt the hot burning sensation on his tongue and sucking in air to soothe his lips, broke the silence.

'Storytelling time,' he said chomping on the homemade bread as he spoke.

The thirteen-year-olds snapped out of their reveries and drew closer in anticipation of a good ghost story to end the night.

'Yeah.'

'Who wants to go first?'

'Nice.'

'I want to tell you about the *jamban* incident!'

'Do you all know the truth about that oily thing?'

'Wait, wait, I have a better one about the nightbird that calls your name!'

Ser Ling lifted his eyes from the dazzling fire and glanced at the boys who were trying to outdo each other for the limelight. 'Why don't we go clockwise?' he asked. 'That way, everyone gets a chance.'

'How about anti-clockwise?' The boys laughed heartily, the full meal in their bellies buoying up their spirits.

'Ser Ling can start,' suggested one lad.

Although Ser Ling knew them all by their faces, their names had a tendency to slip his mind. This excursion was almost called off due to inclement weather, but they had made it anyway, through gale force winds and thunderstorms. The flickering light made uncanny masks on their curious young faces and their eagerness seemed almost ghoulish in the dead of night.

Ser Ling took a sip of the freshly-brewed coffee and wondered which story he should tell the juniors. Being three years their senior, he had to be the responsible adult and remember where to draw the line. Although it was already 1976 and superstitions and fear of the unknown were a thing of the past, he didn't want to scare them silly. He wanted to entertain them with a good ghost story that was naturally enhanced by the sound, sight and touch of their current surroundings.

Ser Ling thought about the tale recounted by one of the voluntary teachers from India. She was the wife of a renowned heart specialist who was working at the Taiping hospital at the time. She was one of the many who stayed behind because she fell in love with this idyllic town.

'Mrs Ramanathan was a matronly woman who spent most of her time tutoring the weaker students in schools. She told us that she would have loved to stay to the end of her days in Taiping if she could. She kept reminding us of how beautiful and special this town was and that we should cherish everything wonderful about it—the Lake Gardens, the hills, the tranquillity and the incredible biodiversity of the fauna and flora.

'She said that if we couldn't appreciate the magnificence of our own backyard, we would never really appreciate anything wherever we went. Although I didn't know her personally, I did hear a little bit about her and the haunting of the headless trishaw man.'

1

The Haunting of the Headless Trishaw Man

'Has anyone heard of the headless trishaw man?' Ser Ling asked, as he introduced his story in a low rumbling voice.

'Yeah, yeah. I have heard about it.'

'Me too.'

'Scared the shit out of me.'

'They say he was killed in—'

'Are you telling the story or am I?' Ser Ling cut in.

'Okay . . . okay,' everyone agreed in unison and piped down to allow Ser Ling to continue.

'They said he was killed in Burmese Pool,' Ser Ling whispered and the tree tops rustled eerily.

'For several years, every single day, just before dawn while it was still dark, he cycled down here to wash his trishaw. The town was always considered safe and no one expected anything but the mildest of criminal activities in this area. Until one day, someone discovered the trishaw man's corpse by the bridge. The head was missing.'

'I think it was *under* the bridge.'

'How could he go under the bridge? He was an old man. He couldn't have wheeled the trishaw down the steep bank on his own.'

'You never know—'

'Beside, under, above, who cares! Let's continue with the story.'

'Why was he murdered?'

'Black magic. Someone needed a decapitated head for a spell that they were casting. The unfortunate old man was at the wrong place at the wrong time.'

'But some people say it was revenge.'

'Nonsense.'

'That's not what I heard.'

'Guys, do you want to hear the story or not?' Ser Ling shushed them to get back their attention.

'Yes, please.'

'Do go on.'

'From that day onwards the old trishaw man has often been spotted walking around Burmese Pool, looking for his head. For a long time, no one dared to come here, especially in the early hours of the morning.'

'How can he look for his head when he has no head?'

'That's true. How can he see? Wouldn't he be blind?'

'There was a rumour that the old trishaw-puller cycled into town to find his head,' Ser Ling ignored the boys and threw them another scenario to spice up the tale.

'Whaaat!'

'Yeah, right,' scoffed another lad.

'Right. It happened like this . . .'

* * *

The thunderstorm swept into Taiping town with an unbiased and impartial savagery when everyone was unconscious, either fast asleep or in an inebriated stupor. It bludgeoned the earth with a torrential downpour that tore into both man-made and natural edifices, dislodging chunks of soil that precariously clung to slopes and eroding the river banks. Some folks woke up in alarm and rushed about frenziedly to keep the rain from deluging their homes, shuttering windows and bolting doors securely. Others slept peacefully through the storm in their air-conditioned, sound-proofed bedrooms wholly oblivious to the cacophony of nature at her destructive best.

Burmese Pool swelled up to thrice its size and transformed into a river, gathering miscellaneous debris in its wake: dead leaves, discarded plastic bags, Styrofoam containers, bottles and cans. A bicycle wheel protruded out of the swirling water along with the other slimy objects and was spinning round in the eddying current.

* * *

'Taiping's weather has become extremely unpredictable,' Mrs Ramanathan cocked her head sideways as she nibbled at her fingertips. 'Was it always like this?'

'Sometimes,' Miss Claire Eng fluffed up the pillow and placed it under the elderly woman's head. 'There's nothing to worry about.'

'I don't like to be alone when it rains. Especially when it's a thunderstorm like this,' Mrs Ramanathan reached out to touch Claire's hand to reassure herself that she wasn't alone.

'I'm right here, Mrs Ramanathan,' Claire smiled and gently patted the old woman's wrinkled hand.

'It's just that, when my husband was alive . . . he was always there for me.'

Claire sat at the edge of the bed and tucked Mrs Ramanathan under the covers. 'Try and get some sleep.'

'I can't, my dear,' the old woman quavered, 'the thunder is frightening. I'm sorry I woke you up.'

'It's all right. Would you like something warm to drink? Perhaps it will help you fall sleep. Milk? Cocoa?'

'Cocoa, please. Milk tends to upset my stomach.'

Claire Eng nodded and said, 'I'll be right back.' She got up to leave but Mrs Ramanathan caught at her arm.

'Claire, don't leave me here, please.'

Claire could see how terrified Mrs Ramanathan was—despite the drawn curtains, the lightning lit up the darkest corners of the room in brilliant flashes and the peals of crashing thunder that followed reverberated through the house There were times when she herself hid from them; especially when the entire sky seemed to be electrically charged, as it was tonight. It was almost as if an apocalyptic battle between good and evil was underway.

'But I have to go to the kitchen to fix your hot cocoa.'

'Can I come with you?' the old woman pleaded.

Claire tried to quell her frustration at being disturbed in the middle of the night. Having to care for the seventy-something-year-old woman had not been by choice.

'Are you sure you're up to it?' Claire asked.

'Yes, yes. I don't want to be alone.'

Mrs Ramanathan swung her legs out of bed. Although Claire reached forward quickly to help up the old lady, she was a little too late. Mrs Ramanathan's unwieldy feet hit the cold cement floor with two loud thuds. She was obviously more worried about being left alone than the shooting pain from her ankles.

Claire drew up the folded wheelchair to the bed and levered it open like one would a wilted flower. Long years of usage had peeled off the PVC plastic and rubber casings, but the main frame was still intact.

Mrs Ramanathan reached for Claire like a toddler waiting for her mother to lift her up. Claire knew exactly where to place her arms to deftly hoist the elderly woman with one heave because she had been nursing the septuagenarian since that ill-fated day long ago.

The double tragedy had happened when Selvam had walked out on both her and her mother-in-law after a dramatic argument. Mrs Ramanathan had never approved of their inter-racial marriage and Selvam, the classic cat on the wall, refused to take sides. Since he was trying to be fair to both parties, together they pushed him further away with their shrill accusations and demands.

Claire was packing her bags to leave in a huff, when her mother-in-law slipped and fell in the porch. While she was dithering on whether she should help the old woman, a neighbour rushed in to inform them that Selvam had met with a fatal accident a few blocks down the road. Ironic as it now seemed, the two women were all that was left of their dysfunctional family.

Mrs Ramanathan squirmed to fit her ample backside more comfortably into the wheelchair which was getting tighter by the day. She grabbed Claire's arm when another flash of lightning lit up the sky casting strange shadows through the windows.

'You won't abandon me, will you, Claire?'

Claire could not look at the old woman's face without tearing up, remembering the past when they would go at each other like feral animals. It was painful to dredge up memories of the nasty things they said to one another. This truce had come with a wrenching forfeit.

'I won't, Mrs Ramanathan,' Claire smiled and patted her hand reassuringly, 'I'll always be here.' Having been orphaned at a tender age, she had lost every form of security even before she could learn to speak. No foster home could fill the void of her fear of abandonment. Selvam was the best thing that had happened to her, but fate had cruelly intervened.

Claire gently wheeled the old woman out of the large bedroom, passing through the hall, and into the dining area. She manoeuvred her mother-in-law into the designated seating space where a dining chair had been removed to accommodate the wheelchair.

'Would you like to eat something?'

'No, no, I'm fine.'

'Okay. I'll put the kettle on then.'

Claire disappeared into the kitchenette. This room was wrong from every logical aspect. There was just about enough room to accommodate two people at a time in it; the poor ventilation meant it was invariably stuffy when any cooking was underway; it was adorned with expensive impractical tiles that were difficult to clean. Although Mrs Ramanathan always regretted her design choices for this kitchen, not once did Selvam complain about it. Claire did. It was one of their many disagreements that quickly spiralled out of control.

Mrs Ramanathan had become fidgety and frail ever since she lost her son. Not even in her wildest nightmares had she imagined that she and Claire, whom she had never liked from the word go, would be keeping each other company on stormy nights like these. Their strained relationship that had begun with the formalities of Selvam's wedding was now set in stone and difficult to undo.

'Perhaps some cream crackers?' Mrs Ramanathan said aloud.

'Can you get them yourself? They're on the counter.'

Mrs Ramanathan silently wheeled herself to the counter by the window. Fat raindrops drummed against the glass. A sudden flash of lightning revealed an intruder at the window who seemed to be peering in. The only thing wrong about the trespasser was that he was missing a head. She screamed, vying with the angry skies for attention.

'Mrs Ramanathan, are you okay?' Claire ran back into the dining area.

'S-someone . . . someone is at the window.'

Claire immediately checked to ensure that the window was securely latched and then peered out into the darkness. Other than the tumult of the storm that showed no signs of abating, she could not make out anything. She drew the curtains firmly together. She wheeled her mother-in-law back to the dining table and sat down beside her hoping to calm her nerves.

'There's no one's there, Mrs Ramanathan,' Claire sighed, 'but, would you like me to telephone the police, just in case?'

'There's no need for the police, dear,' Mrs Ramanathan nervously pumped Claire's hands and released them and then repeated the action a few more times. 'It's him. He has come for me.'

'Who? Why?'

'Claire, do you remember the legend about the headless trishaw man?'

'I heard about it when I was a kid, but I don't think I gave it much thought.' Claire sat back in her chair, allowing Mrs Ramanathan to continue kneading her hands.

'There was this man who would ride down to Burmese Pool very early each morning to wash his trishaw,' the old woman began her story very slowly, her voice soft and quavering. 'Back then, Burmese Pool was isolated from the rest of Taiping town and one had to trek deep into the jungle to reach it. Although it may not seem like a dangerous place, the unfortunate trishaw man was brutally murdered at the pool.

'What most people agreed upon after the gruesome incident was the haunting. On nights like this . . .' Mrs Ramanathan paused as the thunder rumbled loudly overhead, shaking the rafters, '. . . he would return.'

'But why?'

'To look for his head. It started in the neighbourhood when, at the crack of dawn, they heard the squeaking wheel of the trishaw pass by. The closest housing area to the Burmese Pool back then was the army's mess. And then, people in the Aun Say Garden heard it as well. Soon, people living as far as Kamunting claimed to have seen the headless trishaw man.'

* * *

A middle-aged woman peeped out of the window to see what was making that dreadful hair-raising sound at four o'clock in the morning. Her children and husband were fast asleep; she was a light sleeper with occasional insomnia to add to her woes. She had been tossing and turning in bed for hours when the storm broke.

She was contemplating getting up to fix herself a hot drink to help her sleep, but the storm made her bed seem too cosy for her to want to get out of it. Even over the crashing of the thunderstorm she could hear that wretched squeaking noise that set her teeth on edge. If she didn't do something about it, the sound would keep her up until daylight.

She forced herself to relinquish the warmth of the bedcovers to investigate. Since there was already illumination from the porch, the night light and the streetlights illuminated the area sufficiently for her to move around without bumping into anything, so she didn't bother to switch on any more lights.

She walked out of the bedroom and listened intently to the sound, following it from the side of the house to the front gate. It was odd. The sound seemed to be coming from within their compound. The eight-foot fence was a formidable and insurmountable barrier to discourage intruders. She stared out through the window to see if she could locate the origin of the annoying squeak.

There were too many shadows to give her a good view until lightning struck up like a match. The headless man appeared to be cycling his trishaw around the garden. His bloody neck made a loud drip-dripping sound that was accompanied by the infernal squeaking of the trishaw's rusty wheel.

When the headless man noticed her, he got off his trishaw and pointed to the empty space above his neck as though asking for his head. She was in such a state of shock that she could not scream or cry or make any sound. She ran to the bedroom and pounded on the door to wake her husband, gibbering. The ruckus woke her children as well and they scrambled to secure the house before summoning the police.

No one else saw the headless trishaw man. By the time the police arrived, the lady of the house was already severely and irredeemably traumatized.

* * *

'How do you know this?'

Mrs Ramanathan took the mug of hot cocoa from Claire and said between sips, 'One of her sons was in my class. He was the one who told me.'

To Claire, the gentle slurping sounds of Mrs Ramanathan sipping her drink contrasted sharply with the cataclysmic sound of the downpour outside; both equally tested her patience and courage.

'There was another incident with a couple on their way home on a motorbike after a very late supper with friends. Although the ferocious storm had been just a passing cloud, the night temperature had dropped to almost freezing. They were riding on Tupai Road when they saw someone begging for help. They first thought it was a drunk, who had had one too many. But on closer inspection they saw the headless trishaw man stretching out his hands to them, reaching for their heads. They veered off the road, skidded and crashed into a tree. They survived and ran for their lives.'

'Could they have been mistaken? You know how the dark can play tricks on us, especially on a stormy night?'

Mrs Ramanathan replaced the mug on the table like she was in a trance and continued, ignoring Claire's interruption.

'A school boy was riding his bicycle to school at about six in the morning. He was chased by the headless trishaw man on the Main Road. He managed to race into the school but collapsed in his classroom in front of the other boys. He was immediately rushed to hospital. He came down with a very high fever and almost died of it. His parents took him to Kuala Lumpur (KL) and that was the last I heard of him.'

She wept into her hands. Claire felt deeply sorry for her.

'Perhaps you should try and get some sleep now.'

'No, no. Not yet,' the old lady looked into Claire's eyes. 'I have to tell you the stories.'

'How about tomorrow?'

'No. It will be too late by then.'

'Too late?'

Mrs Ramanathan bent closer towards Claire and whispered, 'This went on for a long time. The headless trishaw man was spotted at odd hours and always during a storm. It upset the town's regular routines. Hawkers closed their stalls early and children left for school well after sunrise. The Lake Gardens became deserted as soon as darkness fell. Nobody dared to venture into it unless there was sufficient daylight to penetrate every nook and corner. Although it wasn't on official records or admitted by the authorities, all of Taiping knew about the headless trishaw man's existence.

'Many months later, I forget how long, the sightings grew more and more infrequent. And then one day they stopped completely. People were still afraid of the dark, but their old habits returned.'

Claire placed another steaming mug of hot cocoa in front of Mrs Ramanathan and said, 'Drink up while it's still hot.'

'What happened to the last one?'

'You finished it.'

'Oh? Did I?'

Mrs Ramanathan had become so engrossed in her reminiscing that she hadn't noticed when Claire had made her a second mug of hot cocoa. She was thankful to have a daughter-in-law who could set aside their past differences and still take care of her. She wrapped her aged, furrowed and bumpy hands around the hot mug, appreciating the tingly sensation generated by its heat. The storm's ferocity had diminished considerably and only the last heavy splatters were to be heard now, the thunder now sporadic and receding into the distance. Mrs Ramanathan felt serenity in the hot cocoa drink and was about to count her blessings when she heard the trishaw bell ringing. She wept again.

'Mrs Ramanathan, it's okay. The storm is almost over.'

The old woman took a moment to let it all out and wiped her eyes before looking at her daughter-in-law.

'All the years that I have been nasty to you served no purpose. I lost Selvam because of my stubbornness and arrogance.'

'Mrs Ramanathan, please don't say that. I am just as much to blame. I didn't make it any easier for him as well.'

Mrs Ramanathan clutched Claire's hand and stared at her clear fair skin and small almond-shaped eyes.

'As much as I want to make amends, my time is up.'

'Mrs Ramanathan . . . ma, please . . . don't say that,' Claire used the more endearing salutation to calm the old woman.

'You should have called me "ma" a long time ago, but I didn't let you. Thank you for warming the heart of a cranky old woman. But the headless trishaw man is back, my dear, and this time he is not looking for his head. He's the Grim Reaper although he isn't a skeleton toting a scythe.'

'But that's just an old wives' tale.'

'I thought so too. It wasn't until some of my friends and neighbours related similar incidents to me. Whenever he comes around, ringing his bell, it means that, for someone in the house, their time is up. One stormy night, a house caught fire and the headless trishaw man came to ferry away the entire family of five. Several children, standing around in the rain watching the conflagration, saw him pedalling his trishaw away with the deceased. Some of the adults also bore witness to this strange sighting, but they remained silent for fear of being laughed at.' Mrs Ramanathan looked out through the window and said, 'I know it's time for me to go now.'

'How could you know that? I mean . . .'

'Don't you hear the bell ringing?'

Claire strained her ears and then shook her head, 'No.'

'I do.'

'But—'

'Please forgive me, Claire, for all the times I hurt your feelings. I was labouring under the illusion that I was doing it for my son's benefit and I was hurtful towards you. You know how over-protective and selfish some mothers can be.'

'There's no need for this kind of talk, ma. We've both said and done a lot of things that we've regretted.'

'I must stop running away and steel myself to face unpleasant truths. I've always been afraid of dying, but I'm not anymore. I'm ready now. I'll just finish the drink and go to bed. Thank you, Claire. You have been a wonderful daughter-in-law and you've given me a very good life even without Selvam. I want to share this peaceful moment with you before I go.'

Claire's eyes brimmed with tears at the thought of losing a mother-in-law whom she had come to love and respect. She didn't want to believe that their strange camaraderie was coming to an end. Mrs Ramanathan was the closest thing to Selvam she had. She was family.

'The cocoa was delicious, Claire. I am a contented woman,' she smiled.

Although the thunder and lightning had ceased, the drizzle was incessant. Restraining herself from an emotional outburst, Claire merely nodded like an obedient child.

'I don't have much, but whatever I do have is yours.'

'Mrs Rama—, ma, please don't say that.'

'One can't run away from one's conscience. Everything I did was only to survive as a woman. That was all. I didn't mean to hurt anyone. You know how it is, don't you, Claire?'

'Yes, ma. I do.'

'Sooner or later, in whatever form, he will come for you. The bell is getting louder.'

Mrs Ramanathan saw the headless trishaw man standing outside the window, waiting for her to join him.

'Be patient,' she said to the spectre. 'At least let me go with dignity.'

Claire watched as the old woman spoke to the darkness outside the window. She shuddered at the thought of a supernatural being waiting to take her mother-in-law to another world. She chided herself for being fanciful, put it out of her mind and wheeled her mother-in-law back into the bedroom. After she had tucked the old woman into her bed, Claire sat down in the armchair by her side.

'I'll stay here until you fall asleep.'

'Thank you, my dear. It won't be long now. He's already here.'

Claire didn't dare ask where 'here' was and held the old woman's hands in hers. By the time the morning sunbeams crept in through the window, Claire was fast asleep and Mrs Ramanathan was gone.

* * *

'Are you sure this is true? It sounds suspiciously like an episode from *the Twilight Zone*.'

'Yes, I'm sure it's true,' Ser Ling bridled. 'My aunt told me this story.'

'What happened to the daughter-in-law?'

'How should I know?'

'Why did the headless trishaw man come back as a Grim Reaper? Did he switch jobs? Or was it thrust upon him?'

'Yeah, and how come we never heard of him again?'

'Where did he go?'

'Hey, guys, I don't have all the answers and I don't know why he chose to ferry some people and not others.'

'Do you know why he got the job as the Grim Reaper?' Rao asked.

'Why?'

'Because he was a-head of his time.'

They laughed their heads off at this silly joke and waited for the next person to tell them a better and scarier story.

* * *

'You don't have to be afraid, Carol. It has been over forty years since I learned about the headless trishaw man. There's nothing to be afraid of.' Claire held her granddaughter in her arms and rocked her gently.

'But the man has no head,' the little five-year-old held her neck to demonstrate the lack of head.

'I know, but he will not harm you.'

'Then why is he here?'

'Well . . .' Claire didn't want to frighten the little girl who was already on the verge of tears. 'You see, when you've grown as old as I've done, sometimes you just have to go.'

'But, grandma, I don't want you to go.'

Claire kissed Carol's forehead to reassure her.

'We all have to go sooner or later, and the man is here to take me.'

'But why does he have to look so scary?'

'He . . . he doesn't mean to be. It's just the way he is.'

'I wish he wouldn't stare at us without a head, grandma. It's creepy.'

Claire hugged her granddaughter and wept silent tears. Although she had moved as far away as she could from Burmese Pool, the headless trishaw man had managed to run her to earth in Simpang. She had even considered leaving this quaint little town and settling down in KL, Johor or even Singapore. But there was something about Taiping that drew her. Its allure could turn even primal fear into undying love.

Claire gazed at the headless trishaw man outside the window and said to him, 'At least take me through the scenic route.'

Forked lightning blasted the earth one last time before the downpour dwindled to a drizzle. The ringing of the trishaw's bell grew louder and more incessant until it drowned out all other sounds in the cold dark night.

2

Siloban aka the *Jamban* Incident

'I've been waiting to tell someone this story for a long time,' Rao said and flagged his fingers in front of the crowd to get their attention. 'Do you guys know what a *siloban* is?'

'A what?'

'The Malays call it *penanggalan*.'

'Is that the flying head with the dangling intestines?'

'Yup, that's the one.'

'Isn't it from some old Malay movie?'

'Yes, but this one is real. It happened to my brother and my cousin. We have this KL cousin whom we don't really like. He always puts us down and makes us feel like we couldn't match up to him. Whenever he came over to visit us in Pokok Assam, we dreaded it. Luckily for me, I was too young to keep him company, so my brother had to do the honours. Or dis-honours,' Rao laughed. 'Anyway, he would always tell us about the things KL had and we didn't in our small town—fast food, shopping malls, modern amenities, etc., etc.'

'Enough with the commentary, what about the story?'

'Right, right! Hold your horses! I'm coming to it. I just wanted to give you some background about my cousin.'

'Why?'

'Because he offended the spirits.'

'Tell us the story already, Rao!'

'Fine, fine. Do you guys remember the bucket system that we had?'

'Of course.'

'Yuck.'

'How could anyone forget the "bucket"?'

'*Jamban.*'

'Yes, *jamban.* Well, my cousin from KL didn't know that our *jamban* was outside the house. Late one night he had a stomach ache,' Rao sniggered.

* * *

'Who gets a stomach ache at 4 o'clock in the morning?' my brother groaned, trying to rub away the sleep from his eyes.

'Do you think I want it? Do you think I planned this? I should have gone with everyone else to Ipoh for Cheng Beng, but no-o, I had to babysit you,' my cousin grumbled and punched my brother's shoulder. 'You'd think I had nothing better to do.'

'Okay, okay, you don't have to hit me, you know,' my brother said, rubbing his shoulder and fully awake now.

'Yeah, I do,' my cousin said and showed my brother a fist. 'Where is the freakin' toilet?' He obviously hadn't paid attention to my brother, who had already mentioned its location when he arrived in the afternoon.

'Outside.'

'Outside? Outside, where?'

'Outside the house.'

'Why is the freakin' toilet outside the house? Why is this town so backward? I knew I shouldn't have come here. I told mom I didn't want to, but she insisted. Like I had nothing better to do in

KL than to come to Taiping,' my cousin ranted, clutching at his growling stomach. 'I need the toilet, like, just now!'

'But . . .'

'But what? I'm dying here!'

'Can't you hold on? It'll be morning soon.'

'Are you stupid or something? I have got food poisoning and you're asking me to hold on?' My cousin raised his fist and my brother cringed.

'Okay, okay.'

My brother ran to the kitchen, switching on as many lights as he could along the way, and grabbed a flashlight before unbolting the heavy wooden back door. He peered out into the backyard through the grille set in the doorframe. The rambutan trees which looked sinfully delicious during the day, looked alarmingly sinister in the dark.

'Good god, why is it so dark?'

The fluorescent bulb overhead cast a small circular patch of light around them, but beyond that was utter blackness. My brother reluctantly unlocked the grille with a key and then unfastened the padlock.

'By the time you open all these doors, I'll probably shit in my pants.'

My brother ignored him and said, 'There's a light bulb in the *jamban*.'

'Jeez, only a light bulb?"

'But the bulb is blown.' My brother smirked.

'What?'

'Next, you'll tell me is that you don't use toilet paper.'

My brother wanted to say 'yes' just to needle my cousin but realized that he would see the toilet paper hanging behind the door anyway.

'Do you?' my cousin grabbed the flashlight from my brother and shone it rudely in his face.

You know, when you get pushed to the limit and let it all out in one burst? My brother did just that and said with his teeth and fists clenched, 'Have you heard of the *siloban*?'

'I've no time for your stupid games. Where are the slippers?'

'We only have clogs.'

'How can anyone wear clogs? It's like wearing high heels. And they make one hell of a noise.' My cousin snorted with disgust, shoved my brother aside, jerked his feet into the wooden footwear and holding his knees together, walked awkwardly to the *jamban*. One hand clutching his stomach, the other balancing himself like a tightrope walker.

My brother stood at the kitchen door under the flickering fluorescent bulb adding dread to my cousin's frustration, 'It's a head that flies around at night looking for blood. It makes a hollow sound. Like two coconut shells knocking together. But some say it's actually it's teeth chattering.'

'Yeah, yeah, I'm so scared of your silly superstitions,' my cousin said in a silly little girl voice to put my brother off. 'In case you've forgotten, these are modern times. Oh, I forgot . . . Taiping is still stuck in the '50s. Do you think the *orang minyak* is still running around? Your schools are haunted. You ask the dead for numbers. What else?'

'I'd be careful if I were you,' my brother shouted out to him.

'Of your backward sensibilities,' my cousin continued to rant as he wobbled away with cold sweat and stomach cramps.

'I won't wait for you!'

'You can wait in hell for all I care.'

'Don't get entangled with the intestines. It feeds on blood and shit and dead things. And it also has a vinegary smell.'

My cousin ignored my brother and ascended the cemented steps to the *jamban* that looked almost regal like an exclusive gazebo. The stench of human waste churned his stomach even more as he pushed open the door.

'Aargh! For crying out loud! How can anyone live this way?'

My cousin shone the light at the hole in the ground and saw some familiar looking shapes and thousands of squirming maggots. He gasped and felt like throwing up. He turned the torch light upwards and saw carcasses of dead insects stuck in dusty cobwebs. There was no way he was ever coming back to visit us again. He undid his pyjama bottom and squatted over the hole very carefully. The thought of falling in crossed his mind and filled it with dread and disgust.

The relief of the first excretion swept over him like a cold shower on a hot afternoon. He sighed with relief, but whatever had upset his stomach was not completely gone. It came in bouts of projectiles that echoed with the gas that escaped his anus. The pain and pleasure were both a torment and a relief as he groaned like someone praying for divine intervention. While he was in the middle of cleansing himself, the door rattled, and he heard a strange knocking sound travelling around the *jamban*, from left to right. He could vaguely see a shadow moving about through the gaps between the wooden boards. He thought it was my brother getting back at him and he yelled, 'Hey stupid, leave me alone!'

There was no answer.

The hollow sound continued to drum from plank to plank, shaking them loose with the insistent taps. My cousin was enraged, annoyed and also a little afraid of my brother's retaliation which he had never expected. He had always been the bully so it wouldn't do if my brother stood up to him.

'Stop it! I'll complain to your mother that you made my stay here difficult and gave me hell!'

It went completely silent and whatever was outside stopped moving altogether. My cousin peeped through the gaps, but he could not see anything in the dark. It was pitch dark except for the nightlight at the kitchen door. His stomach seized up again and he relieved himself a few more times. The smell that followed was worse than the whiff from the bucket. He thought it came from him until he heard a squelchy, sploshy sound that could mean only one thing—the entrails of a *penanggalan* draggling over everything in its path. He switched off the flashlight, covered his mouth with his hands and breathed as quietly as he could.

The shadow moved back and forth in front of the door again. Was it real? Was the creature really looking for blood? Faeces? Rotting carcasses? He wanted to call out to my brother, but he was too scared to move or make a sound. His eyes started watering, when he heard the rustling and crunching of dead leaves. Someone or something was approaching the *jamban*.

He groped in the dark for the toilet paper but touched something gooey and immediately wiped it on the wooden wall.

'Yuck! Eww!'

As soon as he had smeared the goo away, he reached again for the toilet paper and managed to drag down a long strip of tissue. Just as he was about to clean himself, the bucket below him was dragged out of the hole over which he was squatting. He scrunched up the toilet paper and stuffed it inside his open mouth and dropped the flashlight into the empty space. The night was going from bad to worse. He peered down to see if something would jump out of the hole but it was completely empty.

He waited for a long while, but nothing happened. He was about to run out when the whole *jamban* shook with the howl of an unexpected wind and the sound of splattering liquid. Some of the wetness dripped through the holes and uneven planks of the roof and splattered over my cousin. A shadow went by quickly and he wanted to scream, but he was all choked up with fear. He tried in vain to convince himself that it was my no-good brother up to his usual antics, but he didn't quite believe it. He didn't think my brother had the ability to pull off this kind of a feat.

My cousin peered through the slits and saw the backyard light but this time the grille door and wooden door were tightly shut. He checked the surroundings as far as his eyes could see and saw a massive object hurtling past. It seemed to be some kind of an elongated silhouette that was dripping with slime.

My cousin pressed against the back of the wall, trembling like a terrified child that had gotten lost in a crowd. He didn't want to believe that whatever was outside was slathering itself with the gunk from its entrails, but he couldn't help imagining the worst.

The hollow sound continued but grew fainter by the minute, reminding him all the while that whatever it was, was still out there. My cousin could not see any other way out of the loo except through the large hole where the bucket was a moment ago. He pulled his pyjama bottom up, not caring whether he had cleaned himself properly or not, and then waited for a few more seconds.

Slime started to ooze through the many breaches in the weather-worn planks; it dripped from the zinc roof and poured in from the crevices in the walls. He cringed, feeling the panic of extreme claustrophobia setting in. If he didn't get out of the *jamban* soon he might not live to tell the tale. And there was only one way out.

He dreaded the idea, but the hole was big enough for him to crawl through. It didn't seem as bad in the dark, but he knew he had to keep his hands off anything that felt suspicious. The ominous presence outside gave him no other choice. He didn't want to encounter whatever was waiting for him, so he jumped into the hole to make a quick exit. He winced at the foulness caked around the edges of the hole, but he manoeuvred himself through it carefully, making as little contact as possible. It was a short crawl under the *jamban* until he reached open space. He didn't know where he was. A long and narrow path seemed to lead to everywhere and nowhere at the same time . . . it was a never-ending labyrinth. It was then that he gave up and shouted for help.

'Kee! Where are you?'

The wind whistled around him and he could hear the sound of his own teeth chattering. The sploshing entrails sounded like they were painting everything that they touched with the gooey stuff. The night felt as empty and eerie as an office building *at night*. My cousin now felt that it had been a huge mistake to have descended through the hole; he felt he should have kept quiet and stayed put. But it was too late. Suddenly, all the terrifying sounds resumed simultaneously, and an incandescent green light glowed a short distance away.

'Oh shit!' My cousin began running blindly.

'You're going the wrong way! Turn back! Turn back!' My brother's voice reached his ears.

'I can't go back. It's blocking my way.'

'Follow my voice.'

'But your voice is everywhere,' my cousin said desperately trying to locate my brother. 'I don't know where I am.'

'Hide. I'll come and get you.'

My cousin could no longer see the back door to my house. It was gone. He was in the middle of a dark passage filled with dead leaves and overgrown shrubs. The green light was the only thing he could see now and it was moving towards him. There was no other way to go except further away from my house.

He wept uncontrollably, fearing for his life for the very first time. The maze-like path led him deeper into the unknown, where everything was unfamiliar, almost as though he had fallen into another dimension. He tripped on something that protruded from the ground and fell flat on his face. The *siloban* that was emitting the green light, caught up with him and stopped. He could not see what it looked like in the dark, but he could vaguely make out elongated growths sticking out of its head. The thing drew even closer to him, making a hideous chattering sound, and then wrapped its slimy intestines around him.

My cousin didn't fight back and shut his eyes because he knew it was pointless to resist. The thing extended a worm-like tongue and started to lick my cousin's face. He trembled like a leaf in a storm and soiled himself when something fell to the ground with a thud.

'Let's go!'

My cousin sobbed with sheer relief at the sound of my brother's voice and he opened his eyes. He saw my brother throwing something at the *siloban* and he was suddenly free of the nasty entrails and tongue. Completely speechless by now, he raised his hands to my brother, mutely begging for help. My brother hooked his hands under my cousin's arms and hauled him up to his feet.

'We have no time to lose.'

The thing wailed, screeched and fought to get out, but it was pinioned beneath the weight and intricate weaving of the net that my brother had flung over it.

'I don't know if it will hold.'

'B-but, shouldn't we kill it? What if it comes back for us?'

'You can't kill it. We don't know where the body is.'

'So . . .'

'So, let's run!'

My brother took the lead and made his way back through the night soil man's path. He knew the way by heart because we had often explored it from end to end looking for shortcuts around the house. My cousin was panting heavily and flailing his arms like a drunk. My brother had to turn around to grab him every time he fell behind. They ran as fast as their legs could carry them and the shortest way back to the house was through the *jamban* hole again. My cousin couldn't believe he had to endure another demeaning and disgusting passage through the hole again, to save his life.

'Isn't there another way?'

'Too far.'

My brother slipped under the hole and jumped out through the *jamban* effortlessly. My cousin followed suit, but had to crawl on his hands and knees, touching surfaces that he never would have if it weren't for his current predicament. His regrets for visiting us mounted higher than Maxwell Hill, but there was very little he could do about it at this time.

They got out of the *jamban* just in time to hear loud shrieking in the night. It was as though the *siloban* was right behind them. My brother had left both the back door and the grille wide open for easy access. They ran in and my brother quickly locked the barriers in quick succession and not a minute too soon. The howling winds thrashed at the door and shook its bolts as though something gigantic was trying to break in.

'What the hell was that thing?' my cousin asked.

'I told you.' My brother was also trembling because he had never had any first-hand experience with the *siloban* either. They staggered into the house and my brother said, 'You smell like shit!'

My cousin was in no mood for jokes. He was on the verge of tears and would have sobbed had my brother not taken it upon himself to comfort him.

'It's over. Go clean yourself up.'

My cousin must have spent an hour in the bathroom washing off every minute particle out of his hair and skin.

After washing up, my brother staggered to his bedroom where he felt safest, still trembling from the encounter with a being he had known about all along but never really believed existed. When my cousin finished scrubbing himself into a red lobster, he joined my brother in the room. They lay on their respective beds without speaking or acknowledging the cries that were obviously coming from the *siloban* trapped in the fishing net.

They lay there a moment longer and my brother checked his watch to see if daylight was coming anytime soon.

'What will happen to it when the sun rises?'

My brother glanced at my cousin and wondered about that himself. According to legend, it would die. My brother's eyes widened at that very thought and said it out aloud.

'It will die.'

'That's great. Good riddance—' my cousin started to say.

'No, it's not!'

'Huh?'

'If it dies, another one may come and hunt us down. If it doesn't die, it will come for us as soon as it gets out of the net.'

'What kind of logic is that?'

'The paranormal kind. I think we had better free it.'

'What? No way! I'm not going back there. You do it . . . alone!'

'Do you want it to follow you back to KL?'

'Shit. Of course not.'

'Then we'd better go and release it before the sun rises.'

'Do we have to go through the *jamban* again?'

'That's the fastest way.'

'Why won't this nightmare end?'

They retraced their steps to the backyard and to the *jamban* which had now become a portal between worlds. My cousin cringed at the thought of crawling through that despicable hole, but he had no choice. Since daylight was fast approaching, he could clearly see the stains and muck for what they were. His stomach made a leap every time he touched something slimy. My brother had only one thing in mind and raced against time to free the *siloban*. It was bad enough catching one, but much worse if it survived and returned for revenge.

My brother was about to jump into the hole when he saw a new empty bucket blocking his way.

My cousin peered over his shoulder to see what the hold up was. 'It's back?' my cousin shouted. 'Where did it disappear to in the first place?'

My brother rolled his eyes. Even a child would have understood the simple logic behind the disappearing bucket.

'The *oop oop* man replaces it with a new one every other day.'

'What's an *oop oop* man?'

'The night soil messenger.'

'What's a night soil messenger?'

My brother rolled his eyes again.

'The shit carrier,' he enunciated as clearly as he could. 'The waste courier. The crap bearer. The poop transporter.'

'Okay, okay, I get it! Jeez. But why do you call him the "*oop oop*" man?'

'Every time he places the bucket in the lorry, he calls out "*oop oop*" to the driver to move forward.'

'You mean they carry the buckets in the back of a lorry?'

'Of course, sometimes when the driver takes a particularly sharp turn too fast the buckets spill their contents all over the road.'

'Oh my goodness!'

My brother kicked the bucket aside and jumped into the hole before my cousin could ask another question.

They were soon back at the scene of crime, so to speak, as they stood over the creature which was thrashing about, wailing and shrieking simultaneously, sounding both like a cat's mating caterwaul and a dog's yelping for help. The thing was covered with its own hair and it was still too dark to make out the finer details.

'Grab one end of the net and I'll grab the other,' my brother said and picked the nylon rope carefully with his finger tips.

'What if it—'

'Just shut up and do it. Make sure you don't get too close.'

My cousin had a fleeting glimpse of the thing struggling in the net and he shuddered as he reached for one of the corners of the fishing net.

'Get ready. As soon as we pull it off, we run.'

'But—'

'One, two, three . . . pull!'

They tugged with all their might but the *siloban* remained hopelessly entangled in the net.

'Run!'

They ran for their lives and never looked back.

* * *

Everyone looked at Rao when he stopped at this climactic scene.

'And then?'

'And then what?'

'That's all my brother told me.'

'What? How can you end a story like that?'

'I can't help it . . . that's all I know,' Rao laughed.

'What a bummer.'

'It was really scary.'

'I don't believe it. It sounded too ridiculous.'

'Well . . .'

'You spoiled the story with that ending. It would have been much more memorable if you had a better ending.'

'Yeah. It's like Radio Televisyen Malaysia (RTM) cutting off the TV shows before they end.'

'And like a TV series taken off the air midway through the season.'

'Like *Potong stim*.'

'Actually, there's more,' Rao giggled. 'I was just testing you guys.'

'You're terrible. You had better tell us everything.'

* * *

My brother stopped when he heard the *siloban* resume its wailing. He expected it to swoop down on them but that never happened.

'Why are you stopping?' my cousin was still running as he gasped out this question.

'It hasn't been freed yet.'

'What?'

'It's stuck,' my brother explained and hesitated for a moment before adding, 'we have to go back.'

'Why? No!'

'We've got to put it out of its misery.'

My brother went back and again grabbed one end of the net and started hauling it.

'Help me,' he called out to my cousin.

'Where are we taking it?'

My brother didn't reply and they silently lugged the head all the way back to the *jamban*. It was still shrieking and squealing when they left it inside the *jamban* and my brother set fire to the wooden outhouse.

'That's the end of the *siloban*.'

'And also the *jamban*.'

They watched the fire engulf the only toilet they had, drowning out the cries of the creature that haunted the entire neighbourhood.

'We have a lot of explaining to do.'

'Where are we going to shit?'

* * *

The boys burst into uncontrollable laughter that was both infectious and delirious.

'So, they murdered the *siloban*?'

'Cool.'

'They were lucky to have survived.'

'How are your brother and cousin now?'

'I don't know. I haven't seen them for a long time.'

'Were they affected by the incident?'

'I guess. Wouldn't you be?'

'So, it's absolutely true?'

'That's what my brother said.'

* * *

Kee and Cyren sat at the dining table, covered in all manner of filth, and cried until the sun came up. They swore never to tell anyone about this. That was why Kee only told his brother a small part of the whole incident, leaving out the fact that they had freed the *siloban*, for fear of being called wimps. Besides, it was too complicated to tell his younger brother the whole truth. It was almost noon before they decided to take another shower to get rid of the nightmare that was still troubling their minds and clung to their skin.

As soon as they were thoroughly scrubbed and felt like they were purged of the previous night's ordure, Kee noticed the trail of grunge they had tracked into the house.

'Look at that mess we've made! My mom will freak out if she sees it.'

'Oh, man, I just took a shower.'

Kee did not respond to that statement. He was frustrated, exhausted, revolted and scared shitless. He grabbed a couple of mops, a bucket of water, and floor cleaner to wipe out the anguish that was gnawing at him. There were too many unanswered questions. He was beginning to see how wrong it was to let the *siloban* go, but he didn't want to frighten his cousin.

Cyren, who had never lifted a finger to help with any housework in his entire young life, must have hated this moment more than anything else. But he relented and picked up the mop when he realized that it was nothing compared to what they had just gone through. He couldn't remember how long he had cried, but he felt drained, emasculated and thoroughly demoralized as he set about doing the menial house-keeping work that he was now compelled to do.

By noon most of the family members returned home. The house filled up with people of all ages. The boys kept aloof from them because they still occasionally trembled, their trauma showing through in small jerky movements and chattering teeth.

'Let's go do something before we go insane,' Kee suggested to his cousin.

'Yeah, yeah, great idea. Where do we go and what do we do?'

'*Mee rebus* and ice *kacang* at the casual market would be nice.'

'Sounds great!'

'Tastes better.'

* * *

Cyren gobbled up his *mee rebus* with gusto and then cooled himself down with the colourful ice *kacang*.

'I am so full,' Cyren said.

'Welcome to Taiping. One of the best pastimes here is to eat till you drop.'

'You can say that again. But I feel like eating something more.'

'Ice *bobo*.'

'What's that?'

Kee was already waving to the aunty who was serving drinks when he saw a beautiful young girl in a flowing dress walking towards him. He was transfixed like a wild animal caught in the headlights. Cyren noticed Kee's dumbstruck look and tracked his eye line to see the gorgeous girl heading their way. The minute she reached their table she stopped and tossed her hair over her shoulder. The two boys could not take their eyes off her and felt strangely drawn to her. She batted her eyes and seductively smiled at them before walking away.

As soon as she was out of sight, the boys stared at one another but refused to admit to the elephant in the room.

'Why is there such a strong vinegary smell?' a man at the neighbouring table remarked and confirmed their horror.

'Did someone spill vinegar?' another person asked.

The boys stood up simultaneously. Kee dropped some money on the table and both boys hurried out, abandoning their tastefully presented ice *bobo*. They walked out of the casual market to look for a phone booth. The first was broken, the second had a missing receiver, and the third merely ate all of their money.

'What are we going to do? They promised to pick us up in an hour,' Cyren asked anxiously.

Before Kee could answer, a vinegary scent wafted through the air and made them panic in broad daylight. They could see her watching them from a distance.

'Sh-she's coming for us.'

'Shut up, Cyren,' Kee said and shoved his cousin to get a move on. 'Don't let her know we know,' he whispered in Cyren's ear and drew him away from the phone booth.

They raced up the stairs to the Larut Matang supermarket to kill time and to lose the girl, looking over their shoulders occasionally to see how far behind she was. The girl was soon out of sight but not out of their minds.

They manoeuvred between the narrow aisles in the departmental store but the girl was once again visible in their peripheral vision.

'She won't go away,' Cyren said.

'I think we should just go back.'

'By bus, again? We waited for what ... like hours ...'

'We'll take a *sapu chia*.'

'What's a *sapu chia*?'

'An illegal taxi.'

They ran to the opposite exit of the supermarket. At the taxi stand, they quickly clambered into an available cab.

As Kee said, 'Pokok Assam,' he noticed a girl sitting in the passenger seat, beside the driver. These communal taxis were usually shared by strangers, so he didn't give it another thought.

Before they could set off, the man behind the wheel sniffed at his sleeves. Cyren was petrified by the man's odd behaviour. The familiar vinegary smell overwhelmed him and made him cringe. He nudged Kee and they both stared at the back of the girl's head. Both of them silently prayed that the girl would not turn around and make their worst nightmare come true. The man didn't say anything, but turned up the volume of his radio and sped through the town and on to Tupai Road without a care.

The boys felt as if their lives were slipping away with the same speed as the world that flashed by past the taxi's windows, made that much worse by the jarring Hokkien song. They sat as far back as they could so the girl's hair wouldn't accidentally brush against them in case it was as disease-ridden as her intestines. Their minds were wholly seized by the thought of their impending doom.

In the exceedingly hot Taiping afternoon, in the taxicab that didn't have air-conditioning, the two boys looked like they were sitting in a sauna. The taxi driver glanced at them through the rear-view mirror and stifled a laugh—with all the windows rolled down, he didn't think that the weather was all that humid.

'Why are you guys sweating so much?'

'Can you drop us off at the market?' Kee said, ignoring the cabbie's question. He pointed to the kerb long before they were at the periphery of the township. It was a long walk back to the bridge where their house was, but Kee didn't want the girl or the *siloban,* that she most likely was, to follow them back.

The man grunted and continued driving with one hand on the steering wheel and the other flagging the wind. The girl hardly moved. The boys wondered whether the taxi driver could actually see her, but they didn't want to know.

Kee noticed how timid his boisterous cousin had become and he felt bad. He missed the bratty and hyper-critical person that Cyren used to be. Cyren seemed to have no more of his fighting spirit left and this was bad news especially with the *siloban* tailing them back to the house. It was his job to now protect his hitherto annoying cousin.

The taxi driver screeched to a stop unexpectedly at the marketplace. He didn't say a word when Kee handed him a dollar. Kee got out of the taxi as fast as he could, but Cyren seemed mesmerized by the back of the girl's head.

'Come on,' Kee said and half-dragged his cousin out of the back seat. 'Snap out of it.'

'What?'

Kee slammed the car door and stepped back to see if the girl would follow, but the taxi sped off into the setting sun.

'Shit, I lost track of time. It's evening.' Cyren stood by the side of the road, feeling disoriented, weak tears welling up in his eyes. 'What's going to happen tonight? I can't bear to go through it all again. Is she coming for us?' He clung to Kee's shoulder for support.

'We had better get back while it's still daylight. But first, let's find some *menkuang* leaves and pineapple leaves.'

'Leaves? What for? Our lives are in danger and you want to dabble in horticulture now?'

'If not for this crisis, I'd shut you up with my fist!'

Cyren gazed blankly at Kee and then timidly raised his hands to protect his face from the forewarned threat.

On their way back, they noticed a lot of pineapple plants by the side of the road, probably planted by the local residents. Kee didn't know whether it was to ward off evil or to make the most of the unattended land, but he only knew that he was immensely thankful that they were there. He fished out his pocket knife and started hacking at the plants randomly and passed the serrated leaves to Cyren.

'Ouch. Oww. Ooohh.'

Kee ignored his cousin's anguish and headed for the bridge and pointed to some *menkuang* trees growing on the banks.

'We need to get those leaves too.'

'How? It's overgrown with *lalang* and that grass is as sharp as knives. Besides, we don't know what's down there. Snakes. Frogs. Centipedes.'

'Someone threw a dead pig in the river once. It was all bloated and was stuck in the reeds by the bank. It stank up the whole neighbourhood and no one did anything.'

'Oh my goodness! Why do people do that? Why is there so much garbage in the river?'

'The *oop oop* man used to dump the shit he collected in there too.'

'Eww, I'm definitely not going down there.'

A *lang-ting-tang* man stopped his bicycle beside them out of curiosity, 'So many pineapple leaves!'

The boys were taken aback by the stranger's abrupt intrusion, but Kee nodded politely hoping he would go away.

'*Siloban?*'

'How did you know?'

The *lang-ting-tang* man sighed and brought out his *erhu* to play a classical tune.

'This is the tale of a young girl who had a child out of wedlock.' The man closed his eyes to imagine the tragic scenario and lowered his head. 'The man left her. The family shunned her. And she was forced into a back-lane abortion. But it went wrong. It went so horribly wrong. She suffered the pangs of infection and the loss of a life.

'Three days and three nights she called out to her lifeless unborn child. She begged the heavens to take her instead of her child but fate . . . fate would not listen to her entreaties. So, her hatred grew day by day. She swore she would drain anyone dry . . . anyone who dared to offend her.'

The *lang-ting-tang* man ended his ditty, opened his eyes and bowed to the two boys. He slung the *erhu* on his back, smiled a toothless smile, and cycled off into the dusking sky.

'What just happened? Who was that crazy old man?'

'He's a fortune teller. He sings you a song and then tells you your fortune.'

'Taiping is weird, I tell ya,' Cyren said and watched the man blend into the sunset. 'Hey, I—' he turned around but Kee had vanished into thin air.

'Kee, where are you?' he yelled, not bothering to disguise the rising panic in his voice. He stopped shouting when he saw Kee coming up the slope, holding a bunch of *menkuang* leaves.

'Isn't that a bit much?' Cyren used sarcasm to hide his embarrassment about the unnecessary anxiety attack.

'Better safe than sorry.'

Cyren didn't argue and hugged the pile of leaves without complaint although their razor-like edges cut into his hands and arms making him bleed.

* * *

Night couldn't have come sooner. The two boys studiously avoided the adults and surreptitiously looked over their shoulders every chance they got. Kee decided to double check the doors and windows although he was well aware it gave him only false hope.

The *siloban* could slip through cracks between floorboards and wooden walls if she so desired. Before he locked down the house, Kee scattered the pineapple and *menkuang* leaves all over the house to ward off the evil spirit. He even stuck some of them into the ground so they protruded like spears.

They holed up in Kee's room as early as eight o'clock that night. It was already bedtime for Kee's parents and for most of the people in the neighbourhood. Kee and Cyren perched on their beds, looking dazed and confused. Kee lifted the edge of the curtain behind his bed and peeped out of the window. The street was empty and partially lit as some of the streetlights were not working—it had always been that way, even after innumerable repairs. Pokok Assam was famous for blackouts, water shortages, gangsters and drugs.

'Is she going to take revenge?' Cyren asked.

Kee twitched the curtain back into place and tucked it under the louvre. 'I don't think so. We didn't leave it out to die.' Kee picked up a lighter, flicked the lid open and clicked it alight. He watched the flame quiver before his eyes. He killed it by flicking the lid shut and then repeated the entire process over and over again, until the flicking and clicking got to Cyren.

'Would you stop that? It's driving me nuts. What do you think it wants?' Cyren rocked back and forth with his hands sandwiched between his thighs. 'I mean, if it wants to kill us, we would already be dead, right? Do you think what the crazy old man said is true?'

Kee pondered on the *lang-ting-tang* man's ditty. A sad and tragic end that created a monster.

'I don't know.'

'Or does it just want some of our blood?'

'We'll find out soon enough.'

They heard the hollow clacking sound outside, moving from one corner of the house to the other.

'You spoke too soon,' Cyren gasped. 'I thought the pineapple and *menkuang* leaves would keep that thing away,' Cyren pulled his feet up from the floor and tucked them beneath the covers although it felt like an oven in the room.

'We'd better hope they do,' Kee turned back to the window and drew the curtain aside.

'What are you doing?'

'I just want to see how close she is.'

'Don't do it, Kee.'

'I'm only taking a quick look.'

'I don't feel good about it. Just don't do it.'

'Shh . . .' Kee placed a hushing finger on his lips and drew open the curtains wide enough to get a good view of the outside. He pulled the louvre windows down to clear a path for his line of sight.

'She's not here.'

'Because she's at the other window!' Cyren screamed.

Kee caught a glimpse of something slimy slither through the gaps in the window without the mosquito netting. But the moment Cyren cried out, she vanished from sight.

A thunderous knocking on the door shook them both up badly and Cyren let out a suppressed scream.

'Are you boys okay? What's with all the screaming?'

'We're okay, pa. Cyren had a nightmare.'

'Go back to sleep then and try not to have any more nightmares.' They heard Kee's father walk away with tired footsteps.

'It's trying to find a way in! Oh my goodness, oh my goodness. What are we going to do?'

'Here,' Kee passed a blade of the pineapple leaf to his cousin. 'Wield it like a sword. There's no sleep for us tonight. So, stay alert.'

The boys fell asleep with their makeshift swords in their hands. When the clock struck four, the *siloban* enchanted Cyren by whispering his name. He twitched, agitated by the sound of the teeth-chattering call. He dropped the leaf, sprang out of his bed and started walking out of the room in his pyjamas. Kee, unaware of these goings on, slept right through. Cyren found his way to the back door and he managed to unlock every barrier as though he had been living there all his life. He knew exactly where the keys were and he knew which one would fit the lock without having to figure it out.

The cold night air was tantalizing. Cyren's skin broke out in goose pimples from the frigid air but he was fast asleep in his dream state. He stood in the middle of the garden and the *siloban* appeared out of the darkness.

Its entrails painted the moist grass with a deeper tone and its hair stretched upwards, outwards and into the trees to form a web. With the distortion of a fun house mirror, its image had the appearance of being able to petrify a living being into a pillar of salt. Its forked tongue shot out of its mouth and wrapped itself around Cyren's neck, drawing him closer for the feeding.

'Let him go!' Kee struck on one of the creature's entrails with the leaf and the *siloban* squealed, chattered its teeth at Kee like a wild animal, released Cyren and shrank back into itself like a coiled spring, readying itself for another attack.

'We didn't harm you the last time. We won't hesitate to do so now if you don't let us go.'

Kee raised a bunch of *menkuang* and pineapple leaves tied into a bundle with all the pointed ends aimed at the creature. It hissed. Its intestines and hair convulsed in defiance and anger. Kee felt like his heart had dropped into his gut and purged out of his body. His knees buckled but he stood his ground. Saving his cousin was the only thing on his mind. The *siloban* made rattling and chattering sounds, thrashing its hair and tongue in fury. Kee swung the makeshift weapon in the air in a twirling motion as if he were summoning the gods.

The creature lunged forward and snapped its fangs at Kee, but he managed to deftly evade the nasty bite and gave it a swift kick. It fell to the ground and Kee immediately thrust the sharp-edged leaves into it, lacerating its intestines. The creature shrieked and Kee threw a net over it. The creature's terror at being snared reduced it to a state of frenzy. It tried to dart out through the open weaving of the net, but only ended up getting even more entangled with each attempt to break free.

Kee quickly twisted the diagonal ends of the net together and dragged the *siloban* towards the *jamban*. It fought in vain to escape, but that only made matters worse for itself. Its intestines and other innards were inextricably knotted up and enmeshed in the fishing net. With all his strength, Kee swung the thing into the *jamban* and slammed the door shut, latching it from the outside. He retrieved the lighter from his pocket and clicked it open, ready to strike up a flame. He hurriedly gathered up a bunch of dry *rambutan* leaves in front of the *jamban's* door and set it alight.

Kee ran to Cyren and checked to see if he was still alive. Drained by the momentary enchantment, Cyren was in a daze, but he was unharmed. He saw the fire, but his confused mind could not piece the information together.

'What's happening?'

'That's the end of the *siloban*.'

They watched as the conflagration engulfed the *jamban*, the screams and squeals of the creature resounding across the neighbourhood.

Kee suddenly had a change of heart and ran back to the *jamban* to kick down the door.

'What the hell are you doing?'

Kee did not answer and used the long stick used for *rambutan* harvesting to drag the net out. The *siloban* was slightly singed but otherwise unharmed. Kee tore the net apart to release the creature. It rolled out of the net and shot up in a green illumination, chattering away. It darted back towards Kee and Cyren as the fire engulfed the *jamban*. The charred and furious head growled and screeched at them, flailing its tentacled intestines violently. The boys hugged each other and waited for their end.

The creature bared its teeth and snapped at their faces, but it retreated when it saw the boys cringing and in tears. The terrifying monstrosity that was the *siloban* transformed into a pretty face with sad melancholic eyes. She was no older than the boys were. For the first time, they saw her for who she really was. Without the rancour. But with an innocence that was ravaged by madness. As soon as she had calmed down, she floated off into the night like a Chinese paper lantern.

'Why did you do such a stupid thing?' Cyren asked.

'It was something about the story the *lang-ting-tang* man said . . .' Kee bent his head and felt the weight of the world on his shoulders slip away. 'Understanding the reason why she became this thing in the first place, I just couldn't hurt her anymore.'

'What made you think she would spare us?'

'I didn't think. It just felt right to stop hating and fearing something we didn't understand.' Kee wanted to bring their own cousinly relationship up as a comparison, but decided it would have sounded too awkward to even mention it. 'Hate makes monsters of us.'

Cyren nodded in silence, agreeing with Kee although he didn't want to go through another nightmare with the *siloban*.

'We could have died, though,' Cyren said and shuddered at the thought.

'Yeah, but we didn't.'

'What are you going to tell your parents about the *jamban*?'

'That you caused it. You dropped the candle and burnt the whole filthy thing down.'

They cracked up and watched the fire devour the only toilet they had.

3

Curse of the Papaya Tree

'This is a tale of a man who took his own life in the most bizarre manner. You may even think it impossible, but everything I'm about to tell you is true,' Jackson jumped into his storytelling without preamble when everyone had done laughing after the previous story. 'No one could have imagined it. Everyone asked the same question when they found out about the mysterious death of Mr Bok. How could a fragile septuagenarian, who had developed arthritis from the long hours of preparing meals at his noodle shop, have done it?'

'Done what?'

'Killed himself.'

'How?'

'Hanged himself.'

'That's not too difficult.'

'Yeah, but not the way he did it.'

'Tell us already!'

'He hanged himself on a papaya tree.'

'No way.'

'Impossible.'

'Are you kidding?'

'See, I told you, you wouldn't believe me. The papaya tree was as frail as he was, but he managed to hang himself from it. It was mind boggling.'

Jackson saw how eager the boys were to hear the rest, so he skipped the other teasers he was planning.

'Everyday, at four in the morning Mr Bok hopped on his cargo bicycle to fetch the *mee*, *beehoon*, *niau chu hoon*, *keow teow*, and other condiments and ingredients to make his famous curry *mee*, *laksa*, *kwan loh* and *ching th'ng* at the shop. The variation of noodles he could prepare, cook and serve alone was beyond admiration.

'With no help or support from his family, come rain or shine, he made his way to the market. He stayed there until all his noodles were sold out, which was usually around 7 p.m. He invested his meagre savings in real estate and rolled the rest on the stock market. He didn't intend to grow any richer than he already was, but money came easily to him and multiplied beyond his dreams. Although it should have made him happy, he felt even more alone and isolated than ever in his own little world. He didn't know what to do with his wealth and he didn't think his children deserved any part of it since they had done nothing to help him in his business. He knew they were only waiting like hyenas to inherit everything he had so tirelessly worked to build up all his life.

'After retiring at the age of seventy due to failing health, he grew extremely tight-fisted and gave no more than what was absolutely necessary to his family. This angered his wife, children and his other relatives. Distant or not. He lived a frugal and quiet life, cycling around the town to get to where he wanted to go, wearing his white pagoda t-shirt and over-sized old-uncle trousers. He usually had supper at Siang Malam with a few of his acquaintances, but sometimes, when he felt like treating himself and craved western food, he would dine at Kwong Wai Sang or at Yat Sun.

'These little pleasures were soon lost to him when the inflammation of his joints swelled to become unbearable knobs and he lost his ability to cycle. Although he felt pain in every part of his body, he was reluctant to consult the doctors. He felt it was unnecessary and preferred to suffer a little bit of agony rather than waste his hard-earned nest-egg on medical fees.

'No one spoke much to him at home because he didn't want to make conversations with anybody and everybody. He led a spartan lifestyle: slept on a thin, worn-out mattress on his old wooden bed, ate small portions of rice and soup, and sat in his rattan chair on the porch and watched the world go by.

'The Indonesian maid was the only person who was kind to him. She attended to all his basic needs every day. The two things that kept him alive for as long as he did were the maid and the papaya trees. He loved eating papaya and the maid propagated as many seeds as she could around the house in Aulong, growing the papaya trees all along the fence and every other available spot. It gave Mr Bok hope whenever he saw the trees laden with humongous papayas waiting to be harvested every day.

* * *

Upon learning that the old man was planning to leave all of his possessions and wealth only to the maid, his ten children, who were greedily waiting for their inheritance, grew desperate and furious. They conspired to send the maid back to Indonesia.

'Father has gone mad,' child number one said to the rest of his siblings. 'I have no more faith in him.'

'He and his Indonesian maid are probably having an affair,' child number seven said and scrunched up her face in disgust.

'I wouldn't be surprised. No wonder he wishes to leave everything to her. Father is not a very wise man. I rather think he could be going senile,' child number two said, combing her slender white fingers through her long lustrous hair.

'It's all ours. Everything he has is rightfully ours. I want what's mine,' child number ten raised his hand to make his point because he was the shortest. 'How could father do this to us?'

'Stupid, goddamned moron. There's no fool like an old fool,' child number three chanted in his husky voice.

The twins, child number eight and nine, spoke in unison, 'The maid's a liar and a thief. We don't know how much she has already pilfered from our legacy.'

'I hate to have to say this, but father has never truly been a good father to us. How can we honour and respect him if he treats us this way?' child number five piped up.

'And he never spends any time with us. He would rather open his noodle shop even on Sundays,' child number four said. 'It's more sinful than not keeping the Sabbath Day holy.'

Child number six, who was known for his instigative and cowardly nature, stepped in at this juncture with the ultimate suggestion, swaying the rest to the truth that was begging to be spoken. 'We should have had the maid killed. Father would have been so heartbroken that he would have lost the will to live and would have left all his possessions to us. Since we did not do that, perhaps we should consider ending a senile old man's unproductive life instead.'

The other siblings pondered on this Machiavellian scheme that none of them had been brave enough to voice, although they had all heard that little voice in their heads suggesting the exact same thing.

'If that's the case, we'll just have to do it ourselves. No one else needs to know,' said child number six.

'But who?' child number one asked.

'A lottery. The one who picks the slip of paper with a black dot will deal with father, in any way they like,' child number six said.

No one agreed, but no one objected.

Child number six used a biro to mark a black dot on a piece of paper. He then crumpled ten similar sized papers, concealing a blank one under his thumb and cupped the rest in his chubby white hands and shook the paper balls as one would do with dice. He then offered these to his siblings, 'Everyone, take one.'

The brothers and sisters took turns to pick up a scrunched-up paper ball and waited for the rest to do the same. As soon as each had one, they unfurled their bits of paper simultaneously. Some doing it quickly; some taking their time.

'Goddammit! This is not fair,' child number three swore. 'Let's vote again.'

'No, the voting's done.'

* * *

Mr Bok woke up one dreary morning to find that his heart ached for no good reason. He knew that a bad day was coming and that it was to be one of the many bad days to follow. He noticed that there was nothing on his bedside table. It was completely empty, which was very strange because Asih always placed a glass of fruit juice here every morning. The juice would always fill him with the hope that he was worth the trouble and that his existence was acknowledged; he wasn't a mere figment of someone's imagination. But, on that dreadful day, he was erased from the world as he knew it. Asih was gone.

He wanted to disown all his children then and there for having done the unthinkable, but he was too weak to even fend for himself. Devastated by the cruelty of his children, he locked himself in his bedroom to bemoan his tragic life. Had he but known the repercussions of having children, he would have remained single and celibate from the start. Now, he didn't know what he could do to get his covetous children off his back. They were like vultures circling around his dilapidated body, hungry for the taste of carrion.

Three days after the disappearance of Asih, he emerged from his bedroom and walked to his garden on a bright beautiful sunny day. The sun was already searing everything in its path at seven in the morning. It was going to be one of those very hot and humid days. With the help of a walking stick he trudged to the largest, loveliest papaya tree with the rope of interwoven raffia strings in his hand. He looped one end into a noose and fastened the other end around the trunk. As soon as it was secured, he stood on the tips of his toes and reached for the noose which hung slightly above his neck. As he inserted his head into the noose, his eyes filled with tears remembering how wonderful it had been when Asih had been around; telling him stories; sharing the laughter; nurturing the garden and harvesting the fruits of her labour.

Long ago, when his first savings had multiplied through fixed deposits, he had bought his beloved wife a gold necklace as a treat. He didn't know then that it was to be the start of a horrendous journey into an abyss. His wife's simple disposition had transmogrified into a monster of avarice. She wanted more. What started out as a simple gift became a compulsion for all things gold. She collected, hoarded and gloated over them like an obsessive collector of rare and expensive artefacts. The idea was to have more, not just to have.

At some point Mr Bok gave up trying to please her and continued with his husbandly duties of merely providing the essentials and keeping the home fires burning. Other than that, he maintained an aloof distance from her. She tried her best to win him back by producing one child every year, but Mr Bok remained impervious and distant. His love for her dwindled with every purchase, with every transaction and with the birth of every child.

Mr Bok shed his last few tears and tightened the noose around his scrawny neck. The raffia strings ate into his flesh as he lowered his head down, waiting for gravity to kick in. Although he was an emaciated old man, the papaya tree bent down with his weight until his feet once again touched the ground. He held on to the raffia rope and raised his legs up as high as he could.

He choked, went into a fit of coughing and his breathing grew laboured. Each time his feet touched the ground he struggled to curl them back up again. He continued with this gruesome exercise repeatedly because he did not lose consciousness immediately. His feet rose and fell as he struggled in this macabre dance of death. He didn't want to be found half dead and then revived at the hospital. It would be a cruel joke indeed if he ended up surviving.

After battling against gravity for a while, he finally lifted his knees and locked his hands beneath them. He swayed with the momentum of his body as he was tossed about like a bottle lost at sea. By now, the raffia strings were cutting into his skin and drawing blood. He endured the agony by closing his eyes and dreaming of a time when his life was simple but full of magical moments. He focused on those fleeting instances and surrendered to the final throes of death. The pain that ate into his neck and cut off the air supply was gone. It didn't hurt anymore. And while rigor mortis set in, he held himself in the foetal position until he was frozen in time.

Child number three was a nervous wreck when he woke up the next morning. The only way he could think of committing this murder was to lace his father's food with rat poison. He didn't know how long it would take to end his father's life. He hadn't a clue whether it tasted bad, had an aftertaste or if it left a residue behind that could be discovered by the pathologist during the autopsy. He was, after all, not a murderer. He psyched himself up and mixed the poison into a bowl of oats. He didn't know whether his father liked oats and whether he ate them at all. None of his siblings knew much about their father. Their only mistake was not asking Asih for information before sending her packing. It would have helped a great deal.

'Shit.'

What if father knows what I am about to do to him?

'Dammit!'

What if the others use me as a scapegoat and blame me when the police come to investigate?

'Bloody fool!'

I had better get this over and done with before I lose my nerve.

He sneaked into the kitchen and saw the mess that his siblings had left behind. There was no maid anymore to tidy up after them.

His shoulders slumped and he heaved a sigh tinged with regret. If they didn't resolve this minor issue of cleaning up immediately, it could escalate into a full-scale family dispute. None of them wanted to hire any kind of help if it meant they had to pay for it out of their own pockets. He had no choice but to ignore the chaos in the kitchen that wouldn't have been there if Asih had still been around.

He picked out a clean bowl with a chicken design on the sides and filled it with oats. He picked up one of the many flasks to get some hot water, but every single one of them was very light—obviously empty. And that could only mean one thing—no one had bothered to refill the hot water in the flasks. Still half-asleep and extremely frustrated by now, he reached for the last flask, muttering under his breath, 'If this one is empty, I'm going right back to bed. And to hell with poisoning father!'

He didn't expect it to be full and he almost dropped it in surprise at the sheer difference in weight. His heart skipped a beat at the near accident and then skipped another beat at the thought of now having no choice but to go through with the patricide. He hurriedly poured the hot water into the bowl and stirred the oats into a broth. When the consistency was right. he added the liquid rat poison. Unsure of the right quantity of poison to use, he poured in a generous dollop into the porridge, that unfortunately made the consistency of the oats too watery.

A chilling cry wafted through the cold morning air. It made him jump and he accidentally spilled some of the oats on to the table. He didn't know whether he should carry the bowl with him or leave it on the table and go out to check on the commotion. After walking back and forth a few times indecisively, he finally decided to take the bowl with him in case someone inadvertently ate the porridge in his absence.

'Who stole my gold? Which one of you stole my gold?' screeched Mother Bok, standing in the middle of the courtyard, her high-pitched shriek nearly shattering the window panes of the house. 'One of you is a thief!' Mother Bok screamed repeatedly like a broken record until all her children and in-laws gathered around her in alarm. Her eyes searched wildly for the two people whom she had come to loathe, but they were both absent.

Everyone living under the roof lumbered out of their rooms lazily, knowing very well that Mother Bok had to have her little drama every day. They poured out of the fifteen-room mansion in their night clothes, heavy with sleep and frustration.

'Mother, what is wrong?'

'My gold. All of my gold is missing! Which one of you took it?'

Mother Bok saw the guilt in all their eyes, young and old. She knew they wouldn't dare do it, but she was also aware that they were all opportunistic sycophants.

'The guilty party had better own up or I will call the police.'

Wild accusations flew in all directions. Every envious ill-feeling harboured against one another erupted like a punctured pus boil. In a torrent of foul words and vituperative curses, dark secrets were revealed. Extra marital affairs, sexual deviances and immorality were aired like so much dirty linen for all to see. It wasn't until child number three suddenly remembered his assignment that he left the family feud to look for his father. He was afraid the racket would wake him up and he would lose a golden opportunity to euthanize the old man who was teetering on the brink of dementia.

Bowl in hand, he crept as quietly and as quickly as he could to his father's room. When he knocked softly on the door, there was no answer. He peered around the door, but the room was empty. The bed was clean and well-made.

'Father?'

He peeped into the bathroom, but that was empty as well.

Where could the old man have gone? In his condition, it couldn't be too far.

He left the bowl of oats on the bedside table and returned to the squabbling family to make the announcement.

'Father's gone! Father's gone!'

'What are you talking about?' Mother Bok demanded.

'He's not in his room.'

'So? He could be in the garden. Why are you bothering us now? My missing gold is more important than a missing old man.'

Child number three retreated and the family carried on with their marathon of finger-pointing and fault-finding.

Having second thoughts, Mother Bok decided to seek out her husband for some answers too.

'Has anyone seen father?'

All her children stole a quick glance at child number three, but he shrugged.

'He may know something about the missing gold,' she snorted and swept into the garden. 'I'm going to get to the bottom of this right now.'

Her children dispersed in her wake to search every inch of the large garden. It was demarcated by several varieties of papaya trees.

Mother Bok spotted her husband in one of the taller trees but couldn't, for the life of her, understand why he was standing in such an odd position.

'Bok,' she called and headed straight for him, 'where is my gold?' She noticed that he seemed to be swaying in the light breeze and she huffed at the peculiar tableau. 'What are you doing?'

The large papaya leaves screened Mr Bok partially and she had to crane her neck up and sideways to figure out why her husband was contorted in such a weird manner.

'Bok, answer me!'

When she drew closer, she stumbled on the Cthulhu-like roots of the papaya tree and only then noticed the raffia rope around his neck gleaming in the morning sun.

Her screams were stifled for a moment as she gasped and then the loudest and strongest screech ripped through the neighbourhood.

The two policemen who arrived at the scene were baffled at the way Mr Bok was curled to allow the raffia rope to work its way around his throat and obstruct his air passage. It was almost like a fluke that the cord fitted so perfectly into the folds of the old man's neck. But death hadn't come easy. It would have taken a lot of effort for him to hang on while the raffia ate its way into his throat.

Before long the police backup arrived to help them bring the corpse down from the tree. However, not all the scissors and knives in the world could cut through the taut raffia. They even tried to bring down the papaya tree with a *parang* (a Malayan machete), an axe and a saw, but somehow the trunk withstood all assaults and proved to be tougher than buffalo hide.

The strange phenomenon attracted the neighbours, the press and more police officers as word spread about how old man Bok had managed to hang himself from a papaya tree. While this was underway, the family kept to themselves and sequestered themselves inside the house to avoid inquisitive people. Mother Bok's heart was broken thinking about her missing gold and the way her children were already staking their claim to the one and only visible property: the mansion they called home.

'Now that father's gone, I will take charge of everything. After all, I am the oldest,' child number one said and raised a clenched fist for all his siblings to see. 'This mansion belongs to me and my family.'

'What gives you the right?' child number ten argued. 'What about our share.'

'There is no "our" share. Father said he was leaving us nothing and even the gold is gone now,' child number seven said. 'That hussy of a maid must have made off with everything when she left.'

'Let's just sell this mansion and split it ten ways. That's only fair,' child number two said. 'I need to maintain my beauty until I can get rich suitor who can take care of me.'

'Goddammit! I don't want to sell this house. I want to live here. There's not going to be another place like this. Besides, I almost did father in if he hadn't beaten me to it,' child number three protested, 'I choose not to sell.'

'Over my dead body,' child number six said.

'I am ruined!' Mother Bok screamed at the top of her lungs and her children quietened down when they noticed the lighter in her hand. 'All my gold is gone. Your father left us nothing but this mansion. And if none of you can agree on what to do with it then we shall all own nothing.'

'Mother, why are you doing—'

'Gas, I smell gas.'

'Get out! Mother's going to burn the house down.'

'Mother, no!'

'Run!'

Mother Bok clicked the lighter and tossed it at the handmade, embroidered drapes over the French window.

* * *

Everyone who had gathered to see old man Bok hanging from the papaya tree said the explosion was spectacular. They watched the family rush out, carrying Mother Bok. The magnificent mansion, adorned with knick-knacks and ornaments from all over the world—most of which were made of fire hazard materials—was engulfed in flames of crimson and scarlet, lemon and gold, silver and ebony. The rubberneckers stood around in awe watching it burn and crackle beneath a cerulean sky and forgot all about poor Mr Bok. In a matter of minutes, the mansion, along with the bowl of poisoned porridge, was reduced to a pile of ashes and debris, and no fire hydrant or fire truck could save it.

In all the excitement and confusion, a five-year-old boy noticed the raffia rope slowly give way in the intense heat. It eventually snapped and Mr Bok fell to the ground amidst the chaos.

After the triple tragedy, the Bok family went their separate ways and broke off all family ties with one another. Mother Bok stayed with the eldest son because it was a traditional norm. For years after the incident everyone talked about the mansion that had been burnt to the ground on the day that Mr Bok hanged himself. No one could explain why, but Mr Bok was soon included in Taiping's inventory of nightmare legends.

* * *

'People who knew this story never planted papaya trees in their garden. And if they noticed one bent at the top, they would immediately chop it down and uproot it. It was rumoured that a bent papaya tree was inviting you to hang yourself,' Jackson said, wrapping both his hands around his neck.

'I'm going to stay away from papaya trees from now on.'

'Heck, I'm going to stop eating papaya altogether.'

'Whatever happened to the Indonesian maid?'

'Beats me,' Jackson said. 'Some people say she put a curse on the papaya trees before she left. But it's anyone guess what she did, or didn't, do.'

* * *

Asih continued planting papaya trees in honour of Mr Bok who gave her a good life in Malaysia although it was short-lived. When she learnt about his suicide, she cried to herself for several weeks, all alone in her room. No one understood what she was going through. They assumed that she had had an affair with the old man because it seemed unlikely for a young woman and an old man to have anything in common. They never understood her invaluable friendship with the old man who taught her to appreciate the little things in life. Even when they did, they were sceptical of such a friendship. Only she knew how wonderful he was as a friend and a confidant.

She decided to remain in her village, although her family encouraged her to return to Malaysia with the hope of finding another kind employer like old Mr Bok. She didn't tell anybody about how Mr Bok's family had conspired to dismiss her without notice, compensation or references. It would only worry her family.

She took a few weeks' break from work and stayed at home to gently nurture her small kitchen garden of herbs and vegetables and try to restore it to life. It didn't produce much and wasn't sufficient to provide for her family, leave alone generate a surplus to be sold at the market. But, secretly, she was delighted to see the plants grow from seed to harvest; from cuttings to fruition. One of the most wonderful trees in her garden was the papaya trees. She hadn't realized that some of the seeds she sowed for Mr Bok had got packed along with her things when she hurriedly departed from the mansion. She planted them in her yard as homage to the old man and they actually took root and grew.

The papayas grew faster than usual and they were bloated as though fed with some super fertilizer. One day she chose one of the fattened, golden fruits and brought it into the kitchen to prepare a dessert. The papaya was extremely heavy and she had to use both hands to carry it. She placed it on the cutting board and sliced it open with a sharp knife, but the knife got stuck half way through. She carefully re-angled the knife and tried again a couple of times before she could finally split open the large fruit.

The papaya seeds glinted in the sunlight; there was only one metal that could glow this way. She scooped them up with her hands and felt the weight of the golden seeds. She had so many questions, but she knew the answer in her heart; it was a simple one that needed no explanation.

4

Jaga Jaga

'My brother said his friend's friend told him this story and then he told me,' said Poh.

'Since the story changed hands so many times, are you sure you'll get it right?'

'Of course,' Poh replied, a smug look on his face, but it was lost in the darkness that surrounded them. Some of the boys giggled, but Poh continued with confidence.

'This boy, Irfan, almost died in our school.'

'What?'

'Really?'

'Who is he? I've never heard of him.'

'Must be our senior.'

Poh weighed in abruptly at this juncture, to stop them from interrupting him, 'He wanted to jump from the third floor.'

'Did he?'

'No. He was saved.'

'Yeah, I heard that the third floor is haunted.'

'He might have become just another statistic had it not been for a ghost.'

* * *

Irfan thought it would be easier this way. It would definitely solve all his problems. He wasn't good in his studies or in sports. He wasn't as sociable and popular as the rest of the boys. Most of all, he had no friends. No one that he could confide in. Especially not about the thing that was bothering him.

He was surprised at how easy it was to get into the school grounds after hours. The badminton and basketball courts looked frightening with innumerable shadows and shapes merging into one another, to make them look like something different altogether. There were usually a few security guards in the vicinity, but that night they were nowhere to be seen, so he didn't even have to creep around. He just walked through the unlocked gate, headed for the stairs to the third floor, and found the corner that he usually went to when he was feeling down. It was the corner that the rest of the boys claimed was haunted, but he didn't care; although, at times, it did feel a bit spooky.

During the many times that he had hung out at that very corner contemplating his life, he hadn't seen any ghostly apparitions, nor had he felt his hair stand on end. The only thing peculiar about that corner was how breezy and cold it was even in the searing afternoon sun. Perhaps there was a scientific explanation for this strange phenomenon. Perhaps it was something architectural. But, paranormal? No, he wasn't convinced.

Now that he was looking down at the ground from the third-floor corridor, he felt a twinge of fear. He thought he could do it without a second thought, but now he was beginning to feel weak in his knees. He scanned the corridor for any sign of security guards, but there was none. If he were caught, he would take it as an omen that he shouldn't go through with it, but if not, this was what was destined. If only he had ideas that would help to turn things around . . . but he didn't and it all seemed quite hopeless. He could see no other way out. He climbed on to the stone balustrade and steadied himself with his back to the wall. It didn't seem like a long drop, but it was dizzying nevertheless. The night sky was resplendent and remarkable as always, but it served no purpose for him anymore.

He stared at the ground that would or would not end his life. He could suffer multiple fractures, but survive anyway, or he could break his neck and be paralyzed for life. Or he could die even before he hit the ground. It was all a game of chance and he was willing to play. He took a step forward, climbed on the balustrade, and dangled his foot in mid-air. His heartbeat was irregular from all the indecision, fear, and vertigo.

'Hey, come down from there!' A huge man in a large white turban signalled imperiously to Irfan. The man's sudden appearance shocked him because he wasn't expecting to see anyone and he hadn't heard him approaching.

'Come down,' the man yelled again and waved to Irfan to get off the balustrade. 'What are you doing there? Do you want to fall over?'

Irfan lowered himself back on to the balustrade. His knees buckling both from the shock of nearly plummeting down and suddenly seeing the large turbaned stranger who had appeared out of thin air. He took a deep breath and scrambled off the balustrade into the corridor. He was a foot shorter than the man.

'Why did you climb up there?'

Irfan was a little annoyed by the man's interference and screwed up his courage to demand, 'Who are you?'

'I'm the school *jaga*, Mr Singh. Who are you and what are you doing here? Don't you know you're not supposed to be here at this time of night?'

Irfan could not see Mr Singh quite clearly in the shadows but from what he could make out, he was a fierce-looking man with beetling eyebrows, a handlebar moustache, and a bushy but well-groomed beard. His eyes began to brim with tears from the inquisition, for the shame of being exposed. The truth was now just a question away.

'I'm sorry. I just want to go home, Mr Singh.'

'You boys are always giving me problems. If you had fallen down, do you know how much trouble I would have been in? Everyone would have assumed it was my fault. I only come in at night to *jaga* the school and if anything had happened to you, I would have lost my job!'

Irfan couldn't hold back his tears back any longer and he let it all out in streams of agony and denial. Mr Singh stepped out of the darkness and patted him on the back. Irfan embraced the giant security guard and cried like a baby. He didn't care whose arms they were, he just needed to confide in someone but couldn't find a sympathetic person who could help him exorcise the demon that was gnawing at him from within. He could smell rancid milk on Mr Singh but it was nothing to the enormous comfort he felt in his presence.

After a hearty bout of tears, Irfan drew away from Mr Singh, feeling embarrassed to have hugged a stranger.

'I'm sorry. I didn't mean to breakdown like this.'

'You do what you must,' Mr Singh replied gently.

Irfan looked at the full moon which illuminated his skin in a surreal glow. He turned to look at Mr Singh and noticed that he had an aura around him, making him look like an angel.

Perhaps he was one, Irfan thought. If it hadn't been for Mr Singh, he would be either dead or dying by now.

'What are you doing here at a time like this?'

Irfan wanted to confess to Mr Singh about his suicidal wish but he didn't want to get into any more trouble than he already was in.

'I couldn't sleep and I . . .' Irfan carefully chose his next few words, '. . . just wanted to hang out.'

'Here?'

'It's th-the safest place I know.'

Mr Singh sighed and said, 'It's not safe for you to be out at this time of night. You had better go back home quickly and take a good rest.'

Irfan nodded and strolled away, not knowing whether he should thank the guard or apologize to him. The long dark corridors were not as menacing as everyone said they were. With Mr Singh keeping an eye on the school, everyone should be able to sleep peacefully at night. Irfan was well on his way down the stairs when he wondered why there was only one guard to cover such an enormous school. There were too many hidden corners and isolated blocks for a solitary guard to inspect all by himself.

When he reached the ground floor, he saw the badminton and basketball courts brightly lit up by the moonlight. He liked the peace and tranquillity that was usually not there during school hours. It did not appear as ominous as it had when he had arrived a little while ago. He was about to walk down to the gates, when he heard voices at a distance. He hid behind a pillar to stake out the source and determine whether they belonged to any hostiles. He saw two other security guards smoking and chatting by the school canteen. He didn't want to go through another interrogation, so he slipped into the shadows to get to the exit. This time he found that the gates were locked so he climbed over them and ran to his bicycle which was stashed in a bush.

The night air was cool and he felt good. The yoke he was carrying was lifted from his shoulders and there was only one person to be grateful to. He wondered whether he should go back to thank Mr Singh someday.

* * *

The school wore a completely different look in the morning and teeming with people. No classroom or corridor was empty. Teachers, students, the administrative staff and other workers milled around everywhere and there was no place to find a moment's solitude to just breathe. Irfan felt uncomfortable knowing that what he had wanted to do was just a few hours ago. If Mr Singh hadn't intervened, he would have made headlines in the school and in the morning news. He couldn't imagine how his suicide might have impacted others. He had always been invisible: one of the average Joes who was easily overlooked. Or more like one of those John Does who could not be identified and remained unclaimed.

'Hey Fan, what are you staring at?'

He started at the high-pitched voice that came at him like a bullet. That voice could be from the one and only Shaz.

'What?' Irfan snapped at him.

'You've been standing there staring at the third floor for some reason. You're drawing everyone's attention to look up with you. What kind of a prank are you pulling?' Shaz chuckled in his bird-like voice.

Irfan glanced around and saw eyes quickly averting their gaze. 'Oh, shit.'

Shaz laughed and asked again, 'So, what were you staring at?'

'Nothing. I was just . . . just daydreaming.' Irfan walked away from being the cynosure of all eyes, but he turned to Shaz for one last question, 'do you know anything about Mr Singh?'

'Is he a new teacher?'

'No, the school *jaga*.'

'They've got a new *jaga*?'

'I . . . uh, never mind.'

'Mr Chew should know these things. He's from Human Resources so he might be resourceful,' Shaz giggled at his own wit. 'Why do you want to know, anyway?' Shaz wanted to squeeze the last drop of juice out of tasty gossip if there was any.

'Curious.'

Irfan didn't want to spice up the conversation any more than he wanted to spark off a rumour with a gossipmonger like Shaz. It had been a mistake to ask him anything in the first place, but at least Shaz had given him a lead—Mr Chew. He liked the administrative staff even less than the teachers and the other students. How was he going to get anything out of Mr Chew?

* * *

Irfan was as restless as a piece of paper caught up in a whirlwind the entire day. For one, he hadn't resolved what was bothering him and it was gutting him from inside, and then there was the case of bumping into Mr Singh that made him uneasy. Although most of the students hardly knew any of the menial staff, he could not forget how the night *jaga* had saved his life. He wanted to thank the man, but didn't want to make a big song and dance about it. It could end up making things even worse for him if Mr Singh told on him. He didn't know whether he should show his gratitude or put the whole incident behind him and forget about it.

At the end of the school day, he decided against it although he had been eyeing Mr Chew like a stalker. He was planning his approach; putting together an innocuous story so as to not raise any suspicions; working on the dialogue with carefully selected words. That was when he made up his mind to come back in the night to look for Mr Singh instead.

'Boy, what do you want?' Mr Chew asked while Irfan was still contemplating his move outside the staff room, 'Do you want to see me?'

'I, er . . . I . . .'

'What's the complaint this time?'

'Complaint?'

'Students only come to me to complain. I am the most unpopular person in the school,' Mr Chew said and bared his teeth in a semi-smile, semi-offended look. 'Come, come I don't have all day.'

'It's about the security guard.'

'We already fired him.'

'What?'

'We found out the claims were true, so we fired him on the spot. You don't have to worry about him anymore. He won't be threatening you boys from now on.'

Mr Chew pursed his lips and pulled his nose a few times to get rid of something invisible.

'Did you find someone to replace him?'

'Yes, didn't you see the two new guards? They would rather have half the pay and work together than to have full pay and work alone.'

'Is one of them Mr Singh?' Irfan found the perfect opening for his question.

'Mr Singh? Mr Singh? I haven't heard that name for a long time,' Mr Chew scratched his head and wiped his nose. 'What about Mr Singh?'

'Does he work here?'

'He worked here a long time ago. But he died when he fell over the balustrade on the second floor when he was drunk. Why?'

Irfan's knees buckled.

'Why do you look sick suddenly?'

'I . . . I think I had better go.'

'What's your name, boy?'

'Ir . . . Irfan.'

'Tell me,' Mr Chew said and paused when their eyes met awkwardly, 'have you seen Mr Singh?'

Irfan felt his world crash around him.

'Come inside my office.'

Mr Chew walked away, and Irfan followed him into the tiger balm scented room with a few tables that had stacks of papers piled high like mesas. The other staff had gone home, but their bored insipid presence lingered on.

'Sit down,' Mr Chew metamorphosed into a completely different person. Irfan obeyed and he picked up the loose sheets of paper lying on the chair and arranged them neatly on Mr Chew's table. 'Where did you see Mr Singh?'

Irfan was reluctant to divulge the encounter because there was going to be a lot of explaining to do. He thought about it and tried to mouth the right words, but he couldn't think of any.

'Okay, let me rephrase that question. You have seen Mr Singh, haven't you?'

Irfan responded with a very faint nod.

'You're not the first and you won't be the last. Some of the staff have seen him too. Most of the time they only see him passing by, but a few have actually spoken to him thinking he was a new staff member. They only realized that he was a ghost when he ignored them and vanished into walls or into thin air.' Mr Chew sighed and cracked all his knuckles simultaneously by bending his interlocked hands backwards.

'You're one of the very few students who have seen Mr Singh's ghost. I guess it's pointless to hide anything from you. I'm not supposed to say this, but we covered up Mr Singh's death.' Irfan didn't seem surprised and this seemed to irk Mr Chew. 'We didn't want the students to ... you know ... be afraid or disturbed by the incident. When I discovered Mr Singh's body in the morning, I couldn't believe what had happened. I had seen him the night before when he came in to start his duty. We even acknowledged each other but I could smell the liquor on him. He confessed to me that he was trying very hard to quit but I guess he hadn't tried hard enough. Sometimes I wonder whether I could have done more to prevent his death.'

'How do you know he fell?' asked Irfan, leaning towards Mr Chew. It frightened the middle-aged man to see a seventeen-year-old boy taking such a keen interest.

'The police said so,' Mr. Chew defended. 'Also, the coroner.'

'How long ago was that?'

'A long, long time ago. I can't remember. Ten years ago? Fifteen years ago? I don't know. But before you even stepped foot into this school.'

'Have you seen him Mr Chew?'

'No! No, thanks! I don't want to. I might just get a heart attack and die on the spot!' Mr Chew flapped his hands like was trying to shoo away the bad luck.

'People who have seen him, did anything bad happen to them?'

'They're still alive, if you must know, so you have nothing to worry about.'

'It's not that. He seemed like a nice man—' Irfan stopped talking as soon as he realized he was giving away too much information.

Mr Chew wiped an invisible cobweb from his face and bared his teeth that could indicate either concern or disgust.

'Look, I know it's not something you want to discuss because of the nature of the circumstances. Other than hearing you out, I can't help you much. If you need to talk to someone, perhaps you could try the school counsellor.' Mr Chew's face sagged with empathy and he pulled his nose a few times to show his helplessness.

'It's okay, Mr Chew, I'm fine.'

'You're braver than the two new security guards. We can't even get them to go up to the third floor. Is that where you saw Mr Singh? He is sometimes seen doing his rounds up on the third floor. If word got out, it could cause a panic or mass hysteria.'

'I understand.'

'I don't know why some people can see ghosts but others can't. Whatever it is, I hope you don't see him anymore.'

Irfan nodded but wasn't too sure whether he agreed. To think that he spoke to a ghost was frightening enough, but Mr Singh hadn't seemed like he was out for blood or vengeance.

'As they say, perhaps it's time to change your luck. Stay away from the place you saw him,' Mr Chew said, but Irfan was already making plans to come back to the school at the right time and the right place.

* * *

Just like the night before, Irfan walked into the school without any hindrance. The two new security guards were prattling away in the open-spaced school canteen and not minding the other floors for fear of bumping into Mr Singh.

The colonial-style building with the Gothic structure, short of gargoyles perched on the corners and ledges, was enthralling by night. The way the shadows cast black-and-white impressions, the elegance of the pillars and the way the corridors diminished into infinity were breathtaking to an artistic eye. But to one who was afraid of things that lurked in the darkness, it was the perfect setting for all kinds of anxieties and phobias.

Irfan felt a chill in his heart at the thought of meeting Mr Singh again. He didn't look forward to talking to a ghost, but he was curious. He wanted to know if the *jaga* accidentally fell or if he was pushed. This little mystery gave him a reason to temporarily put aside his troubles and at least try to solve the enigma. After he got past the guards, he headed for the stairs that led to the third floor.

The stray beams of light from the neighbouring buildings and street lamps paved a sinister walkway of alternating light and darkness between the columns. Irfan stepped cautiously into the phantasmagoric realm, battling mixed feelings about meeting Mr Singh. He darted his eyes from side to side to catch a glimpse of everything that moved. He didn't want to be oblivious to his surroundings for he hated jump scares more than anything else. It was a thing that the other boys played on one another for kicks, like what the horror movies throw at you. It was an unnecessary adrenaline rush. To calm his nerves down he called out to the ghost instead of imagining every rustle and thud to be something that it wasn't.

'Mr Singh.'

His call was like a whistle in the wind. Gone even before it was heard. He shuddered as he approached his favourite corner where the darkness was opaque, calling, 'Mr Singh . . .'

It was quiet except for the occasional solitary cricket or the faint flutter of a bat's wings. Irfan changed his mind. What he was doing was crazy. Nobody wants to see ghosts, let alone communicate with them. The temperature dropped and the chills rose. It felt like a soul trying to re-enter its body after it got sucked out into a nightmare.

The drumming in his chest quickened and was loud enough to be heard, almost simulating a familiar tune. When he turned around to look, it was Mr Singh tapping his fingers on the balustrade to a bhangra rhythm. It wasn't his heart's quickening, after all.

'Boy, what are you doing here again?'

'M-Mr Singh. I-I want to thank you for, for—'

'Saving you? I already know that. If you are not planning to attempt it again, why do you come out here in the middle of the night?'

'How did you . . . know?'

'How could I not? Isn't it obvious?'

Irfan shied away from the question, but his nerves were still knotted by a fear of the unknown.

'Mr Singh . . . you do know that you are—' Irfan could not bring himself to say the word, so the *jaga* completed it for him.

'Dead?'

'Er . . .'

'A ghost?' Mr Singh said and walked into a brighter spot to expose himself in an ethereal glow.

'Then, why are you still here?'

Mr Singh's surreal image blended into the background like a watercolour painting when he walked past Irfan and leaned over the balustrade.

'This is where I died,' he pointed to the ground that no longer held any traces or markings of his obscure death.

'Did someone push you?'

'Did you know that this school is still haunted by the remnants of World War II?' he countered with a question.

'I heard a rumour.'

'It is no rumour. The Japanese killed and buried a lot of people under the school hall. When I was a *jaga* here I used to see the old teachers and Japanese soldiers moving around as though they were still alive. Wounded, limbless, headless, they were unrestful spirits. And not all of them were friendly.

'I needed the job and the only way to get through the night was to drink myself into a stupor. My fall was inevitable because I was drunk most of the time. I should have tried something different, but it's too late now. I used to blame the ghosts for turning me into a drunkard but I was trying to fill a void in my life with an elixir to make me forget.'

Irfan was too young to understand regrets, but he could empathize with Mr Singh. He knew what emptiness felt like.

'Is your life so worthless?' Mr Singh asked Irfan unexpectedly and startled him into a string of stuttering half-responses.

'I . . . I . . . but . . . I . . .'

'Is it so bad that you have to contemplate death?'

Irfan broke down instantly because no one had asked him that question before. They spent the next few minutes listening to Irfan's sobs and sniffles for no words could bridge the lack of communication from either one. Mr Singh stood beside him in support, looking radiant and distinguished in the night.

'I'm s-sorry . . .' Irfan managed to say between sobs and hiccups.

'Apologize only when necessary. You have done nothing wrong.'

'But I feel like I have,' he wiped his nose with the back of his hand and then continued mopping his face with his sleeves.

'When I was alive, I used to wonder if my family loved me for being a lowly, poorly-paid *jaga*. My daughter especially. I had never had a good education and I doubted myself my whole life. I did all kinds of menial jobs to make ends meet. I felt like I had let my daughter down because I couldn't be a father she could be proud of. People always referred to her as the jaga's daughter. That kind of state of mind led me to believe the worst. Don't do that to yourself.'

Irfan listened intently, sniffling only at intervals. He felt as if the yoke he was carrying had been eased a little, and he never felt better in his life since the incident as he did now.

'It was this teacher,' Irfan said. 'He tricked me into going to his house and then started showing me porn.' Irfan shook his head vigorously to stop himself from reliving that guilt-ridden and humiliating experience. 'I feel so stupid. I should have known, but I didn't do anything.' Irfan began to tear up again, making him choke on his words before they could be spoken.

'I know that teacher,' Mr Singh said, and Irfan stared at the image that was dreamlike.

'Y-you know?'

'We all know.'

'But . . .'

'And we did nothing. We all thought it was okay for boys. Boys are tough. Boys can take care of themselves. Boys are never the victims,' Mr Singh said, and stood in front of the moon that looked like a halo over his head. 'I should have done something when I heard that one of the teachers was violating the boys, but none of us wanted to get on the bad side of the teacher. He was, and still is, I suppose, a well-respected man with contacts all over town and could get you out of trouble as easily as he could get you into it.'

'I hate myself for not being strong enough to . . . I mean he didn't force himself on me and . . . and I could have fought him, but I didn't . . .'

'You're just a kid. You don't know any better. That's why they prey on children.'

'I feel helpless . . . like anything I do is wrong and pointless.'

'Find a way to get through this and forgive yourself. Focus on the things you want in life. Whatever we do today affects us in future.'

'But what will become of me? Am I ever going to be able to have a normal life? '

'Killing yourself won't solve anything. If you die, you'll be earthbound like the Japanese soldiers and all the other victims of war and suicide. Do something instead of whining or taking the easy way out.'

Irfan didn't like what he heard. Mr Singh wouldn't understand what it was like to be in his shoes and why was he being so admonitory, anyway, instead of understanding his plight?

'I have to go,' Irfan said curtly and started walking away.

'No one can help you if you don't help yourself.'

'How can I help myself when I feel like shit?!' Irfan halted to make his point.

'If you want to get through this, get help. Do you want to end up as a ghost who relives the same problem for all eternity, but can do nothing about it?'

Irfan shuddered at the thought. He wondered if Mr Singh was now talking about himself. Perhaps this explained his annoyance.

'Did you have something you wanted to do when you were . . . alive?'

'There were a lot of things I wanted to do. So many things I would have done differently. But there is only one thing now that is making me regret every moment that I am still here. My daughter, Gouri.'

The *jaga* drummed the balustrade with his fingers.

'I wish I had been a better father. I wish I could somehow let her know that I did my best to provide for her. And I hope that she was proud of whatever little I did do for her. These are my chains.'

Mr Singh moved back and merged with the darkness, the drumming fading with him.

'Mr Singh wait.'

But he was already gone. The corridor on the third floor was silent although the cold still lingered.

* * *

Irfan didn't know what was real anymore: the fact that he had had a tête-à-tête with a ghost or the fact that he could have died just a few days ago. What he used to perceive as reality was now another illusion. Developing anthropophobia was something he never expected while growing up to be an adult. The distance between him and the people around him increased each day. The self-inflicted and superficial cuts, well-hidden under his clothes, were scaring him deeper each time he thought about the incident with the teacher. If he hadn't met Mr Singh it would have only been a matter of time before a cut sliced through a vein.

He spent his day ruminating about what Mr Singh said. Getting help was the last thing on his mind and in a small town like this, there usually wasn't any form of help—not any that he knew of anyway. The only thing that was stuck in his head was the name, Gouri. She was the last link holding Mr Singh back. He had died a long time ago, so his daughter could be about his age. Irfan needed to know. Even if he could not get his life together, he could at least help deliver a message from the other side. But where should he start?

'Mr Chew,' he said under his breath.

* * *

'Why do you want to know about Mr Singh?' Mr Chew blinked rapidly to get rid of the dry eye syndrome that affected him frequently.

'Can you help me without asking questions?'

'Hmm,' Mr Chew wiped his nose and pondered the question. He wanted in on the mystery, but if he didn't offer his help, the boy could leave him with nothing more than crumbs of curiosity that would haunt him forever. 'It's not illegal is it?'

'No, no, nothing like that.'

'You're not going to disturb the family, are you?'

'No, Mr Chew. I just want to know find Gouri . . .'

'Gouri? How do you know about her?'

Irfan was disinclined to reveal the truth, but he knew there had to be a price even for a small favour. He said, 'Mr Singh told me.'

Mr Chew's eyes almost popped out of his head when he heard that. Irfan was not only seeing a ghost, he was communicating with it!

'Are you sure you know what you are doing?'

'I'm sure.'

'Don't mess around with things you don't know and don't understand.'

'I'm not messing around with anything, Mr Chew. I have a message for Gouri.'

Mr Chew was petrified but the last statement was what he had hoped to hear and he agreed, 'Okay. But . . .'

'But, what?'

'Did you really speak with him?'

'Yes.'

* * *

What were the chances of finding Mr Singh's daughter in the same place and that too after all these years? Irfan was worried that all this madness was merely a diversion to stop him from hurting himself . . . and that, really, he wasn't all that keen to pass the message to his daughter. But before he could second guess himself, he found himself at the door of a terrace house in Golden Hills ringing the doorbell at the pillar beside the gate.

A young girl about his age appeared behind the grille and peeped through the hexagonal patterns.

'Yes?' she asked.

'Gouri? Er, I'm looking for Gouri,' this girl was way too young to be her.

'Who are you?'

'Can I talk to you about something?'

The lanky girl with slender limbs unlocked the grille and approached the gate at the end of the short driveway.

'Are you selling something?'

'No, no, I . . . I . . .'

'Well? Are you evangelizing?'

'No, not that either.'

'So, what is it? Doing a membership drive?'

Irfan imagined hitting the sides of his head with the palms of his. He should have begun the conversation with an explanation, but it was too late to start over. Gouri laughed before he could say another word.

'I'm only joking. What's your name?'

'Irfan.'

'And you're looking for me because . . .?'

'You're Gouri?'

She nodded.

'But, but you're too young.'

'Am I supposed to be older?'

'I mean . . . I . . . I don't know how to begin.'

Gouri took pity on the boy's sad eyes and she stood at the gate to hear him out.

'Why don't you start by telling me what I have got to do with this story?'

'It's about your father.'

'But my father is . . . not with us anymore.'

'I know. He was our school *jaga*,' Gouri's eyes wavered undecidedly. When he added, 'I saw him a few days ago,' she wondered whether Irfan was pulling her leg with a tasteless joke.

Gouri could not believe what she had heard. It was one of the unlikeliest things for a stranger to come up and say, but it was also intriguing. She never really knew her father because he was hardly ever at home. The unwarranted accident that took her father's life had always been a mental drain whenever she thought about it. It didn't make any sense knowing that her father fell to his death due to his intoxication.

'What? I hope this isn't some kind of a cruel joke,' Gouri said, with a piercing look.

'No, it's true. I really saw him.'

Gouri unlocked the gate and ushered him in.

* * *

The silence took them from the gate to the living room and to the sofa. As soon as they were seated, Gouri fixed her eyes on Irfan again but they were both tongue-tied. How do you begin a conversation about ghosts?

'Your father still haunts the third floor of the school,' Irfan deciding to start with the facts. 'Some of the school staff have seen him too.' When Gouri didn't say anything, Irfan felt heat rising from his collar although he was wearing a v-neck t-shirt. 'I don't know why most other people didn't get a chance to talk to him, but I did. He said his biggest regret was not spending time with you. And he wished he had been a better father.'

'When did you see him?'

'In the middle of the night.'

Gouri was trembling with mixed emotions.

'I want to see him,' Gouri said, after digesting what Irfan had to say.

'But I don't know if I can get you into the school. You know the guards can report us, right?'

'I don't care. I want to see my father.'

'I don't know if you can see him.'

'I want to try.'

'I guess—'

'What were you doing there on the third floor of the school in the middle of the night, anyway?' Irfan fidgeted uncomfortably, but Gouri spared him the embarrassment of a long and convoluted explanation by ending the conversation abruptly. 'I'll meet you behind the school at ten tonight.'

* * *

It was just as easy as when Irfan crept in alone. The guards stationed themselves at the school canteen like clockwork, making it a painless effort for them to get in and out of the school without being harassed.

They passed the badminton courts and made it to the stairs when Irfan stalled.

'Are you sure about this?'

'Yes, yes, show me.'

Irfan was a little apprehensive when he thought of what he had done, interfering with Mr Singh's affairs and seeking out his daughter. What if Mr Singh did not want to see his daughter for some reason? What if the reunion made it harder for both of them to carry on?

'What if . . . what if your father doesn't want you to see him as a gh—as he is today?' Irfan tried to dissuade Gouri in case Mr Singh became violent for being cornered in this situation.

'Shut up already,' Gouri whispered. 'I'll be fine. My father will be fine. Don't overthink it.'

Gouri's words struck Irfan like a slap in the face. Perhaps he *was* overthinking things. Perhaps everything would be just fine. He led Gouri to the spot that had nearly become his last place on earth.

'This is it.'

Gouri looked around to see if her father's apparition would appear.

'*Apa?*' she whispered into the deathly silence.

Irfan wanted to help summon the spirit, but he knew that this was a sacred moment between the father and daughter. He wished he had someone in the family who was as close to him as her father was to Gouri, without boundaries.

'If you are here, please come forward. It's me, Gouri.'

Still no sign of the dead.

They waited a while and a cool breeze blew past them. Both shivered but neither yielded to it.

'I just want to see you one last time.'

Irfan could hear her crying in the dark and he wanted to hug her, to let her know it was going to be okay.

'You've always been a good father to me. Not once did I ever doubt you. Whatever you did, right or wrong, I know you did the best you could. I . . .'

Mr Singh came forth and stood in front of Gouri.

'*Apa!*' She wanted to run to him and throw her arms around him, but Mr Singh raised his hand to stop her.

'Gouri,' the resonance of Mr Singh's voice made it seem like a dream.

'*Apa*, I miss you.'

'And I miss you. If I could turn back time, I would do everything right this time,' Mr Singh spread his palms in a sad and helpless gesture that revealed the spectre's immense love and affection for his daughter.

'You have done nothing wrong, *Apa*. You only did what you thought was best.'

'I wish I could have done more.'

'It was sufficient. And I love you for it.'

'I'm sorry for letting you down.'

'You don't have to apologize, *Apa*. Even when you were not around, I knew you were always there for me.'

'I didn't mean to leave such a large burden on your mother.'

'She knows and she understands as well, although she misses you.'

The father and daughter held out their hands, touching only at the fingertips. Irfan watched with brimming eyes and saw the thin line between life and death.

Mr Singh's image wavered in the moonlight and they saw him glow when he smiled.

'I think it's almost time for me to go now.'

Gouri walked towards her father and stood as close as she could get to him.

'Then, go. You don't have to be earthbound anymore.'

Mr Singh turned to face the bright light that was inviting him to cross over and he looked at Irfan and said, 'There is just one more thing I have to do before I leave. Thank you, Irfan.'

'You're welcome, Mr Singh.'

'Promise me you will not come back here again.'

The two teenagers nodded in unison.

Mr Singh waved to them and darkness once again reigned in the corridor.

* * *

'This is a safe space, Irfan. Feel free to start whenever you are ready,' Mr Chew said and offered a warm reassuring smile.

Irfan thought for a long time about how he should open up to the only person he could trust, and he eventually said, 'I don't like to be touched.'

'Haphephobia.'

'What?'

'That's a fear of touching or being touched,' Mr Chew said. 'I like to read up about phobias.'

'It started after this teacher invited me to his house . . .'

Mr Chew heaved a sigh and said, 'Finally!'

'What do you mean, Mr Chew?'

'There have been rumours that one of the teachers molests and sexually abuses students. I have wanted to take action for a long time now, but I had no evidence. No formal complaints were lodged by the victims. When I approached some of the boys, they brushed it aside like it never happened. I think most of them believed it was a rite of passage or something. I couldn't do anything if they didn't come forward themselves. It would seem like a personal vendetta against a popular teacher.'

'I think most of us were afraid that no one would believe us.'

'I know who it is and if you are willing to testify, I will make sure this teacher doesn't work in this school anymore. That is, provided you're willing.'

Irfan nodded. 'Yes, I am. I don't want to live as though I am at fault all the time. I want to purge it once and for all.'

'I am not a psychiatrist, but I can help you look for one. The first thing I will do is call for a management meeting. I am sorry that you and the other boys have had to go through this . . . this horrific experience. I am ashamed of the other teachers and the staff, myself included, who did nothing to make this school a safer place although we all knew about the teacher and his transgressions,' Mr Chew shook his lugubrious head apologetically.

Irfan tried to speak but his mouth kept turning down to prepare for the long-awaited bout of tears that he needed.

'It's okay, Irfan. If you need to cry, you have nothing to be ashamed of. Everything will be all right from now on.'

* * *

'And that was what Irfan told my brother's friend's friend,' Poh concluded his tale with a nod.

'Really? Saved by a ghost?'

'Why not?'

'Well, it wasn't as scary as I thought. I've heard worse.'

Poh felt offended and he asked, 'What story?'

'I'll tell you when it's my turn.'

'So, what happened to Irfan? Does anyone know him?'

'No.'

'Nope.'

'Must have left school a long time ago.'

'And what happened to Gouri?'

'I don't know,' Poh said.

'What about Mr Singh? What was that thing he had to do before he crossed over?'

'I don't know.'

'You don't know much, do you, Poh?'

'Of course, I do! From that day onward Mr Singh was never seen again.' He laughed so loudly that he startled the slumbering creatures in the dark forest that they fell off their perches.

* * *

Mr Varmin could not believe the shoddy treatment meted out by the management after all he had done for their school. He had given the best that he could in terms of education and disciplining the students. He wanted to sue the school, but that one boy who destroyed his life gave courage to the others and somehow they were able to build a bigger case against him. To him it had been nothing but some consensual pleasure between guys. He had never 'forced' the boys but rather 'seduced' them to have a little fun; this was the price he had to pay for introducing the adult world to a weakling, a pansy and a tattletale like Irfan.

When word got out, staff from all levels ostracized him. The management wanted him to go on an 'instant vacation', but he refused to leave. He was concerned about the students' welfare. It would be unethical to leave without completing the syllabus. He only agreed to go because he did not want any more hassle from the so-called 'victims' who, he knew, were no angels themselves. The parents were ready to crucify him even though they had hardly any time for their own children.

He flared up when the principal informed him about the management's decision. He wanted to destroy the school for sullying his reputation and he also wanted to ruin the boy who had started all this nonsense. He thought it would be good if he could teach the boy a lesson, perhaps hurt him a little for ending his long and fruitful career. In the middle of a school day, he crept into the staff room to look for Irfan's file and find his home address, academic results and other such data. Boys like him needed to be chastised and taught a sharp lesson so they would learn to respect their elders.

'He ought not to have squealed on me to anyone. He enjoyed it as much as I did,' Mr Varmin muttered and yanked so hard at the files that were stuck in the cabinet that they flew out into the air and scattered documents like confetti all over the staff room. 'He's going to get what he deserves!' Mr Varmin slammed the table and carrying on with furious monologue, 'he doesn't know who he is dealing with, that lying little wimp!'

Mr Varmin was about to pick Irfan's file that was lying on the floor when he saw something out of the corner of his eye. He didn't expect anyone else to be in the room. He was already making up excuses in his mind when he saw Mr Singh looking dauntingly large and formidable, staring down at him. He backed away hurriedly from the apparition and tripping on the files, toppled backwards and hit his head on the side of the cabinet.

The ghost of Mr Singh came close and pointed at his face. Mr Varmin levered himself up clumsily but the fallen files slid away under his weight causing him to sit down heavily on his behind. No matter however many times he tried, he could not get up.

'You're not real,' Mr Varmin said and shaded his eyes with his hands. 'There's no such thing as "ghosts"!' He closed his eyes and waited for a moment hoping for the spectre to disappear. When he wasn't attacked, he opened his eyes and realized that Mr Singh was inches away from his face. Mr Varmin shouted for help but he was sent flying across the room, hitting the shelves and bringing down everything with him. The noise of the commotion could be heard to the far ends of the school and very soon a large crowd rushed to the scene.

Mr Varmin lay writhing in pain from the bruises and cuts but his physical agony far outweighed his terror upon coming face to face with an outraged ghost.

'What do you want from me? What have I ever done to you?'

'Stay away from the boy!' Mr Singh shouted in his ear.

For a moment there, Mr Varmin failed to grasp the context of that statement and asked, 'What boy?'

Mr Singh continued with his warning, 'I will come for you if you hurt him in any way.'

'But I did nothing to that boy!'

Mr Singh flung the teacher through the door; Mr Varmin bounced off the net in the badminton court before falling flat on his face on the ground. It was only then that he squealed and begged for mercy.

'I will stay away from him. Please don't hurt me any more. Please, let me go.'

'To ensure that you do, I've brought along some friends,' Mr Singh said.

The teachers and students rushed to his aid and heard his delirious rant, 'The ghost! The ghost is trying to kill me!'

Irfan arrived just in time to hear Mr Varmin scream and saw Mr Singh stepping back into the shadows. Strangely enough, there were also Japanese soldiers with an array of weapons and torture devices in their hands, standing motionless around Mr Varmin, almost as if they were waiting for something, or someone, to give them the green signal. It could only mean one thing.

* * *

'I told you never to come back,' Mr Singh said, glowing brighter than before.

'I had to. I want to thank you for saving my life and . . . and for looking out for me. Did you go after Mr Varmin because of me?'

'It was something I should have done while I was alive.'

'No one has ever done anything like that for me before,' Irfan said and reached out to touch the ghostly figure, but he only felt the cold air. 'But I don't want you to stay here on my account.'

'I'm not staying.'

A bright light materialized out of nowhere and Mr Singh gazed at the portal with a smile of satisfaction.

'Why have the Japanese soldiers returned?'

'They're here to do what they must.'

'The last we heard, Mr Varmin had gone out of his mind.'

'Sometimes this world can seem like an ugly place. It is frightening. Vicious. Depressing. But with nice boys like you around, it doesn't have to be. You can make a difference. Don't expect anyone to take care of you. That is your job from now onwards,' Mr Singh walked towards the light.

Irfan could not hold back his tears and waved to the ghost of Mr Singh, 'Thank you, Mr Singh! Goodbye!'

He watched Mr Singh coalesce with the blinding illumination and felt the emptiness in him gradually filling up with emotions he had lost along the way.

5

In a Locked Room in Maxwell Hill

'Er . . . er . . . my turn? I don't really know any ghost stories,' Darshan said and glanced around nervously.

'Everybody knows ghost stories. How can anyone not know ghost stories?'

'Come on, give it a try.'

'It doesn't even have to be scary.'

'It can be funny.'

'But scary is better.'

'Don't listen to them, Darshan, just tell us the first story that comes to your mind.'

'Okay, okay, I think I got one. This is about a girl who was possessed by a demon.'

'Who is she?'

'Do you know her?'

'Er . . . she's my sister's friend.'

'How do you know she was possessed?'

'That was what people said.'

'Stop with all the questions. Go on, tell us. What was it about?'

'Well, these three girls—they are friends, you see—decided to go up to Maxwell Hill for a short holiday.'

* * *

Liz, Iris and I thought it would be nice to have an all-girl trip to the hills. No boyfriends. No parents. No chaperons. To have the freedom to be ourselves and do what we girls like to do best. Have fun without the protocols that dictate the limitations of being a girl.

Yes, yes, we told everyone about our plans; those that needed to know about our whereabouts at least. It wasn't some kind of a secret cult meeting or that we were starting up a coven. We just wanted time off from girly responsibilities, you know, the kind of unwritten laws that stipulate that we girls have to behave in a certain way, fulfil certain duties . . . that kind of a thing. So, we decided to be ourselves for a change.

What do you mean 'what kind of a thing'? The kind where we have to do the dishes, the laundry, tidy the house, set the table . . . that kind of a thing . . . the kind boys never have to do just because they are boys.

Afraid? Of course not. We may be girls, but we have every bit of courage that boys have. Maybe even more. Courage is not determined by gender, haven't you heard?

I don't think I can remember everything, but I will try to narrate the events which changed our lives forever.

We left home at about eleven to catch the afternoon jeep up to the bungalow and found that we were the only three people at the station that morning. I don't know why there was no one else walking up the hill; there are usually large groups of people every day but somehow on that day no one was around. I mean, yeah, there were some people, but not as many as one might expect.

So, we sat around waiting for the jeep in the waiting room. Nothing was out of the ordinary. We were excited. It wasn't our first trip up the hill. We had had a day trip with the school before and also gone on a camping trip to the Tea Garden. But this was our first time at the bungalow by ourselves. I don't quite remember the name, but we had heard about its reputation.

Yeah, we knew about the 'locked room', but didn't think anything of it. I mean, so what if there was a locked room. It doesn't necessarily have to be a bad thing.

When the jeep eventually arrived, only the three of us boarded it. We didn't think that it was strange or anything because it was a weekday and wasn't a holiday.

So how did we get permission to go up the hill on a school day? We didn't. Our school had a sudden infestation of those nasty little hairy black caterpillars. Even thinking about them gives me goose pimples. They came out of nowhere in swarms after a heavy thunderstorm the previous night. They caused us to itch unbearably and some of the girls even developed allergies that made them swell up like balloons. We were told to go home until the fumigators got rid of them and cleaned up the school. With the unexpected time off, we decided to go on this trip.

As I was saying, it was smooth sailing with no obstacles or difficulties to get to the bungalow. It was as though it was meant to be.

When we got to the bungalow, the caretakers were very warm and welcoming. The middle-aged couple showed us to our room and took us on a tour of the entire house. They did mention that one of the rooms was locked and that they didn't have the key. They didn't say why, so we didn't ask. Were we curious? Of course. But what was the point? We were there to enjoy ourselves and not to worry about some locked room.

After a short nature walk around the premises, we sat down for the dinner that was cooked by the caretakers. After this, we spent some time lounging around in the spacious drawing room, making girl talk. Before going to bed, we went out for another ramble. It felt like a foreign country. The air was very cold. The surroundings were extremely quiet and super dark. It was so dark that we could see the stars from one end of the sky to the other, like a sparkling blanket of sequins. It was awesome.

We sat for a while on the bench outside, appreciating the cool atmosphere and admiring the magnificent sky until our noses, ears, toes, and fingers were frozen numb with the cold, and then we decided to call it a day. We each had our own single bed; two adjacent to each other and the third one across the room. I took the one opposite Iris and Liz. Everything was good until twelve midnight; that was when strange things started happening.

I was the first to experience it. I woke up shivering in the middle of the night. I had thought that the blanket I had was warm enough, but my whole body was freezing. I wanted to wrap more of the blanket around me, but it had completely disappeared. I couldn't find it anywhere. I was a little upset thinking that the other girls were playing a cruel trick on me—we sometimes did that to each other. But before I could call out their prank, I realized I wasn't in the room at all. I was lying in front of the locked room. I didn't think anything of it until I once again felt the chill bite into my skin. My hair stood on end when I felt a draft from beneath the door. It was unbelievably frigid.

It was followed by a small faint cry; the kind you think you misheard. Could-be-a-cat-or-a-kid kind of a sound. Worst of all, it seemed to be coming from inside the room. I wanted to investigate, but the darkness creeped me out. I ran back to my room and discovered that one of the girls was gone. I couldn't tell who it was in my panic mode, but one of the beds was empty. I shook whoever was on the other bed and it turned out to be Liz. I asked her where Iris was, but of course she couldn't tell me. She had been asleep all along. Like it or not, we had to go look for her.

We didn't want to wake the caretakers who stayed in the quarters behind the bungalow. I mean, if it was a dire emergency then perhaps, yeah, but we didn't know if Iris just went to the kitchen to get something to eat or to the bathroom. Liz and I searched high and low. In the living room and in the dining room. In the cupboards. In the corridors and even outside, in the pitch-black garden, just in case. She just wasn't anywhere to be found. We were beginning to feel the urge to summon the caretakers when we heard the cry from the locked room again. Both of us were scared out of our wits. Wouldn't you feel that too if you were in our shoes?

We were about to run away from the locked room, when Liz said the crying sounded like Iris. We stopped to listen carefully before jumping to conclusions, and it did sound like Iris crying.

You're asking me? We were asking ourselves what she was doing in there and how she had managed to get in. The padlock was still firmly in place and the door was securely shut. We didn't want to cause any trouble, so we leaned on the door and whispered Iris's name. We called her over and over again, but she didn't respond. Just as we were about to give up and turn away, she called back. She said she was lost. We asked her a whole bunch of irrelevant questions like what she was doing in there, how she had gotten in, just what she was trying to prove and other such stuff.

When her crying grew more intense, we comforted her and assured her that we would find a way to let her out. She didn't even know that she was in the 'locked room'. Liz tried twisting and rattling the door knob to see if it would open, but it didn't. I touched the padlock to see if it had a key or something and, to my astonishment, it simply came off. It was actually just hooked on. We stared at each other, but we didn't know what we should do. I told Liz that maybe we could go in and get Iris out, but she went insane with paranoia.

Liz said something awful must have happened to Iris and that she may not be herself any longer. I was sceptical about these things. Yeah, the supernatural kind. I don't believe in them and I have no patience with them. The whole town is chock-full of weird superstitions. Okay, so Liz waited outside the door while I went in to look for Iris. It was so dark inside than even the flashlight was no use. I could only see dust motes floating about in the empty space.

I was heading in when Liz grabbed me from behind. I would have punched her in the face had I not half expected her to do exactly that. I knew she wasn't brave enough to be left alone, so I took her hand and we ventured in. I mean, how hard can it be to look for someone in a room, right? Wrong. The room was larger than we thought. We couldn't even see the corners. The strangest thing was, when we turned around, the door wasn't there anymore. There we were, stranded in the middle of nowhere. Liz was about to start crying and I comforted her by lying. I told her I knew what I was doing, and I knew exactly where the door was. But, of course, I didn't.

I didn't think that I would be able to handle a paranoid person during this search for a missing friend in an eerie room, but I psyched myself to carry on. With only one flashlight we moved very slowly, one step at a time to make sure we didn't bump into anything. It was already cold when we went inside, but as we proceeded further it got colder. We were freezing and on the verge of giving up, when we saw a light flickering in a distance. Someone was holding a candle in the dark. We called out and rushed to her thinking it must be Iris. She didn't seem to hear us and continued moving away from us. We gave chase.

Liz and I were startled when we realized it wasn't Iris, but a girl about our own age walking around in her pyjamas holding a lighted candle. She ignored us, shuddering away in confusion. We could tell that she had been crying a lot. It frightened us even more thinking that she might be a ghost. Before we could even decide on what she was, another girl in her nightgown walked past us. Her hair was braided into pigtails and she was holding a different kind of a candle. Like the red ones used in Chinese ceremonies for the gods and spirits.

By now Liz was hanging on to me like a limpet. We didn't exchange a single word, but we knew just how frightened both of us were at the supernatural turn of events. More barefooted girls came forward in various kinds of sleeping attire and each held a candle in her hand. Although they didn't say anything, we could tell they were lost.

We made our way past them, but it was difficult to know where to go since we didn't know in which direction the exit lay. It grew even more disorienting now that the group was moving in circles. On top of that Liz pointed to a girl who was bleeding through her nightgown, dripping on to the floor for others to make scarlet footprints everywhere. As if on cue, or in sympathy, some of the other girls began to bleed simultaneously, almost as if it were a menstrual period party. Liz and I tried to shoulder our way through the bleeding girls, but it was impossible. One by one, they were all gushing out blood like several leaky taps.

The ground was covered with a film of crimson liquid that made it hard for us to walk. We must have just about made it out of the bloody perimeter, when we saw the girls slipping one by one in the ankle-deep blood, accidentally putting out their candles. That was when the screaming began. Screams of agony and despair. Perhaps there was also hysterical laughter, but we weren't sure. In that moment of madness, the flashlight went out and tumbled to the floor but the screams continued to overwhelm all our senses.

Liz and I held on to each other and crouched in the middle of the darkness until the screams died. The flashlight suddenly came back on and, although it was faint, it still shone like sunlight in the pitch-black room. I helped Liz up and we looked for the door, calling out to Iris at the same time. It gave us a purpose instead of second guessing ourselves all the time and thinking the worst.

Now we had to walk on water, or something liquid that squelched underfoot, and I knew it could only be one thing. I shone the light on our feet and sure enough it was the blood that oozed out of the girls' bodies. Liz was too distraught to notice it and I kept the information to myself.

We were still milling around, trying to find our way when something brushed against our feet. I didn't really want to know what it was, but curiosity got the better of me. I shone the light at our feet and saw a foetus floating by. Unfortunately, Liz saw it too and she screamed. When we looked around us, we saw a river of blood surging forward, carrying foetuses at various stages of development in its current. We were terrified at the sight of them swirling around us.

Our first instinct was to go against the flow. We had to get out of the way of the dead babies and the blood that was converging in a corner of the room. We were getting sucked into the black hole of the bloody cascade and although we tried to fight it, it was too slippery for us to resist it. When Liz fell to her knees I went down too because she was clutching on to my arm. I lost the flashlight and that plunged us into complete darkness from then on.

We were taken by the stream with the rest of the foetuses down into the darkest part of the room. Although it wasn't deep, we couldn't stand up even if we wanted to. We stopped fighting after a while, but held each other's hands to avoid getting separated. But, when we felt the ground sloping down, we were forced to let go of each other because we couldn't hold on any longer, and Liz's scream was the last thing I heard. Although I called out to her, it was in vain. I remember thinking that if I ever got out of this nightmare, I would go and find both Liz and Iris. But was this just a nightmare?

When I woke up, I was half submerged in the shallow end of Burmese Pool. I was freezing but the dawn's sun was toasty enough to thaw me a little as I stretched out on one of the giant boulders. The moment I was able to pull myself together, I once again looked for my friends, but they were nowhere to be seen. That was when I headed to the police station.

I'm glad they're okay.

What? They're not?

Liz was never much of a talker to begin with. Now that she has retreated further into herself, I can't see that it has made much of a difference. I mean, she never liked to talk about anything that frightened her or made her sad. She once told me that she doesn't care to think about the bad things that happened to her in the past. I don't know what 'bad things' happened to her; she didn't tell me.

What about Iris?

She's in ICU? She's delirious? Of course, why wouldn't she be? Did you people hear what I just told you? It wasn't a dream. I can't explain it, but everything we went through was real.

Can I speak to her?

Why?

Whatever.

* * *

I don't know what happened. I heard a baby crying. It woke me up. I looked around. Maeve wasn't in her bed. I didn't think it was strange. I mean she could have just gone to the bathroom. I also wanted to wake Liz but then I thought, hey, Liz is not suited for this sort of a thing. Anyway, I was more concerned about the baby crying in the middle of the night than a missing friend.

I checked the bathroom, but there was no one there. Maeve wasn't a midnight-snacker. Besides, we had tons of snacks in our room. So, why would she go out in the middle of the night to look for anything else? When I recalled the time she had sleepwalked during one of our camping trips, I panicked. What if she had walked out of the house in her sleep? And, into the jungle! It was possible.

I sneaked out of the room and stood for a moment in the hallway to let my eyes adjust to the darkness. At the same time the baby's cry could be heard again. God, it was eerie! I rubbed my arms to get rid of the jitters. It was silly, I know, but I could have sworn the sound was coming from the locked room. There were so many thoughts running through my head. I tried to think sensibly. I mean what if there really was a baby that was in pain or in need of help? How could I live with myself knowing that I didn't do anything? I braced myself and started walking towards the sound.

I saw a cloth bundle before the door. I wasn't sure whether I should pick it up. Just in case. But then, I didn't want to frighten myself, so I reached down and lifted up one corner of the swaddling cloth. I couldn't see much in the dark and as I drew the blanket away slowly, I prepared myself for a jump scare. But what I discovered was nothing else but Maeve. How did she get there? Why was she sleeping outside the locked door? That was what I would have liked to know but the baby's cry distracted me.

Between looking at Maeve and then at the door, I realized that the lock was open, just hanging there. Someone must have unlocked it. The crying got louder. I was concerned. So, leaving Maeve behind, I pushed the door open and walked in.

Why didn't I wake her? I would have been wasting too much time if I had tried. She sleeps like the dead and by the time she awoke and I had explained everything to her, it might have been too late. For the baby.

I trained my eyes against the obscurity inside the room. It was something I liked doing. By disciplining my eyesight to the dark, I could get a better sense of where I was going. The flashlight would only create a black film in front of my eyes that wouldn't go away. Without overthinking it, I went in. I was literally blind in that room. This time my superior night vision didn't work. I couldn't even make out silhouettes or shapes.

Anyway, I called out to the baby. Asking it to lead me to where it was. But I was confused. It sounded like it was directly in front of me. And then it was somewhere to my left. When I approached that direction, it moved to my right. It wasn't working. I decided to go back to awaken Maeve to help me. I could see her still bundled up outside the open door. I headed for the exit, but I was intercepted by a girl with a baby in her arms.

Good god! I almost died.

Yes, it was a ghost! How did I know? She was like transparent and all. Or translucent. She was luminous in the darkness, for goodness sake! Of course, I was scared out of my wits and couldn't move. I was dumbstruck. She came at me and I screamed. The next thing I knew, I was running. I didn't know where I was going. I didn't even care if I stumbled over anything that was in my way. I ran in a direction that took me away from the door. I went deeper inside the room.

To make matters worse I stepped into something squelchy. Squishy. The whole floor had become slippery. All I could do was to slosh through it, very carefully. It was ankle-deep, whatever the gunk was. If I had gone any faster, I would have fallen flat on my face. It felt disgusting. I dragged my feet on the floor. Knees bent. Body arched. Legs apart. I skidded forward after every few steps.

I searched for the ghost, but she wasn't there. I kidded myself into thinking that it had all been my imagination. But I couldn't fool my heart. It was drumming to the beat of a lion dance.

I came to a part of the room that felt really strange. If everything had been unreal before, this was ultimately surreal. The weirdest. The darkness was gone. Girls of all ages were just standing around in their torn pyjamas, nightgowns, and other sleeping attires. They were shivering in the cold. Some hugging themselves. Some bent over. Some hanging down like marionettes.

I slipped past them and saw their empty eyes staring into space. As I continued on my way, weaving in and out between them, one of the girls caught at my arm. I squeaked from fright. She looked at me in mute appeal. I shrugged off her hand and ran. The slippery floor didn't matter anymore. I had to leave the room and run from the distraught girls who were now all reaching for me. Every time I slipped, I used them as leverage to grab on to and haul myself up and they fell like dominoes. I managed to get to the periphery of the circle of girls. Just when I thought it was over, I toppled into an abyss. The next thing I knew, I was being rescued in Burmese pool. And then I must have blacked out again.

* * *

'You've gotta snap out of it Liz,' Iris said.

'Yeah, we're in this together. If you don't, they will take you away. And it may be for a very long time,' Maeve agreed, as she gathered her long hair together and tugged it tight before fastening it into a ponytail.

Liz glanced at her friends. She hadn't spoken for months. Her eyes and cheeks were sunken from a lack of appetite and sleep. She was still in the pyjamas that she had been wearing for the past few days. She felt safe, all curled up under the covers in her brightly lit room. She shook her head in response to her friends' coaxing and cajoling.

'You have to speak sometime,' Iris said. 'You're not making it any easier by shutting down.'

Liz kept her eyes focused on Iris's short bobbed hair instead of listening to her.

'Liz, stop playing games,' Maeve seized her hand. 'You know if they take you to Tanjung Rambutan you'll never come back again.'

Liz jerked her hand away from Maeve's grasp and struggled to get out of bed with a bundle in her arms. The pillow, blanket and stuffed toys scattered around the bed when she jumped out. She ran to a corner, cowering from the delirium that had followed them back from the hills. She closed her eyes and covered her ears to try and forget the girl's face and the never-ending baby's wail. She looked like an inmate from the asylum with her cropped hair, unkempt clothes and unwashed skin.

'Perhaps we should just leave her alone,' Iris said.

'No, we can't just leave her to rot away here. They'll have her committed. It's wrong. We're friends. Something happened to her that night which really frightened her and turned her into this . . . this thing. We have to find out what it is.'

'Why is she always holding that bundle of cloth? Do you remember when we saw her at the hospital? It must be her security blanket.'

Maeve approached her friend steadily, with her hands outstretched, 'Give me that blanket, Liz.'

'What are you trying to do?'

'She has never needed a security blanket in all the time that we have known her. This has only started after our trip. Don't you think it might have something to do with her withdrawal?' Maeve said.

'It could be dangerous taking it away. She seems to have placed her entire trust in it,' Iris objected, but didn't do anything to prevent Maeve from grabbing it. She too was curious to see what would happen.

'Give it to me, Liz.'

The dishevelled girl who seemed to have renounced the world hugged her swaddling cloth tighter.

'Don't force her, Maeve. Can't you see it's upsetting her.'

'Perhaps that's what needs to be done.' Maeve was close enough to take the blanket, but she said one last time, 'Don't make me do it, Liz. Give it to me and I won't snatch it from you. I only want to take a look.'

Liz pressed herself against the wall and then turned her back on Maeve.

'I won't ask nicely again.'

'Maeve, nooo . . .' although Iris gripped the edge of the bed, she kept herself from getting involved in the tussle.

Without hesitation Maeve grabbed the tail end of the blanket and ripped it out of Liz's grasp. It came away quite easily because Liz hadn't been her athletic strong self for a while. Liz screamed. It was the exact same scream that Maeve had heard when she had ventured into the locked room.

Iris covered her ears and shouted, 'Stop! Liz!'

Maeve did not expect Liz to react in this manner and she embraced her as tight as she could.

'It's okay Liz. It's okay. Snap out of it. Please.'

Liz struggled to free herself from Maeve's arms but she was too weak. Defeated by her own obsession, Liz let herself go limp and then wept.

For the first time, after months of silence she spoke, 'Give me back the baby.'

Her friends were shocked to hear her utter words that made no sense.

'Liz, it's only a blanket.'

'My baby. Please give me back my baby.'

'Liz, you don't have a baby,' Iris said.

'Give her back. Give her back. Give her back!' She shoved Maeve and made her rock back on her haunches. Liz grabbed the blanket and stuffed it in her arms again, rocking it gently.

'Oh, Liz,' Iris said sadly as she helped Maeve up. 'Whatever happened to you that night?'

Liz walked back to the bed and tucked herself under the covers.

'She came to me,' Liz said, and her friends gathered by her side to hear the bizarre tale for the first time.

'Who?' Maeve asked.

'The girl in the room.'

'Th-the ghost?' Iris said and cringed from the memory.

'What happened to you after we got separated?' Maeve asked.

'I was in her room. She was unhappy. She was pregnant, but she was alone. She stood on a chair, threw one end of the rope over the fan and looped the other end around her neck. She kicked the chair away and she swung. Back and forth. Back and forth. She held her stomach. The baby was coming. She changed her mind, but the rope was already taut. She couldn't do anything. She was dying. The baby was coming out.

'She gasped her last breath and the baby fell to the floor. It was unhealthy. She never really took care of herself because she hadn't wanted the child. That man who made it didn't want it either. The baby's cry was weak. No one knew anything until they forced open the door three days later. It was too late.

'She begged me to take care of her baby until she was ready, so I took it from her. I'm taking care of her baby now as I promised.'

Liz cradled the blanket in her arms and cooed softly. Maeve and Iris were speechless. They couldn't see any baby in the bundle of cloth and what they had heard was beyond comprehension.

'But why you?' Maeve asked trying to figure out how Liz had become thus unhinged. 'Why did she choose you and not us?'

'No offence Maeve, but I'd rather not know,' Iris interjected.

Maeve placed a finger over her lips, motioning to Iris to stop interrupting her gentle interrogation.

'Because she knew I felt the same way.'

'Felt what the same way?'

'When I was fifteen, I also got rid of my baby. She knew.'

Maeve and Iris exchanged stupefied glances.

'But,' Iris said, 'you never told us anything.'

'I was waiting for the right time, but it never came.'

'I am so sorry, Liz,' Iris hugged her. 'I never knew.'

'No one did. It was my secret.'

'You could have told us,' Maeve said. 'We could have helped.'

'I was afraid. But not anymore,' Liz said and lulled the cloth in her arms to sleep.

'But you have to start acting normal in front of others. Don't talk about the baby. Don't behave like a crazy person. If you continue to do so they will send you away,' Maeve implored.

'That's my plan. I have to take care of the baby until her mother comes back to claim her. The only way I can do this without interference is to behave this way and get sent to a place where we will be left alone.'

'But your whole life will be wasted in the asylum,' Iris said.

'Not to me.' Liz smiled and rocked the baby in her arms with fondness. 'Not to me.'

* * *

'That's it,' Darshan said.

'It started scary, but it ended so sadly.'

'I heard about the locked room in Maxwell Hill, but I didn't know the whole story until now. It is incredible.'

'But is it true?'

'I don't know.'

'Who told you this story?'

'I overheard my sister talking about it.'

'So, you eavesdropped?'

'No. I overheard.'

'Same difference.'

'You mean your sister is one of the girls?'

'Huh? I don't think so. She didn't say anything to me.'

'Did the ghost mother ever come back to reclaim the baby?'

'I have no idea.'

'So, did Liz remain incarcerated in Tanjung Rambutan for the rest of her life?'

'I don't know.'

'Poor thing.'

'She actually believed she had to take care of the ghost baby?'

'Something like that.'

'I wonder whether a ghost baby can grow up?'

'That would be awesome!'

'I guess we'll never know.'

* * *

The baby's laughter permeated through the neighbourhood. It was neither too loud nor too soft. It was negligible at most times since they lived in the quieter and hillier residential area in Taiping with only the pristine primary jungle in the backdrop.

The sound of joy came from a single-storeyed bungalow built of concrete and wood. It was first erected in the '50s and it was still standing strong. The three people who inhabited the house nourished it with love and shrouded it in mystery. In all their years of being together, their neighbours knew nothing more than they should and nothing less than they shouldn't. The fence was adorned with bauhinia coccinea, Rangoon creeper, butterfly pea, bougainvillea and other vines and shrubs to protect the privacy of their home.

In the serenity of the congenial home, three middle-aged women surrounded the apparition of the baby they had found many years ago. While two of them gazed at her in awe the third stroked her gently on the head.

'Why couldn't we see her before?' Iris asked.

'You didn't believe,' Liz replied and kissed the baby's hands. She chuckled and waved them about. 'You can't see the things that you don't believe,' Liz continued.

'I can't believe . . .' Iris said and giggled. 'I mean she feels so real. Like any human baby.'

'No matter. She's still a baby,' Maeve cooed to draw her attention.

'I'm so glad the two of you are here,' Liz said and carried the baby closer to her bosom. 'If it hadn't been for you guys, I don't know what I would have done.'

'We made a pact to stick together.'

'We couldn't just leave you alone to bear the brunt of the problem. After all we've been through worse together—like getting lost in the locked room,' Maeve said.

'You guys could have had normal lives.'

'Define normal,' Maeve said.

'Like what? Love life? Marriage? Family? You know they're badly over-rated when you reach a certain age,' Iris laughed. 'Besides, we're a family by choice.'

'Been there, done that. There's nothing like nurturing a friendship that keeps us youthful,' Maeve added.

'It was nice of you to offer your home to me Maeve. I was all set to spend the rest of my days in the madhouse.'

'I wish it could have been sooner. But, you know how life is.'

'It's already soon enough for me,' Liz said.

'Yeah, for me too,' Iris said with a contented grin.

The temperature dropped quite suddenly and the three friends felt a presence enter the living room. The fluorescent light flickered and the night seemed to get quieter. They examined the room and then shared a knowing look with one another.

The girl from the locked room materialized before them with her arms opened wide. The three middle-aged women braced themselves to meet the child's mother after such a long time, neither afraid nor perturbed. They knew this day would eventually come. They had lived with their ghost baby all their lives and seeing her mother was something they secretly wished would never come to pass.

'Are you here for Audrey?' Iris asked.

The spectral mother lifted the baby from Liz's arms, cradled her and kissed her on the cheek.

'We call her Audrey since you never told us her name,' Liz said but the girl was too preoccupied with her baby to care.

After cuddling the baby for a while, the ghost said, 'Not yet,' in reply to Iris's question.

She laid the baby down in Liz's arms, and gradually shimmered out. 'After *Chap Goh Meh* (the fifteenth night of the Chinese New Year),' she whispered before she vanished completely.

'Why such a specific time?' Maeve asked, still astounded by what she had just seen.

'What will we do when the baby is gone?' Liz was anticipating the empty nest syndrome which would take a lot of getting used to.

'We've been a family to each other for a long time. We'll get by somehow,' Maeve replied. 'We can still go for walks in Maxwell Hill.'

'But it won't be the same without Audrey.'

'She's different Liz. She has never been a day older than when you first adopted her. The only thing we need to do now is to entertain her although she is unlike real human babies who eat, shit and cry most of the time,' Iris said, an irrepressible giggle escaping her throat.

'At this age, we had better not be adopting any more babies. Ghost or not,' Maeve said and stirred up a mild laughter. 'They will outlive us before they're old enough to take care of themselves.'

'How is it possible that no one knows about the girl in the locked room? We tried everything to find out something, anything, about her, but no one seemed to know a thing. I had hoped that we could perhaps help her find some peace,' Liz said.

'Someone's lying. That's it,' Maeve said, and they nodded in silence.

'I hope she finds justice for the pain and agony she endured when she was alive,' Iris said. 'I wonder what it has to do with *Chap Goh Meh*.'

6

Chap Gore Mare

'What a coincidence! My story is about *Chap Goh Meh*. I heard this story from Ah Saw,' Toh said, his eyes opened wide. 'It has something to do with *Chap Goh Meh*. But he calls it *Chap Gore Mare*. As in G-O-R-E and M-A-R-E.'

'What is it about?'

'Murder.'

'Do you mean someone was murdered?'

'Is someone about to get murdered?'

'No, this is about revenge,' Toh knitted his eyebrows together to create a sinister look.

'Huh? Which is it . . . murder or revenge?'

'Both,' Toh sneered grimly and whispered in a low ominous tone, 'it's murder and revenge.'

'In Taiping?'

'It was on the eve of the fifteenth day of the Chinese New Year when the bodies began to float out of their watery graves in the Lake Gardens,' Toh said. 'The first person to spot this strange anomaly was an old man while on his morning walk at five o' clock. Although his eyesight was debilitated by glaucoma and cataract, he could still clearly see the bodies because the lake was usually clear of debris and other floating objects, especially large ones. At first, he thought they were branches and twigs that had fallen from the rain trees surrounding the lake, but upon closer inspection he noticed limbs and faces—some were in advanced stages of decomposition, while others seemed more recently deceased. Floating among them were fresh, plump oranges.

'The old man looked around to get someone to help him decide what to do, but there was no one around. Usually some of his acquaintances joined him on his constitutionals, but not so that morning. The first person he telephoned was his son who was still asleep at home. Before the old man knew it, the sun rose, his family rushed to the garden, rubberneckers gathered around and the police also arrived at the scene.

'They couldn't be too sure just how many floating corpses there were, but they said the number was between eight and ten. That part of the lake was quickly cordoned off by the police, but curious bystanders still hung around, waiting to see them being fished out of the water although that did not seem like it was going to happen anytime soon.

'The first group of police tried to go into the lake, but they were almost sucked into the muddy lake bed. They knew the bed was likely to be soggy but hadn't expected it to be this bad. One of the policemen said that it had felt like the lake was bottomless.

'Next, they attempted to use poles, nets and even fishing rods but somehow, they either failed to get a grip on the corpses or their implements got entangled in the process. There was nothing else to do but wait for the special rescue unit to come with their gear and equipment. It took them an hour to arrive and another hour to set up their boats, and paraphernalia.

'One of them said the bodies looked female but he couldn't tell for sure since they were bloated and deformed beyond recognition. And that was how the legend of the *Chap Gore Mare* began at the Lake Gardens.'

* * *

It was a strange day at the Taiping Lake Gardens. Dark and heavy storm clouds gathered and threatened the area with impending doom and gloom. A thick velvety mist enveloped the surrounding area, making it seem more like dusk than daybreak. Some of the kids referred to the fog-like atmosphere as 'whitewash' instead of whiteout since a whiteout wouldn't have done justice to this unique phenomenon that could only occur in a town like theirs.

The firefighters, ambulance, police, and the special rescue unit team soon ran out of ideas. Other than barring the public from getting too close to the evidence, there was nothing they could do. Everything was working against them. The weather, the unknown depth of the lake, and the mist. They were accompanied by curious spectators who stood by and watched as the bodies bobbed gently to the rings made by pond-skaters. Although it was revolting, they couldn't take their eyes away from the long-legged water bugs nibbling on the putrefied flesh.

* * *

Old man Ronald had a bad taste in his mouth. He didn't like it one bit. It reminded him of the medications he used to take to keep himself alive. These days he had given up on them as he didn't want to depend on pills and spend hundreds of ringgits every month at the pharmacy. He realized it was pointless trying to prevent a bad thing from happening to him when he still ate unhealthy food and drank and smoked without giving any of it a second thought. He wanted to ignore the despicable flavour, but it wasn't just in his mouth. His whole body felt weird. Like rancid curry or mouldy bread on his skin. When he checked his seventy-plus-year-old limbs he noticed new red splotches that had not been there before. They looked like boils and pimples, some about to burst from the taut protrusion.

He scratched a few of the bulbous swells and they popped, oozing a thick yellow slimy substance. He didn't want to alarm his family, so he kept quiet about the symptom. He wore long sleeves to cover up the pustules, but the contact of the fabric against his skin only made it worse. They merged together like an extra layer of epidermis.

Even with the revulsion occupying his mind, he couldn't help but think of revisiting the Lake Gardens. He hadn't been there for ages. He checked the sky to see if it was feasible to cycle there, but the ominously dark overcast storm clouds threatened a heavy downpour soon. He waved his bodyguard away, telling the hired hand he didn't need any protecting that day. Without another moment's hesitation, he walked out of the house and towards the garage to get his bicycle. The handyman he hired for menial work kept it working at its optimum capacity, although no one in his family ever used it.

Manoeuvring the bicycle past the Mercedes, the BMW and the Volvo, he wheeled it past the automatic gates and clumsily mounted the bike and settled his derrière into the saddle. As soon as he stopped wobbling and was slightly steady, he rode it as though it were his first time on a bicycle. The breeze was exhilarating and the distant thunder was comforting. He didn't know why he needed to go to the Lake Gardens, but he felt the urge to go there for some strange reason.

* * *

Peng had a severe and throbbing headache, something he had never had before. He had heard complaints from his girlfriend, his mother and his friends about the sharp pounding pain in the head that drove them insane, but he had always thought that they were exaggerating. He thought only women and weaklings had headaches. But now *he* had them. This one even came with a burning smell. It throbbed all the way to his eye sockets, jaws, gums and teeth, making it impossible for him to eat. His teeth enamel became extra sensitive to touch and temperatures. He had already skipped breakfast and now he would have to skip lunch as well.

He was waiting as patiently as he could at the doctor's, but it was ridiculously packed. It would take another hour or more before his turn came. He hated this doctor, but he was the best in town. He felt that the doctor spent way too much time with each patient thus delaying the long queue and causing the extended wait. The people around him looked very ill and he dreaded having to look at their deathlike appearances.

He heard the storm brewing from afar and thought it would be a good idea to go to the Lake Gardens to kill some time before his turn came. He walked out of the clinic and into his old faithful Alphard Toyota. With his mind focused on the Lake Gardens, he felt much better. The pounding in his head lessened and he became a little light-headed. He pictured the beautiful lake demarcated by the spectacular rain trees which he had gotten used to ignoring because he had lived in Taiping all his life. It was different today somehow. It felt magical. It was the place he had to go to, so he just did.

* * *

Loon Kee's hands cramped painfully while he was having the famous *koay teow* soup for breakfast. He dropped the chopsticks and startled everyone. The pain was excruciating, almost as though someone was breaking his fingers. He could no longer eat, and he noticed that his digits were twisted like dead twigs. He told his friends that he was experiencing stiffness in his joints and they stared at him with concerned looks. It frightened him to see their tortured expressions, so he laughed it away like it was a joke. He had always been the clown, the joker, the happy-go-lucky guy, the entertainer in the group and he intended to keep it that way.

He hid his hands under the table and told his friends that the *keow teow* didn't taste as good as it used to. Some of his friends agreed and stopped eating it altogether. Loon Kee was held in very high esteem among his peers. His word was considered gospel and his personality was perceived to be godly. He thrived on that.

As he surreptitiously massaged his hands under the table, he had the sudden urge to go to the Lake Gardens. He needed to be there for some reason. He imagined the beauty of nature that emanated from every corner of the magnificent lake and longed to be in her arms. He had never felt this way before towards the fauna and flora that flourished in that tranquil garden, but today, he wasn't going to fight the affection that was bursting out of his heart. As soon as breakfast was over, he would come up with an excuse and head there all by himself. This was something he had to do alone.

* * *

Cheem could not see where he was going. It was as though someone had splashed dirty water on the car's windscreen. He skidded, but managed to pull over to the side of the road before anything untoward happened. He got out to check the windscreen but it was just as clean as when he had washed it earlier that very day. His car was his pride and joy and he loved nothing more than his old reliable Volkswagen Beetle. His lovebug.

He cleaned his spectacles with his handkerchief but the whole town appeared foggy because of the mist and that was making him disoriented. It was not unusual for the town to be enveloped in condensed vapour, but it wasn't this bad usually. This felt peculiar. It had a scent. A floral scent that had been in the air ever since he woke up. It was sweet. Delectable. It reminded him of something, but he couldn't recall the significance of that angelic essence.

He sat in his car and twiddled his thumbs to see if he could recollect the fragrance from his memory bank. It was only a matter of time before the jigsaw fell in place. He was reminded of the aromatic bouquet of the Lake Gardens and decided to drive there and relax under the humongous rain trees. He didn't care if he was going to be late for work. He didn't enjoy working at the bank anyway, and he owed it to himself to take it easy for one day and not deal with other people's money.

* * *

The itch was unbearable. He tried cleaning his ears with his little finger, but the itch went beyond the part that was safe to reach and not even a cotton bud q-tip did the trick. He would have to go to the barbershop to have his ears checked. Mr Sen was the best ear-cleaner in town, way before someone had alighted on the great idea of starting an ENT clinic and charging exorbitant prices. Clement had to do it soon because the itch was irritating the hell out of him and he could not focus on anything else.

He rushed out of the house before his wife could say anything to upset him. She did this every morning like clockwork. His children were no different. They were always screaming and shouting in the morning as they got ready for school. It was a madhouse he had never intended to move into, let alone build. If there was one thing he would have done, had he been able to turn back time, it would have been to embrace his bachelorhood again in a heartbeat.

The only two things that he was about to do differently today was go to the barber to get his ears cleaned and then ride around the Lake Gardens on his faithful Honda C70. He didn't know why he felt like cruising around the Lake Gardens but his furniture shop could afford to stay closed for a while longer. The workers could wait. There was a time when he could be late by an hour, but no one dared to say anything because he was the boss. He wasn't making as much money as he used to. People here were turning stupid and not wanting to use timber-based furniture any more, while the rest of the world was trying to be environmentally friendly by avoiding plastic. Clement once told a customer to sit on the grass when he queried about the origin of the timber. He had no patience for people like that.

All he wanted now was to get rid of the ear itch and get to the Lake Gardens as fast as possible.

* * *

Nam Kok's tooth fell out while he was chomping down the *kueh kak* and accidentally bit into something hard. He wanted to throw the plate of *kueh kak* back at the vendor and accuse her of carelessness about hygiene. He spat out the foreign object into his hand to retain as evidence. It ought not to have even been in this soft and scrumptious fried rice cake in the first place. As soon as he cleared the semi-masticated glutinous mess that remained of the cube noodle, he saw the ugly shape of his own tooth. It was just as well that he had not given in to his ill-tempered impulse; he was known throughout the town for his temper. The embarrassment of becoming a laughing stock would have been unbearable. He would never have been able to return to the *kopitiam* ever again.

He dropped the tooth on the table and continued with his meal when he heard another crack. He spewed everything out on the table and saw another tooth sticking out of the mushy meal he was trying to consume. He stuck his fingers in his mouth to feel the stability of his other teeth and they all moved easily from side to side. He panicked and pushed the plate away, creating more of a mess as it glided over the stuff he had spat on to the table.

He knew he was old, but this was ridiculous. He raced to his old jalopy, jumped into it and honked at the car that was blocking his path. He dithered between going back home to check on his teeth himself and rushing to the dentist immediately. And then on second thoughts, he drove casually in the direction of the Lake Gardens because it felt like the right thing to do.

* * *

By the time the six impromptu visitors to Lake Garden arrived, the extremely cold weather, not to mention the poor visibility caused by the mist, had dampened the thrill of their spontaneity. The darkening sky made it seem like nightfall had prematurely set in. Other than a few authorities who were stationed at the perimeters to keep the public from endangering themselves, the place was deserted.

Cheem liked what he saw of the Lake Gardens. It looked like a hill resort. He had always loved Genting Highlands when he was raking in the cash but had hated what it stood for when he went bankrupt. It was different in Taiping. He was realizing only now that there was a unique serenity about this place. Only when he was knee-deep in the water. Only when he saw her again.

In the beginning, it had bothered him a lot that he had caused the death of a girl he was stalking at school. She didn't want to have anything to do with him, but he was head over heels in love with her. How could she reject him when all he ever wanted was to demonstrate his undying love? He managed to convince her to meet him at the abandoned building behind the school. He only wanted to kiss her and that would have satisfied him. He would have agreed to stop stalking her. To stop harassing her. But she wouldn't have it. She wouldn't let him kiss her—not even on the cheek.

She struck his face. She scratched him. He forced himself on her and got kneed in his groin. He reached for her neck and tightened his fingers. All he could think of at that moment was the pain between his legs and how he wanted to transfer that pain to her. When she dropped to the ground like an old dusty book he violated her soft virginal body and then left her for dead. He went back to being a student, a brother, a son. No one knew why he turned into somewhat of a recluse. He waited for the police to come and get him. He waited for witnesses to come forward and identify him. To tell everyone that they saw him killing the girl at the abandoned building. How he had choked her to death.

Heartlessly and brutally. But nothing. He was ready to be taken away, but no one came.

He later found out that she did not die. That although she had somehow survived that night by some miracle, she had kept mum about it.

He cycled past her house frequently to see if she was still around. She hadn't been to school since that fateful night. He wondered whether she would expose him and destroy his life. He wanted to confront her, but she remained sequestered within her house.

While he was still deciding on the best way to get in touch with her to apologize, he heard about her unfortunate passing. They found her in one of the rooms in a Maxwell Hill bungalow. She had hanged herself and her baby did not survive. He continued living his life and read about the girl's tragic suicide in the papers. Everyone talked about her, but not him.

Never had Cheem felt so much at peace with himself. This was the day he had been waiting for. The day to be free of the burden of knowing what he had done. The day of redemption to never again feel guilty about something he had regretted doing all those years ago. It didn't matter that the water was ice cold. It didn't matter that there was no turning back now. All that mattered was to be with the girl, the one and only girl he had ever loved.

Even with her eyes rolled into the back of her head. Even with her tongue flopping out of her mouth. Even with her skin looking pallid and cadaverous, he was happy to see her. He could not wait to get to her at the deep end of the lake as she waited for him with a baby in her arms.

* * *

Peng arrived shortly after Cheem, parked his car and walked towards the water where the decomposing corpses were spotted. He knew he was home even before he waded into the lake. He called her name over and over again to apologize. In the fog, all he could see was his wife crying in the middle of the lake, blood running down from the gash in her head. Every day of his life he missed her and regretted doing what he had done to her.

He had believed that a woman's place was in the kitchen. That she was to be treated like a slave and sometimes as an object of desire or frustration. He didn't consider her beautiful, nevertheless she was the kind of woman who made a good wife: one who obeyed his commands and requests, and kept the house comfortable for him. He had believed that she was someone who would bring his seeds to term and give him a brood of healthy children.

Every time he hit her, he felt a part of his heart grow cold. He didn't like seeing her cry or bleed, but he couldn't help himself. She was not as pretty as she used to be. She was putting on weight. She wasn't a very good mother either. She was beginning to get on his nerves. He lashed out not because she did him any wrong but because he just couldn't stand the sight of her. How and why had he fallen out of love with her?

He lamented to his dead wife about the times he had taken out his frustrations on her and had made her cry, but she just stood in the water and wept.

He told the police that she had suffered from very bad headaches and that her sudden death was nothing more than a health condition. Perhaps an aneurysm, perhaps a tumour, but he made sure that there was no autopsy that would have determined it was actually a very hard blow to the head. He never meant to kill her, although he had thought about it. She was a nobody, no one cared whether she lived or died. Even her parents were relieved to get her out of their hair. Her children were not bonded with love or compassion to her. It was easy to get rid of someone who didn't amount to anything much. Someone who would not be missed. At the same time, he made sure he left no marks or incriminating clues behind.

He kept this secret buried deep in the recesses of his mind. But there were always nightmares. Reminders. Guilt. They came in waves, but he managed to stay afloat all this time.

He found his dead wife with the familiar contusions, bruises and swellings as she stood shaking with fear. He splashed across the lake to embrace her, feeling a special kind of love for her for the very first time as he began to sink into the slimy ground below. He could not help apologizing to her repeatedly for all the times he had made her feel worthless. From now on it was going to be okay.

* * *

Loon Kee's hands were gnarled into a contorted and indescribable shape by the time he was knee-deep in the water staring at his dead mother. He hated everything about her. He had hated the way she had incessantly nagged and humiliated him. Undermining, crushing and diminishing his self-worth so much so that he had grown diffident and timid. Everyone in his family hated her as well, but she picked on him the most. His siblings ignored her and stayed away from home as much as possible. His father had taken the easy way out, opting to embrace death when Loon Kee was only twelve years old. Loon Kee was the last child and left alone to be with his mother.

He looked forward to flying the coop after completing his form five in school. He planned to go to the city, take up a course and start over. All he wanted to do was to leave. But his mother made it so bad for him that he didn't even have the courage to run away from home. His anger was building up. He was like a rat looking for a way out of a burning house. He was going mad, but he saw an opportunity when his mother was at the top of the stairs of their double-storeyed terrace house with him behind her. He wanted to push her down but couldn't do it—he was too weak. But when his mother took a misstep and fell, he watched her go down. Tumbling and rolling. Cracking and shattering.

Until she reached the bottom of the stairs. He continued to watch and observe. Waiting.

His mother called to him in a broken voice. Her voice was hardly a whisper from the pain and her body was horribly contorted, but he just stood there. On the one hand, he was very afraid, on the other, he wanted her to suffer. He waited for another minute and then he walked back into his room and locked the door. He cried into his pillow—not because his mother was hurt or could die from the fall, but because he would get into a lot of trouble for not doing anything about it. It was too late, anyway. His mother would always hold that against him if she survived.

He didn't dare go down and he didn't know what to do. Day became night and there was still no scream, no cry, no siren. By the time he was ready to meet the fate that awaited him it was almost eight o'clock at night. It was dark. His mother usually switched on the lights in the living room, porch and backyard. But she wasn't able to. He came out of his room and looked at that dark lumpy thing at the bottom of the stairs. It was still there. He flicked on the lights and his mother was lying there motionless. Perhaps it was time to call someone.

He dialled his uncle's number and wept. His uncle said he would set out immediately. His uncle would know what to do, but he himself didn't dare go near the body. He stayed where he was. Upstairs and far away from his dreadful mother. His uncle came in with the spare set of keys and found his mother dead. The rest was a blur. The ambulance came. The police came. His relatives came. The house was filled with strangers, friends and neighbours. The episode was over, but he kept seeing his mother in his nightmares. Sometimes in his daydreams. Sometimes at the bottom of the stairs.

It took him a few years to recover from the ordeal. He knew he could have made a difference had he called for help. He knew that that truth would haunt him to the grave.

His mother looked angry and ominous in the lake. He was afraid. He had always been afraid of her. He wished he didn't have to be with her again, but he had no choice. He had to obey her every wish, her every command and bidding. As he got deeper into the lake, his mother just stood there and watched him drown without blinking or batting an eyelid. She just watched with her cold, unforgiving, and bloody eyes while her head dangled at the end of her broken neck.

* * *

Old man Ronald appeared in the mist like a white knight to the rescue. He saw the little girl shivering in the freezing water and he just wanted to put his arms around her. He had always liked her until the day she threatened to tell her mother about her uncle's strange behaviour. He was fortunate that his sister hadn't had time to spend with her daughter. She was too exhausted from work to listen to her little daughter's inane complaints. Old man Ronald, who was in his twenties at the time, decided he had to do something about his niece and very soon, before someone actually believed the child.

That night, when everyone was asleep, he went to the little girl's room as usual, but this time with a different intent. Instead of climbing into bed with her, he grabbed a pillow and pressed it down on her face. It was quicker than he had anticipated. When it was all over, he hugged her one last time before leaving her to be discovered by someone else.

The little girl still looked the same, but he had aged poorly. He could feel the boils erupting as he stepped into the lake's vinegary water. He wept and called out to his niece, begging for forgiveness but he was already waist-deep in the water and had almost completely disintegrated.

* * *

Clement's ears were bleeding by the time the barber finished cleaning them for him. He shouted at the man for not having been able to resolve the problem. He could still feel something trapped in his ears. Possibly a cockroach, a cricket or one of those small insects, seeking sanctuary in a warm dark place and crawling into someone's ear. But this time, he could hear a groaning sound deep inside his inner ear.

He could hardly put on his helmet as he straddled his bike. It was getting worse, but he managed to insert his ears into the helmet before riding off to the Lake Gardens. He could barely see anything when he reached the cordoned-off place. The police didn't seem to notice him as he walked past. He even nodded to one of the officers, but there was no acknowledging nod. He didn't have to look far and almost immediately saw his first wife standing on the surface of the water in the middle of the lake in the moonlight. He would have recognized her anywhere. She was as big as they came.

He knew he had married her for all the wrong reasons, but it was a mutual arrangement. She was a tycoon's daughter but born without the appropriateness of a woman according to societal norms. Despite the proverbial silver and gold spoons in her mouth, she had no beauty to outshine any metallic glitter. She refused to undergo corrective surgery to make herself as close as she could get to the cover girls in beauty magazines. She didn't care about how hideous she looked. She only wanted true love.

Clement, like many other suitors, tried his luck to win her over with true love. She had seen through the charades of all of the others and even Clement's, but somehow settled for him. They both knew love did not figure in the picturesque landscape of their matrimony, but they pursued it anyway. It was a case of having someone being better than having no one. But as the years went by, they began to despise each other, and the edges of tolerance began to fray. She learned that being with someone she didn't care for was so much worse than being alone. Especially when there was a third party involved. It was no big secret that he was cheating on her with the other woman. She wanted a divorce and that would mean the end of Clement's carefree lotus-eating existence, without having to work for a living. All he ever did was throw his weight around in his wife's furniture shop. He never did any heavy lifting to help the business prosper—neither did he sell any products nor did he help with the accounting and other paperwork that was needed. He only collected the profit and stuffed as much as he could in his pocket, but it was all going to be over soon.

He pleaded with his wife to reconsider, but she said she had made a mistake and had short-changed herself by marrying him instead of waiting for a better opportunity. The harsh confession led to an argument and it quickly escalated into a physical fight. He swung a punch and missed her face when she turned away, but his fist landed on her ear. She screamed, fell to the ground and held the blood from gushing out but it still flowed through the gaps between her fingers. He panicked and he struck her with a gear lock on the other side of the face. She was barely breathing when he tied her up and gagged her. The last thing he heard was her distinctive groan which sounded like something that came from a being that could not die.

It was nightfall when he staged the kidnapping. He drove her to the nearest estate just off Kamunting and left her there to die. Days turned into weeks but no one found her until the stench grew too much for the villagers around to bear. It was one of the hottest months of the year where even the hardiest of plants began to wilt and anyone out in the sun for too long were struck by heat stroke.

She was ripe and funky when they found her. She was so advanced into the last stages of decomposition that no one could do anything but pack her up in a container and send her off to the other world with a lavish funeral. Everyone suspected Clement for her demise, but no one could prove it.

His ears bled and painted his shoulders as red as the colour of his wife's eyes on the day she died. Eyes that spoke of vengeance.

Clement stood in the lake face to face with his dead wife for the longest time. He had gotten away with murder all his life but now, he was too tired to fight any longer. He waded into the water and all the while the groaning grew louder and stronger, drowning out everything he knew about life.

* * *

Nam Kok could feel his other teeth throbbing all the way to his temple, tugging at the nerves and making them hypersensitive to touch. He could not control the tears that were streaming out of his eyes because of the sheer agony and there was nothing he could do. The dentist said he couldn't find anything wrong with his teeth and there was no need for any dental work, but no one could feel what he felt. They didn't understand. The spasms were excruciating unlike anything he had ever felt before. Worst of all, it hopped from one tooth to another with a specific shooting pain as though the dentist was stabbing a needle into his gums without anaesthesia.

He was banging his head against a rain tree when he saw the Indonesian maid who used to work for him. She was in her work clothes, a pair of extra-large Bermuda shorts and an over-sized used t-shirt, both of which were obviously hand-me-downs. She was looking around the rain trees like she was lost, cupping her hands together and shuddering from the cold water, which was ankle-deep.

Nam Kok remembered the day he first had the excruciating toothache. It was the day the maid discovered his activities with the young boys he brought back from Sunday school. He had tried to explain to her that he was doing nothing wrong and that although the boys may have been underage, they knew what they were doing. Although she didn't say anything, she may as well have been the judge, the jury and the executioner, all rolled into one, as her eyes spoke volumes of her utter contempt. He felt that the condemnation in her eyes had transformed her into a horrendous creature.

He confronted her when he could no longer stand her searing unforgiving gaze. She finally told him that she wanted to leave, return to her home and have nothing more to do with him. He didn't take that as a sign of good faith to stay quiet, but as an opportunity to announce what she had witnessed to the world at large as soon as she was safe from potential harm.

He pushed her into the swimming pool and held her head down for as long as he could. Although she had already stopped moving, he continued to hold her down just to make sure she stayed dead. Having no friends or family in the foreign country made her vulnerable. Almost invisible. With a small compensation made to her family, no one pursued the matter and it was unanimously agreed that she fell into the pool and accidentally drowned.

The day she died, his toothache flared up again. As before he could feel the aggravating pain transferring from tooth to tooth every time he tried to get a fix on it. His whole mouth was racked with unbelievable and indescribable pain. The mouth-burning sensation was the last straw. It made him so agitated that he lost his appetite. There was nothing anyone could do for him. He gradually slipped into a depression that lasted a few months before he was summoned to Lake Gardens.

He recognized the maid, shivering in the cold and standing, rooted to a spot and glaring at him with her unforgiving gaze. He felt his lungs gradually fill up with water. Dirty, foul smelling, sludge-like water. His breath quickened and grew shallow. His teeth were having a spasmodic tug-o-war with each of the nerves in his body as they shut down, one by one, for good.

* * *

'There was a total of thirteen men ranging from a teenager to an octogenarian. They were found in the Lake Gardens when the smog cleared the next day after *chap goh meh*. The police couldn't understand how they had slipped past the blockade without being noticed. They blamed it on the mist. And the strangest thing of all was that each of them held an orange in their hand with their names written on it.'

'No way!'

'Yes way!'

'You said thirteen, but you only told us about six of them.'

'I know. The others were a coroner, a policeman and a bodyguard. They were involved with covering up some of the cases. The most I got of their stories was that they sleepwalked straight into the lake on that fateful day.'

'What about the remaining four?'

'Those were the ones with unknown background stories. The only thing that linked them together was their friendship and how their bodies were blackened as though they were burnt to death.'

'You mean someone burnt them and threw them into the lake?'

'Wouldn't we like to know!'

'How come the killers were all men?'

'I heard there's another version where all the murderers were women. But that's another story altogether.'

'Do you know that story?'

'No.'

Everyone laughed.

'I wonder what the four friends did to take them to the Lake Gardens. Could they have been doused in petrol and then burnt in the water?'

'No one can explain it. But whoever or whatever did that to them must have been really pissed off.'

'So, these ghosts were taking revenge?'

'Wouldn't you if it happened to you?'

* * *

'I saw her.'

'It's not a her. He's just dressed like one.'

'I am not going to argue about that at a time like this. She is back to claim us.'

'How? As a ghost? I don't believe in ghosts.'

'Didn't you see her?'

'I . . . it was late. I don't know what I saw.'

'How do we make it right? How do we get out of this?'

'There is nothing to get out of. He was asking for it.'

'Stop confusing us. Whatever it was, we killed her.'

'So what? She was a prostitute; disowned by her family. No one would miss her.'

'Yeah, and he didn't have to behave that way. He could have stopped all that fake life he was leading and acted normal.'

'Why are you guys bad-mouthing her now? She's dead—because of us. We bludgeoned her to death. I know there was nothing that linked her death to us, but she is back. Don't you guys get it? She is back!'

'When did you see her?'

'Last night. She was still in the same state we left her. Charred and in flames. She grabbed my hand. Look. Her handprint is seared into my skin.'

'And my face.'

'I got it on my back. I was trying to run away when she touched me.'

'What about you?'

'Ahh, bullshit. You guys are crazy. I didn't see him and I have no burns to show you.'

'Y-you.'

'What?'

'Y-your hair.'

'Your hair is on fire.'

'D'you think I'm ten? What kind of a stupid joke is that?'

'You hair is really on fire.'

'Uh, what? Oh, oh. Help me guys. Make it stop!'

'W-why are we in the lake?'

'What? We're waist-deep in the Lake Gardens? How did we end up here?'

'I can't stand that screaming! Someone help him!'

'My hands are on fire. No! My hands!'

'My face. My face!'

'We're sorry for what we did. We didn't mean to kill you. We just got over-excited, got carried away and . . . and . . . and . . .'

The four boys illuminated the Lake Gardens like a beautiful bonfire at the stroke of midnight when *Chap Goh Meh* marked the final day of the Lunar Chinese New Year.

7

When the Nightbird Calls Your Name

'"Tok tok tok". That's how it goes. "Tok tok tok". The nightbird is sometimes called the graveyard bird or the toktok bird. But those of us who know it, know what it does. You had better not answer when it calls your name, because it is telling you that your time is up. Wherever you may be. Whoever you may be. It will find you and it will only go away when you answer it,' Ter Son attempted to describe its malevolence as best as he could, but the rest were not impressed.

'Yeah, yeah, I've heard that one before.'

'It's not even scary. It's just a bird.'

'Isn't it supposed to be an owl?'

'But an owl doesn't go "tok tok tok". That's a nightjar.'

'Er, well, it's not really a nightjar and not really an owl . . . but something in between,' replied Ter Son.

'What is it?'

Ter Son continued his story to avoid questions to which he had no answers. 'It started when the poacher took a strange and unusual baby bird from its nest. That was the first time he found out people would pay to own it for fun or to turn it into something medicinal.'

'He ran a pet shop in KL, but he got his supplies from small towns like Taiping. He paid his runners to trap all kinds of wildlife and insects to sell to his regular customers. His motto was: if you can pay for it, I will get it for you.

'He started his trade in exotic animals that were not meant for tropical weather. They were brought in from all over the world but most of them did not make it. Those that did, lived a short and tortured life trying to adapt to the hot Malaysian weather.

'When the losses were too great and his customers complained more than they appreciated his services, he turned things around by poaching locally for the international market. There was less risk in poaching from small towns. The tropical animals could survive long journeys; and bribing the officials was far more conducive for making a quick buck.

'Selling animals that he trapped for free and exporting them was a more lucrative enterprise. He started with arthropods and arachnids. They were easy to handle and the jungles were literally crawling with scorpions, spiders, beetles, and bugs. But the profit was not as attractive as he would have liked it to be.

'So, he went on to trade reptiles, before moving on to mammals and birds that brought higher returns. He found ways to conceal them in false-bottomed suitcases, sewn into secret pockets of clothes, stuffed into water bottles, car seats, wheels, and into every kind of unsuspected tight space he could think of.

'Everything was going like a breeze until one night he heard the nightbird call his name.'

'How did the bird know his name?'

'That . . . you have to ask the bird.'

* * *

Darren woke up to the same sound he had heard the previous night. It was as though someone was calling his name in the wee hours of the morning. As a sceptic, he did not believe in the hokum of superstitions. The creatures that he removed from their natural habitats were very real and not abstract concepts. He had always assured himself that there was no such thing as a 'rare' species because once he found them, he would breed them to make them as common as the housefly. But he made sure the demand was always higher than the supply by culling the offspring if the numbers got out of hand. Business is business.

He looked out through the window and saw the main gate from where the voice was coming, but there was nothing that suggested the paranormal, let alone inexplicable. The peculiar shadows of mismatched shapes swayed with each breath of the zephyr. Other than that, it was a beautiful, cool night with a full moon and it was tranquil.

When Darren saw how comfortable his girlfriend was beside him, he discounted the experience as one of those ridiculous nightmares. He didn't like getting these bad dreams. They were pointless and he hated how some people associated them with spiritual interpretations or things that went bump in the night. It was a frivolous escapade for people who couldn't face reality. In real life you take what you want. Sometimes by coercion.

There was only one thing he believed in: if poaching animals made the collectors happy, he would do it in a heartbeat. Animals go through natural selection anyway. Besides, he shouldn't be held accountable for a few missing animals since they already had to battle with the wilderness everyday just to stay alive. He did not create that law, but animal lovers blamed him when all he was doing was helping Mother Nature to keep the population in check. He had been fortunate to avoid the animal activists so far but he knew their paths would cross someday.

He tried to get back to sleep, but it was elusive since his head was now filled with random thoughts. He got out of bed, careful not to wake his girlfriend, and tiptoed out to the living room to catch something on TV. It was three in the morning but the 24-hour channels that he subscribed to may have something to keep him occupied, at least until his eyes grew heavy with sleep.

He walked around in the dark as he always did when he stayed in the Airbnb he rented for the job. He used to let the runners deliver the merchandise to him but ever since they raised their fees, he decided to take the pleasant drive from KL to Taiping himself. With assurances from the bribed authorities, he knew he would never be caught. Besides, it was a food paradise to him because he ate everything under the sun and had no qualms about where the meat he devoured came from as long as it tasted good.

Taiping was too quiet for him. He could hear everything from the lizards chuckling to the crickets chirruping. But what was most disturbing of all was the nightjar tok-tokking as though it were knocking on a door with an unusual resounding echo. He hated the natural noises and longed for the city sounds with which he was more comfortable. The constant hum of traffic, the non-stop shuffle of people's feet and other uniform auditory sensations calmed him, so the irregular cacophony of nature just didn't do it for him. One moment silent and the other, filled with birds squawking or insects buzzing or monkeys howling.

He walked to one of the rooms where the birds were kept before the journey back to KL. He would stuff them into special compartments and cages, but some of them suffocated and died during the three-hour journey. These days he didn't need to conceal the animals because he literally had a free pass to go anywhere he wanted. By playing his cards right and greasing the right palms, he could almost get away with murder.

He heard some fluttering and movements inside the room where the birds were boarded up for the night. When he opened the door and switched on the lights to check his cargo, it frightened them for they had never known what it was like to be caged in a space that was barely sufficient for them to move. He had learned from previous experiences that, in sheer panic, the birds would attempt suicide by crashing at the sides of the cage, fatally injuring themselves. This time however, he safeguarded his money-making cargo by drugging them and confining them in smaller enclosures.

The peaceful doves were always in demand for their tuneful cooing. Some of the better singers could fetch a very high price. Darren also had bulbuls, orioles, black-rumped flameback woodpeckers, kingfishers and munias. But they were all very disappointing to him. He needed to up his game. Not just larger in numbers. Not just exotic. But unique in every sense of the word. His regular customers were filling up their mansions with one too many birds that were similar. It no longer mattered how colourful or magnificent the birds were, but how hard to acquire they were. He had yet to trap a nightjar and other larger-sized species like the milky stork, brahminy kite, sparrow hawk, and maybe even the rhinoceros hornbill. They were in high demand and were next on his list.

He quickly glanced around to ensure the birds were all alive. Then he decided he would be better off getting some shut eye. He switched off the lights, shut the door, and walked back to the bedroom, heavy with the hollowness that usually came with being rudely awakened. He was drowsy and exhausted, so he wasn't sure if he heard the nightbird call his name again.

Although he was not affected by the distraction, his skin broke out in goose pimples. Something as unnerving as this could not occur more than once. Hearing his name being called out two nights in a row was not only unsettling, but puzzling. He took a deep breath and braced himself to go to the window to check the dark surrounding the house. His front gate was located halfway between two distant street lights, making his front porch darker than the rest of the street.

The nightjars were still at it, talking to each other tirelessly somewhere in the neighbourhood. How did people even get to sleep with the racket? He felt the chill when he thought about it, but he shrugged off the idea before it could twist itself into a wild figment of his imagination, for which he had very little patience. Before he could withdraw from the window, he noticed a figure as dark as fear itself moving in the shadows.

He squinted, blinked a few times, and looked again. It was hard to make out the various shades of silhouettes and shadows. When his mind started making up stories, without missing a beat, he made a beeline for the bedroom. He almost covered his ears with his hands, but he didn't want to be a lesser man for admitting his dwindling bravado. What good would that do? Before he could take another step, someone—or something—called his name for the third time that night.

He tried to calm his nerves by flicking on the porch light. The darkness beyond that could not be penetrated. He had been wanting to tell the owner about the fluorescent light that flickered as though it were on its last legs, but he had not stayed long enough to have that conversation. Half of the things in the terrace house did not function as they should. He wasn't keen to make anyone's acquaintance in Taiping. Having even one person know about his illegal activities would be devastating. He may have paid off a few people, but it was impossible to pay everyone.

He peered through the gap between the dusty louvres and wondered whether he should check it out to keep his sanity. He walked to the front door, unlocked it and threw himself into the cold embrace of the night. He didn't know why he did what he did. Unprepared. Undressed. Unhinged. He had cast himself into the role of a foolish person in this unpredictable situation. There could be a felon at large. Someone looking to make quick money. He couldn't control himself but continued walking into the night without even a makeshift weapon.

'Darrennn . . .'

This time it was clear. There was no room for doubt. The person or thing that was calling him stood in front of the gate. It looked human in the confusing patches of light and darkness. But that person or thing had things protruding from its body. Feather-like. Wings, beak, talons perhaps.

'What do you want?'

He had heard about the old wives' tale of not answering a call at the witching hour, but he could not help himself.

'Look at what you've done.'

'What have I done?' he countered. He didn't like to hear about animals being sentient beings or that our compassion should also extend to them.

'Darrennn . . .'

He was close enough to reach out to the stranger who had come calling, but he still could not see who or what he was talking to. Two ruby-red lights glowed from the stranger's face, making him very nervous, and yet he could not stop looking.

'Leave me alone! I've done nothing wrong!'

A giant claw-like hand with talons lunged forward and seized his head, puncturing his scalp and cheeks and forehead. He lost his footing and nearly lost consciousness as well, but the thing that had a hold on him shot up into the sky. Its wings spread out like a cloak and covered half the celestial sphere from his view.

With another flap of its wings they flew so high that they reached the stratosphere. Darren felt lightheaded from the shortness of breath due to the altitude and the dizzying view of the town far below, but the pain was by far the worst of all. Once they reached space the bird-like creature released Darren from its grip.

He spun like a plastic bag caught up in a whirlwind. The world below him was as spectacular as the night sky above. It was almost as though the city lights were a mirror image of the stars. When he stopped struggling, he felt himself drift between worlds. The speed at which he fell began to compensate with the force that kept him afloat. While in that state of tranquillity, a void grew from the pit of his stomach and swallowed his entire being. It saddened him to the point of madness. But when the realization overwhelmed him, he fell to the ground and woke up on the bedroom floor.

He sat up and wept, hoping his girlfriend would wake up and console him with her love and kisses, but she was fast asleep. It was unlike any dream he had had before. Even as a child he had never had bad dreams or nightmares. And he was proud of this positive attitude that he had brought with him into adulthood. But now, he wasn't sure if he still had it. He knew that growing old meant change. But to him it was more like loss. Losing sight. Losing the ability to hear well. Losing the stamina to do something that only youth would allow. For the first time in his life he wasn't sure whether he knew what it was like to live anymore.

'Darrennn . . .'

He stood up and felt the familiar routine. He had done this before. Time and again. His girlfriend was in a deep sleep as she always was, and he was shaken by something that called his name. Had it been a dream? Was it all in his head? It couldn't have been real, could it? He didn't dare dig any deeper for answers. It was the start of another long night debating on his mental health.

He left the bedroom and went straight to the kitchen to get himself a drink. A shot of whisky usually helped despite what people said about liquor disrupting sleep. He poured himself a stiff peg and gulped it down. He shuddered at the strength of the liquor and the caress of a cold draft. It was a dreadful night to be awake. He had a long trip back to the city and deliveries to handle. The faster the goods were shipped out the better, in case the animals died in transit. He got out of the kitchen and wandered into the living room, feeling restless. Displaced. Contemplating the dream he had had moments ago.

'Darrennn . . .'

The call came again. He was getting tired of it. It was like a childish game. Someone toying with him. He walked to the front door, unlocked it, and once again found himself outside the house in a mystical world where anything was possible.

'What do you want this time? Another one of your cowardly nightmares?' Darren shouted at the night while positioning himself in different directions. 'You don't scare me! You're not real. You're my imagination. Or maybe someone else's imagination. Are you going to show yourself or do I have to—'

Hundreds of birds swooped down out of nowhere, flapping their wings in a frenzied circle around him. He shielded his face from the strobe light of birds against the moon and the stars. They were flying at maddening speeds and he could not get out of the enclosure. He felt a sharp pain on his arm and he saw a gash open up and blood begin to ooze out. Another knife-like wound tore on his calf. He cried out in agony, but the pecking and clawing continued to rip, slice and puncture him all over.

'Darrennn . . .' it called again and he woke up in the exact same location where he had his last dream.

He checked his arms, legs and body but there were no wounds. He traced the contours of his face with his fingers, fearing the worst, but there was no disfiguration. He wept into his cupped hands and shook the bed with his sobbing, but his girlfriend slept peacefully through it all. All his life, he had never felt as vulnerable as he did now.

He glanced at his girlfriend, needing to wake her up, to keep him company, especially at a time like this. He hesitated and thought long and hard about it. She had always been there for him despite everything. Sure, they had fights and tantrums and tongue-lashings, but he believed every relationship had to have them to keep the fire burning.

'Cora,' he whispered softly in her ear so as to not alarm her. He placed a hand on her shoulder and rocked her gently. 'Cora.' She was a deep sleeper, but he was determined to share his night terrors with her. If he could confront his fears by saying them out loud, they may go away. 'Cora, wake up.'

His girlfriend finally turned to face him, her eyes still shut tight, 'Whaaat?'

'I've been having nightmares.'

In the room, illuminated only by the streetlight outside the window, he could see that she wasn't interested to know.

'Cora,' he called a little louder, his voice echoed from one end of the house to the other.

'What time is it? Why are you waking me up?'

She stirred reluctantly and rubbed her eyes to get back to sleep, but Darren was unrelenting in his plea.

'Coraaa!'

'Fine! Fine! I'm awake! What do you want?'

She opened her eyes and gazed at him and then screamed, shattering the peace and quiet of the entire neighbourhood. She scrambled out of bed before Darren could understand what had made her go crazy.

'Cora,' he called, but she had already gone out of the room and he heard the front door slam. 'Cora, wait . . . what's wrong?'

He got up to go after her when he caught sight of himself in the mirror at the dressing table. For a moment there he forgot where the light switch was, but what he saw reflected in the mirror was enough to convince him. He could barely make out his face that was covered with feathers. He tried to pluck one out, but it was embedded deep into his skin. His hair had thinned away and his features had taken on a bird-like appearance. Dead eyes. A protrusive beak. A bald head. And spasmodic twitches characteristic of birds.

It had to be another nightmare. He pulled up his t-shirt and saw how delicately smooth his body was, carpeted with extra fine feathers. This nightmare was getting more and more demoniacal. He heard his girlfriend scream hysterically outside the house and he ran out of the room to get her. To explain to her that she needn't be afraid because it was not real.

Lights came on around the neighbourhood. Insomniacs and light sleepers were the first to be awoken by the frightful sound emanating from a young woman in her nightgown. If they had not sighted Darren or what he had become they would have easily gone back to bed and ignored the entire event.

Darren was about to shout out for Cora when he realized that his voice had become hoarse. His throat had tightened, and he could hardly speak. What came out of his beak-like mouth was a squawk instead. He heard someone scream 'Lei Gong!' and he knew he had to get out of the area or wake up from this nightmare as quickly as possible, before things got worse.

* * *

'And then?'

'That's it. He ran away and hid in the jungle.'

'Where?'

'How?'

'What happened to his girlfriend?'

'As far as I'm aware, she said she didn't know that her boyfriend was operating without a licence.'

'No, we don't want to know about that. We want to know what happened after that?'

'Did anyone see him?'

'It sounds like a Hitchcock movie. Are you sure you didn't exaggerate it?'

'I may have embellished the story a little but the facts remain the same. He did change into some kind of a bird creature according to the witnesses. They were willing to substantiate what they had seen with their statements. But strangely, no one has sighted him, or it, again after that night.'

'Thank god for that.'

'So, when the nightbird comes calling your name, you will turn into some kind of a bird creature?'

'Maybe.'

'Wait, wait. What's a Lei Gong?'

'Lord of thunder! It's a half-man, half-bird creature. You can see the statue in the temple.'

'Which one?'

'Go find out.'

* * *

Tong heard about the strange phenomenon from his sister who lived in the area where the incident took place. The man behind all the animal-trafficking was not caught because the authorities didn't know where to find him, but Tong knew. He himself was somewhat like the animal trafficker—the only difference was that he hunted wild animals for restaurants. People would pay anything for wildlife delicacies. Blood, bones, organs; the rarer they were, the better. He didn't need any middleman or poachers to get him what he wanted. Their ways were outdated, and their resources, limited. With the use of black magic, Tong managed to catch more than anyone else could in their entire lifetime.

In his humble home he had the two headed snake, a goat's foetus with a human face, a flying fox with human genitals and all kinds of albinos steeped in herbal soups in humongous jars. He knew about Darren whom he had bumped into in the jungle, but they always kept a distance without acknowledging one another. It was sort of an honour among thieves or in this case, traffickers. But like all laws, it could be broken.

It wasn't hard to track Darren down since a creature like that would stand out in the natural world. When Tong found him, he was still in a transitional form. Weak and vulnerable. Tong managed to trap him just as he was about to disappear into the thick forests of Maxwell Hill.

With this prized possession in his menagerie, he would have all the time in the world to enjoy hearing about that strange-looking humanoid bird. But best of all, the strange and unusual specimen would be good for bile and blood extraction and other parts of its body to be used for medicinal purposes. He knew this find would astound the world, but there was no way anyone was going to take it away from him when it was more precious than gold. He patted the humongous Chinese dragon pot where Darren was kept alive for routine harvesting.

'Better than diamonds and pearls,' Tong said to Darren who could only make a melancholic sound that could be misconstrued for a song.

He was careful about the curse of the nightbird that called the name. He protected himself with the dark arts of shielding himself from them so that he would not be affected. He got a medium to help him burn special talismans on to his body to keep the birds at bay.

Tong looked out of his window and saw all kinds of birds perched on his gate, fence, and anywhere else that they could roost around the house. He knew he was safe and that none of the birds would be able to call his name because they were impeded by the black magic.

The owl that was sitting on the fence was watching him closely, waiting for the thinning film of protection to gradually fade away. Only the birds could see that it would be soon, as they prepared to call his name to reveal his true nature.

8

The Confessions of a Gambling Man

'My story is about a gambling man. Someone who believed in high-stake wagers,' said Jacob. 'Money was always a thing with Philip. Even as a kid, the only thing he ever wanted was money. The more the better. That's what he told everyone.'

'Sounds like someone we know.'

'Shh, the story . . .'

'When Philip, as a teenager, learned to play with numbers he became obsessed. He would lose hundreds of dollars in one go and then win back a smaller amount to start all over again. At the beginning he spent his own pocket money but that wasn't enough to sustain his habit. The next thing he did was to borrow from his friends. Before long he started stealing small amounts wherever he went—from his relatives' houses, from students in school, from strangers and so on.

'Soon he got into a trouble with the law, but each time his parents bailed him out. His habit continued into his adulthood and eventually to the end of the road.'

'What end of the road?'

'Let Jacob tell the story.'

'The very end of the road in the middle of a cemetery.'

* * *

Yes, I am a gambling man. I have always been attracted to numbers. Luck or science. Economics or Feng Shui. Beauty or deformity. Life or death. It's all about numbers. That's how everything works. Since childhood, I've wanted to understand the Fibonacci Sequence. I wanted to figure out the golden ratio. I wanted to decipher H.P. Lovecraft's stories. Pythagoras. The human symmetry. The Devil's number. I wanted it all. But the one thing that side-tracked my fascination of them was gambling.

I loved calculating risk most of all. Everyone is born a gambler whether they like to believe it or not. People like to take chances, but we are constrained by time, age, seasons and weather. We think we can out-fox the control of numbers, but we are bound by them in the cruellest form. Too young, too old, too late, too early, too poor, too rich. We calculate the dates for the trees to bear fruits. We calculate our daily expenditures. We calculate the right time to approach someone, to launch an event, to celebrate a festival and we are always speculating to see how much return or benefit we get out of it.

That's us. Gamblers at the mercy of numbers. I don't steal. Okay, not anymore. I don't go around intentionally hurting people. I don't make it a point to create misery and drama. I only want to take my chances and play every card game, every lottery and every race in town. I mean what's the big deal in playing mahjong or *chor tai ti* or three cards or even betting on the rain? It's just for fun. But fun lasts only as long as it lasts. I know that. I know sometimes that it can be too late. By the time we realize we could actually hurt someone, it is already done. Like how I hurt the dead.

How? It's from the things we do. The despicable things we do out of greed! I wasn't sure if I wanted to try it, but my friend convinced me. Leong said he knew a medium who could help us get a winning number from the dead. I was afraid of the repercussions, but I was tempted as well. A winning number could mean a turnaround from my gambling losses. My debts. My anxiety. My disrupted life. My screwed-up existence. Or so I thought.

The medium, we called him Or-Lang, or black man, was the opposite of what his name implied. He was as light-skinned as powdered sugar. Pale as a corpse. In fact, he looked like one.

We met at 11 o'clock one night at the cemetery and brought him a steamed chicken, a strip of roast pork, some fruits and packet drinks. He supplied the joss sticks, incense and candles. Leong and I were sitting in a corner watching the thirty-something-year-old man twiddling with the offerings and the prayer paraphernalia. He laid them out systematically on the floor and then cracked a homemade whip around them. He strutted around the altar barefoot as he chanted inaudible incantations to summon the gods or the devil. Or maybe both. He didn't tell us what exactly he was doing. I was afraid that he might actually slash his tongue with a knife, drip his blood into a cup, and tell us to drink it. Thank goodness that wasn't a part of the ceremony.

But with a big fat *ang pow* or red packet waiting for him, he could do the hootchy-kootchy and tell us it was one way to get blessings from the gods and we wouldn't be any the wiser. We let him deal with the ritual while we dealt with our patience card but I was nervous as hell. I checked my watch worrying that he would miss our targeted time when he was supposed to wake the dead to ask for the winning number. At about quarter-to-twelve he came out of his trance and gestured to us to gather around the altar.

* * *

'A girl who died a violent death was brought in. She is the one we will summon to get our winning number,' the medium said and circled the altar with his whip. 'The undertaker left the grave open for us. We have to do this now before he buries her. The body is considered "fresh" and although she has been dead for three days, she will still be very fertile.'

'How did she die?' I asked, like it would make any difference.

'We don't need to know that, Philip,' Leong said and the medium pointed a finger at his face.

'No names. Numbers. I am one, you are two,' he tapped my shoulder, 'you are three. If the ghost knows your name, she will follow you home.'

I regretted being there the moment he said that. I felt a chill run through me. The sounds in the cemetery suddenly felt terrifying. The darkness was real. The only light source was from the candles and incense. We were told not to bring any identification that we might accidentally leave behind. Identity Card, driving license, name tag, ring or watch with engravings. Not even a flashlight. I was already scared shitless. I wanted to discontinue this idiotic charade, but I was too embarrassed to say anything.

'She was raped and murdered. Stabbed fifteen times and her throat was slit from ear to ear.'

I felt disgusted with myself. I was appalled at our action. I wanted it to stop. 'Can't we use someone else?'

'There is no one else as good as her. Besides, the more rage they have in them at the time of death, the higher our chances are. Since she wasn't ready to die yet, her spirit will still be very strong. She is between worlds. If vengeance was the last thing on her mind, she will return no matter what. This is good for us. That's why we have to take advantage of it while we can.'

'Won't she attack us?' The danger finally woke Leong up from his apathy.

'If she gave in before she died, she will just be a lost and listless earthbound ghost. If she fought for her life right to the very end, she will be unrestful for as long as she can hold her anger. Wear this. This will protect you.'

The medium passed us each a talisman. It was a yellow strip of paper with red Chinese characters written on it and folded into a triangle.

'Keep them with you all the time.'

Leong stuffed the talisman into his shirt pocket and I tucked mine into the pocket of my jeans.

'Let's go to the grave now. We have to conjure her at midnight.'

The medium threw in a few camphor tablets into the incense holder and created a smoky ambience. He fanned it in all directions, grabbed a long bamboo stake, and led us away from the altar.

The short walk to the grave site felt like a longer journey than I expected. I was at my wit's end trying to figure out a way to wriggle out of the stupidity that brought me to this pass. What kind of a senseless fool would go to the extent of asking for a winning number from the dead and not expect a backlash? I shuddered at the thought of encountering the ghost of the dead girl who had died violently. No telling what she would look like. Much less what her disposition would be.

The mound of earth that was left untouched was a marker for the gravesite. There must have been some palm-greasing between the medium and the undertaker to leave the girl unburied for three days. That was how people got things done the way they wanted, at the speed they desired.

'Whatever happens, stay calm. Don't run. Don't panic. Don't do anything stupid. Understand?'

Leong and I nodded and signed our own death warrant. By getting a warning to not do what was considered stupid, I couldn't help wanting to do exactly that.

The medium went on to chant his indecipherable incantations while smoking up the entire grave. After confusing us with some disorienting gestures, he disappeared into the thick fog he created. Leong and I were preparing to do everything he told us not to do. But the only thing that we did do was to let our hearts silently sprint out and run off in hysterics while we remained glued to the unholy ground upon which we stood.

When the smoke from the incense dispersed, we saw the medium standing over the coffin. He lit up two candles, gave us one each to hold, and pried open the lid to expose a pretty girl who looked like a teenager. Although she was made up and embalmed, she still had a frown that was visible in the faint light that flickered with our breaths. I was hoping the medium would not ask us to join him because this was about as close as I wanted to get to a dead stranger while manipulating her spirit.

His watch alarm went off and gave us a start. We were about to laugh it off when he stabbed the girl in the heart with the sharp end of the bamboo stake. We heard the crunch and squelch that came with it and my knees went weak. My stomach roiled. I felt numbness all over my body. What on earth did he do that for?

The medium mumbled something under his breath and drove the stake deeper. I began to feel dizzy and held on to Leong's shoulder for support. He gently pushed my hand away and continued observing the ritual without appearing concerned.

The medium stopped what he was doing and put his hands together in total silence. We waited and I noticed that the entire cemetery had gone quiet. Whatever insects or birds or animals that hunted at night were gone. I looked at the full moon that was just above us and it seemed larger than usual. It was as though it was watching us. I wanted to forget the whole thing and go back home. It was at times like this that I wished I had a wife and kids to go back to, even though I had never wanted any of them.

The wait was draining my strength and essence. I decided to squat down before I fainted or fell into the hole. After a tiresome wait, a hollow-sounding respiration finally turned the night even more dreadful. The medium stepped back and I stood up and away from the grave. Soon a stringy vapour rose from the top end of the bamboo stake. We were unsure of what it was, but I knew it was to be the beginning of long rueful days that were to come. The vapour accumulated into a cloud and hovered over us like a huge umbrella. We didn't know what to do and we kept looking at the medium who seemed as terrified as we were.

When the medium shuffled his feet, we prepared ourselves to make a dash. It was then that we saw what must have been the most peculiar and amazing sight. We saw numbers in the cloud of smoke or vapour or spirit or what-have-you. They were swirling around. Leong was the first one to substantiate our sighting.

'Do you see that? Can you see the numbers?' He shook me out of my stupor, but I was mesmerized by the strange phenomenon.

'Yes. Yes!' I replied anyway.

'318,' Leong shouted. 'Are you taking this down?'

I dug into my pocket for the cigarette packet and a set of house keys. I scraped the packet with one of the sharper keys since they were the only things available at hand.

'016, 965, 337,' Leong continued to chant out the numbers full of enthusiasm.

'Why are there so many numbers?'

'Shh . . .' Leong shushed me and read out the last number, '462, I think.'

I doubled-checked the numbers. I couldn't see what I had etched on the soft cardboard of the cigarette packet but I was confident I had gotten them all.

We waited a little longer to see if any other numbers would appear in the smoky cloud but they dissipated as soon as we got the numbers.

'Too many numbers,' the medium said with a hollow voice.

'Isn't that good? That means we will be rich! Perhaps they are some random numbers we could play for Toto 6D.'

'They usually never give out so many numbers. I don't understand,' the medium sighed and shivered from the intensifying cold. He stepped closer to the coffin and yanked the bamboo stake out with a resounding slosh that ended the session. Leong and I felt our blood going cold and we squirmed.

The medium climbed out of the grave and walked away when Leong called to him, 'The grave . . .' he pointed.

'The undertaker will settle the rest.'

We hurried to his side and trudged on like allegiant soldiers ready to lay down their lives for some cause. I glanced back at the grave reluctantly for I had to know that nothing was following us.

* * *

'We went our separate ways the moment we got to our cars. It was up to Leong and me to decode the numbers and invest some money in Magnum, Damacai or Toto. Needless to say, Leong and I couldn't sleep that night. We telephoned each other to talk for a bit, but I forget what we talked about. It had nothing to do with the excursion to the cemetery or the significance of the numbers. We each just needed to assure ourselves that the other had reached home and was still alive and kicking.

I sat in the living room in front of the TV to keep myself distracted from the stray and unwanted thoughts that were troubling me. It was bad enough that we did what we did but knowing how the girl died made me sick to the pit of my stomach. Who does that? What the hell is wrong with people? What kind of a world are we living in? I kept wondering what if the girl was my sister or daughter or friend?

I dozed off a few times to catch fragments of a horrific nightmare where profanities were hurled at me. I couldn't see the man's face, but he was blaming me for his actions. It didn't feel like me and yet it was me at the same time. I was wearing an unusual skin as it were. I was that girl.

I thought I had finally fallen asleep, but I woke up with an extremely painful sensation in my groin—something I had never felt before. The muscles were having a tug-o-war and the nerves had become hypersensitive. The only way to describe the pain was to imagine arrows being shot at my genitals.

In the morning, I called Leong to see whether he was experiencing a similar discomfort, but it was too embarrassing to even mention it. Instead, I just said same place, same time and he replied with a grunt that sounded like 'hmm'.

* * *

By the time I arrived at the *kopitiam* where we usually hung out, I saw him at the table listing down the numbers in the sequence he wanted to place his bets.

'All set?'

'Yeah, yeah, waiting for Ang Bee.'

She was the *pah gee* woman who went around to buy numbers on the punters' behalf. Although it was illegal, she ran quite a lucrative business that was left unnoticed by the authorities. I was about to sit down to get my list ready, when a fifty-something-year-old woman appeared behind me.

'Anything today?' she asked.

'Yes, got, got,' Leong said abruptly and shuffled the papers together for her.

She sat with us and glanced at the stack of numbers with the utmost curiosity and almost shrieked, 'So many numbers? Where did you get them from? Must be either gods or ghosts!' She laughed and for a brief moment we didn't know what to do. She noticed our confusion and snapped impatiently, 'Time is money. Quick, quick.'

We obeyed her and explained to her what kind of betting we wanted. She jotted the instructions down, calculated how much we owed her, and left as abruptly as she came in. Occasionally, people who run illegal gambling rackets like her were hauled up to the police station for questioning that lasted a few hours; being on the move all the time seemed like a strategy that had been agreed upon to keep both parties sated.

After she left, Leong and I ate our curry *mee* and *wan tan mee* silently. We both knew we wanted to talk about last night, but something held us back. I didn't know if it was the fear or the fact that we did something we might regret for the rest of our lives.

As soon as I finished eating the noodles, I could no longer stand the silence and I said, 'I've got this pain . . .'

'Me too.'

We looked at each other with our jaws dropped. Leong pushed his half-eaten curry *mee* aside and leaned closer to say, 'I found blood.'

'Blood?'

'Didn't you?'

'No. Just pain.'

'Where?'

I didn't like discussing private matters with anyone let alone in the open, but in this case it was necessary.

'Where I pee.'

'No blood?'

'No.'

'I couldn't pee since last night and this morning, when I tried, there was blood.'

I cringed and felt a phantom hand grab my crotch.

'Do you think it's from . . . you know.'

'Of course!' Leong shouted and immediately turned down the volume to a whisper. 'It's the ghost doing this to us.'

I wanted to say we deserved it since we desecrated her body, but there was no point in rubbing salt into the wound.

'What are we going to do?'

'Wait for a strike. If we hit the jackpot, bleeding like this is a small price to pay.'

'If we don't?'

'We'll ask the medium to send her straight to hell!' Leong fumed like a little boy who knew he was in deep trouble.

'She's already suffered so much!' I actually felt guilty for making her go through this agony even after death. Was it even possible to feel that way for a ghost?

'She's a ghost. What suffering?'

'I don't know but she should have been laid to rest in peace. Not dragged through another horror in hell. She was a victim of rape and murder, Leong! Have you no heart?'

'You're one to talk. Weren't you there with us last night invoking her restless spirit for a winning number?'

'I know I was. I'm beginning to feel really bad for doing it. She was an innocent girl who died too young. She was at the wrong place at the wrong time. She had suffered enough. I feel really, really bad.'

'It's over. Let's just concentrate on the windfall. We'll make a peace offering when we collect our winnings. I'll give her an entire roast pig if that's what she wants! Does that make you happy?'

'It's not about me. You know as well as I do it's . . . it's more than that.' I sighed and got ready to leave. We sometimes did not see eye to eye about a lot of things. Politics. Economics. History. Everything, come to think of it. But we had never differed so badly before—we were just going through the motions now. 'You had better go to the doctor to have it checked out,' I said and rose from the chair. 'I need to go to the pharmacy.'

Leong didn't reply and he continued eating the curry *mee* that had become cold and puffed up. Little did we know that that was just the beginning of a very long and tedious journey to hell. It's not fire and brimstone or eternal damnation that trouble you; it is always the small and insignificant but persistently annoying things that do, especially when you are trapped between life and death.

* * *

'I need something for . . . you know . . .' I blushed in front of the young salesgirl at the pharmacy and I almost couldn't get the words out, 'difficulty in urinating.'

'Do you have UTI?'

'Huh? What is UTI?' I must have sounded really stupid, but I really had no idea what it was.

'Urinary Tract Infection.'

'Er . . .' I shrugged, 'maybe.'

She turned away to locate the medication on the shelf behind her and within seconds she was back with a cheerful smile.

'This is only for pain relief. It will not cure the infection.'

'What?'

'It may go away on its own in a day or two.'

'Is it serious?'

'If it persists you will have to go to the doctor to get antibiotics.'

I was not ready to hear horrific details for something I had no idea about, but the girl continued to speak in an automated mode.

'You can also try drinking lots of cranberry juice and water.'

'Cranberry . . . water . . .' I was stumped by the over-informative girl.

'If neglected, it can cause kidney infection and other complications.'

I wanted to cry like a baby but instead I thanked her and trudged away like it was the end of the world.

* * *

Two days later I began to panic. Leong was right. I started bleeding. The pain was unbearable, but I didn't dare go to the doctor to explain to him that this was a curse from a dead girl. I called Leong to ask how he was, but all he could say was how the numbers were fake. We didn't become overnight millionaires. We weren't even close to hitting any jackpot. It was all for nothing. Worst of all, the ghost made sure we suffered for causing her unrest. And a torturous sensation in my anus was starting to develop.

The medium refused to see us or give us further explanation. He hid in his house for days and nights. From what we could gather from his neighbours, he was in extreme agony, crying and moaning

every few hours. No one could tell us why, but Leong and I were
way ahead of them.

* * *

'I think we're going to die,' Leong chanted about the hundredth
time since we left the medium's abode and parked ourselves in our
regular hangout at the *kopitiam* the next day.

'Why would she give us random numbers that don't mean
anything? She could have outright refused us.'

By now, I was more curious about the reason behind the
bizarre contact rather than becoming an overnight millionaire. But
then again, had I not been suffering, I would have dismissed the
entire thing as a hoax and forgotten about the encounter. For all we
knew, the medium could have staged the whole thing with the help
of his friends. But that couldn't be, because he was suffering as well.

I was at my wit's end when I saw a little girl flipping a picture
book a few tables away from us at the *kopitiam*. The first thought
that came to mind was how rare a scene like that was in the world
of today. If it wasn't a handphone, it wasn't a tablet or a gaming
device of some kind. What struck me as peculiar was that it
brought back a memory of a conversation I had with my grandma.
She used to refer to a little pink book whenever she wanted her
dreams or nightmares interpreted into numbers. The *Chifa* was
essentially a pictorial book back in the days when people believed
that the gods were giving them dreams that could be assigned to
winning numbers.

'Have you checked the corresponding numbers in the
Chifa book?'

'What for? They are numbers directly given to us. A whole lot
of good they did. Not even a consolation prize. I'm going home to
sleep. It feels like I'm on fire between my legs.'

'Did you have it checked?'

'Are you going to do it?'

I hesitated.

'That's what I thought. I have strange discharge coming out from both ends. Another medium gave me some herbs to drink and apply but nothing has worked so far. I think I'm a little feverish. I feel like . . . I feel like vomiting—'

Leong stood up immediately and staggered on his feet. I got up to aid him, when he suddenly dropped like a sack of rice before I could lend him my arm for support. He shocked everyone when he grabbed at the table, sending it crashing down along with everything on it to announce his fall. All I could do was stand there and watch, knowing I would be next.

* * *

I dug out the *Chifa* book which was lying in between many other periodicals, school magazines, and stacks of Reader's Digest, which used to be the most popular little book in every household.

'318, 016, 965, 337, 462,' I read the numbers aloud as I flipped through the book. 318 is staircase. I grabbed a pad and pen to jot down the image references. '016, a swallow. 965, a coconut. 337, a mirror. 462, a rubber band.

They were all random. Unconnected. It was ridiculous to think that the numbers meant anything other than the delusion of a get-rich-quick schemer. I cast the stationery and book aside and felt the sting moving back and forth between my anus and my crotch. If this didn't stop soon, I would have to check myself into the general hospital. And I was worrying more about the embarrassment than what was ailing me.

The fever came in the most unconventional way. I was in deep sleep or rather in the deepest part of hell where the fire was not only eternal but cold. I don't know how to explain it, but it was so hot that it actually felt cold. I knew I was in bed, coming down with something really bad, but I was determined to not give in to the curse, if it was one in the first place.

At first light, I checked to see if I was still alive. The house I had inherited from my parents was still musty and drab. Since I was my only concern, I didn't take much care of the interiors, but I was king here. The pain shot up from my groins when I swung my legs off the bed. A dizzy spell hit me and churned my stomach, forewarning me of what could follow if I forced myself to stand. Cold sweat popped out of my pores everywhere and I shouted to the dead girl, 'What do you want? We're sorry for defiling your body. Haven't we paid enough?'

I expected her to appear and probably scare me with a grotesque look that I would remember for the rest of my life, but nothing happened. Not even a ghostly sign of her presence. No fluttering curtains. No flying objects. No fuzzy images. No drop in temperature. No curious sounds. The only thing that startled me was my own reflection in the full-length mirror. I hate it when that happens. 337. That number came to mind. The image associated with it was a mirror. Could the numbers actually mean something?

I was listless and in pain the whole day. Leong was admitted into the general hospital when I called him. His daughter told me about his worsening condition. Who was I going to call when I got to Leong's condition? I had no one in my life. There was no one that I wanted to be in touch with. All of my relatives were estranged. The only friend I had who would put up with me was Leong.

I drove to the hospital to visit him, but he was fast asleep. His wife greeted me with layers of bags under her eyes.

'He was screaming the whole night. I think he must have woken up the entire neighbourhood. He said he couldn't urinate and when he did, he bled. And then there was pus. How on earth did he get like that? Must have been from some prostitutes he went to. If he hadn't been in so much pain, I would have chased him out of the house. Do you know where he got the disease from?'

I was taken aback by the question. It was not impossible to convince anyone about what we did because most of the people still believed in black magic, ghosts and gods. But it was not my place to trash a fallen man.

'I really don't know. How is he now?'

'The doctors gave him some painkillers and they are waiting for his blood and urine test results. But if he deserves it, he will get worse. He screams as though his bladder is about to burst. If he didn't pick it up from a prostitute, he must have angered some spirits.'

I felt sorry for Leong, but it was difficult to show my remorse and sorrow. His wife had a very keen intuition. She could pick up on things by just watching a person's reaction to her litany of accusations. I looked away from her eyes and gazed at a man who was beaten by his own game of chance and my eyes welled up, ready to break down crying.

'So, do you know anything?' she observed my facial expression as she asked the question.

I was doomed. Just then, my telephone rang. I raised a hand to ward her off and walked out of the room to avoid her.

'Hello.'

No one answered at the other end. I checked the number, but it was unfamiliar.

'Hello,' I said again, but the static only grew louder. I cut the call and sped out of the hospital before Leong's wife caught on to what we had done and kicked up a big fuss about it.

The sky was darkening. Whether it would rain or not was something the older generation used to gamble on. These days we just expect the unexpected.

I was driving out of the hospital when the call came again. It was the same number, but I had to pull up somewhere to take the call. I had seen too many accidents caused by people who thought they could handle a telephone while driving with one hand. Sooner or later fate will end their call for good.

Just before I could pull into one of the parking bays on Main Road, the ringing stopped. It couldn't have been anyone I knew because all my friends had names attached to the numbers on my telephone. As I continued driving, adjusting myself to avoid the pain between my legs the insistent caller attempted a third time. This must be really serious. I found a spot where I could park again and answered the phone as fast as I could.

'Hello?'

'Terrence?'

'No, you've got the wrong number.'

'Eh . . . this is not Terrence?' the stranger said.

'No.'

'Oh, sorry, wrong number,' he repeated what I said and hung up.

I was more terrified than annoyed, what with the agony that was burning me like thousands of ant bites. I put the phone back in my pocket when I saw a man walking out of an exit from a three-storeyed shop-cum-house. The moment I saw his face, everything made perfect sense. He was holding a phone in his hand, looking confused. There was an incessant and jarring recording of swallows playing in the background coming from the bird's nest breeding spots. And beside the office block from which the man stepped out, was a furniture shop. A full-length standing mirror was displayed by the doorway.

318, staircase. 016, swallow. 337, mirror. I chanted. This couldn't be coincidental. Deep down I knew he was the one. The rapist and the murderer. He didn't notice me sitting in the car. What could I do? Tell the police that my allegation that he was a criminal was based on my intuition? *Chifa* numbers? Accuse him outright and perform a citizen's arrest for rape and murder? I was this close and yet there was nothing I could do. I got out of the car anyway and approached him with disgust.

'It was you.'

'Eh? Who are you and what do you want?'

'That girl. It was you.'

'*Chee sin!*' he shouted and waved his hand at me as though he was about to strike.

I cringed, but he walked away. But just before he disappeared around the corner, he adjusted his crotch and I knew I didn't have to do anything. The girl was coming for him and it was going to be far worse than any sentences that could be slapped on him. I was partially relieved that I wasn't beaten up by the guy for stupidly accusing him. Also, I was glad to know that the girl was getting her vengeance.

My phone rang again but this time it was Leong's number.

'Hello.'

'It's gone,' Leong shouted.

My heart fluttered.

'What? What's gone?'

'Everything. The pain. The pus. The ache. It's all gone. What did you do? Did you do anything?'

I froze on the five-foot way. The chill that crept up on me was deathlike.

'What about you? Are you . . .' he lowered his voice to a whisper, ' . . . free from the curse?'

My shoulders sagged and my head drooped in disappointment.

'No.'

'How come?'

'I don't know.'

'So, did you do something?'

'I will tell you in person,' I said and started tearing up. Why was I still being punished? Held accountable? That wasn't fair. 'I'll come by later and tell you the whole story.'

'Thank God, Philip! Thank God it's over,' he said and hung up.

I had to clear my head. Why was he spared? Why wasn't I? I walked to the nearest *mamak* shop to get a drink and wallow in self-pity. That was the least I could do.

I sat in a corner at a vantage point and ordered my *teh halia*. I wanted to break down and cry like a hopeless man. The pain was excruciating. The last time I felt this way was when I had a toothache but that was only a tenth of the agony I was feeling now. When my drink came, I looked up to thank the waiter and saw a heavyset man sitting a few tables away in front of me. It felt strange, until his eyes met mine. On one of his arms, was a badly drawn tattoo of a coconut tree. On the other arm, he wore a bunch of rubber bands around his wrist. The final two numbers. 965, coconut. 462, rubber band. And somehow, I learned who he was and where it took place through the bits and pieces I could gather from eavesdropping on his conversation with his friend.

'I've always been afraid of the morgue. Aren't you even a little scared of working there?' his friend asked.

'Sheesh, it's normal. What's there to be afraid of? Besides, sometimes there's a bonus.'

'That's too gross.'

'This one still looked good.'

'Yeah, but, how could you? Urgh!'

'I could and I did,' the heavyset man laughed out loud in the noisy *mamak* shop.

He was the second rapist.

* * *

'Wait, wait. What do you mean second rapist?'

'He raped her in the mortuary. He works there.'

'Wait, but she was . . . she was dead!'

'Necro-something.'

'Necrophilia.'

'Let Jacob finish the story. There's some more to this story, right?'

'Yeah, just a bit. Philip immediately checked himself.'

* * *

I couldn't believe it. I shook my legs, drawing them apart and then squeezing them back together again. Whatever sting or discomfort I had felt before was no longer there. I tried crossing my legs and it was fine. I was about to celebrate my day with food when the guy who boasted about his exploitation jumped up from his chair. He knocked over one of the glasses and tea splattered all over his friend.

'What the . . .! What's wrong with you?'

'Something bit me. Ants, I think. Oi, *mamak*, are you rearing ants?' He laughed loudly. He hadn't a clue about what was in store for him.

That was the last I saw him. They left to clean themselves up and I was free.

I met Leong at the hospital again a little later and told him the whole story. It was more bizarre than the ritual we did at the cemetery. But who would have believed us anyway?

It took me a long time to recover from the night when we almost gambled our souls away for a momentary gain. I would wake up in cold sweat in the dark checking my groin just to be sure I was spared from the wrath of the ghost we violated. From that day, my UTI, or whatever it was, went away and I never took on another game of chance or wished to become an overnight millionaire. That desire died a sure and certain death. I was never happier knowing that winning isn't always everything.

* * *

'What happened to the rapists?'

'I guess Philip and his friend passed on the disease to them.'

'I think the girl was lost. She needed someone to guide her to them.'

'Yeah, yeah. I think so too.'

'I hope they suffer as much as the girl.'

'What about the medium? Why did he cut off contact from everyone?'

'Who knows? Gamblers don't always tell you the whole truth.'

* * *

The medium checked the doors and windows for the damaged talisman that had protected him all this while. He had not stepped outside his room since that night he invoked the spirit of the dead girl. It was usually a quick summoning to get the winning numbers out of the dead. There were no complications. He had never encountered anything this terrifying in all his life while playing for numbers with the dead.

When he realized that a dark entity rose with the dead girl's spirit, he hurried back to keep himself safe within the confines of the temple. He saw it occasionally even in daylight. A dark shadow passing by the window and appearing underneath the door. It was not death that was worrying him. It was something worse than death that had him arrested with fear. Since then numerous entities had made their presence known. He had no idea what they were, but if he knew, he would have learnt that they were the many dead bodies he had desecrated in his money-making rituals.

He heard about the disease the girl had spread to her victims. And how the two guilty men confessed to the police, begging to be arrested. While in the lockup the two men were unexpectedly cured from their festering wounds in and around the crotch and anus. But like many other punishable sins it didn't end there. They were ravaged by other inmates who found their act of defiling a young girl unforgivable. Although the curse was lifted their true suffering came later. The inmates were never going to leave them alone and the wardens had no sympathy for rapists. Until the end of their days, when they took their own lives on separate days, they told everyone about the whispers. The girl who they killed whispered something to them every night when they tried to sleep. No one was sure what she whispered to them but some said she told them how she had suffered in gruesome detail.

These days the medium could only wear loose clothes like the monk's robe. What he couldn't fathom was how he was still cursed even with hundreds of talismans that were renewed every day and pasted everywhere. From what he could gather, the dead girl's curse latched on to the three of them the moment she rose from the grave to offer the two guys a set of numbers—he still had no idea what they meant.

In the meantime, he had to endure the excruciating pain between his legs and in his behind. The last time he looked down below he saw that most of what he used to have was now an abscessed blob. He didn't know how much longer he could stand the agony or if the girl would get him eventually. Whatever it was he didn't want to take any chances by leaving the only safe place he knew.

9

The Boy who Cried Hanged Man

'Like the previous story, what is unknown should stay unknown. The rules and regulations are simple. Stay away from them and don't provoke them through black magic, invocations or seances for your own selfish reasons. What you awaken from the abyss will stay with you forever,' Ray said as his opening sentence.

'So, what is the story about?'

'Yeah, why do you have to give an introduction to this story?'

'Because the boy who started this was playing with fire and he didn't know when to stop.'

'Yeah, like some people who carry a joke too far even after it stops being funny.'

'Until it's too late.'

'That's right.'

'As the story goes, you could say Alfie had it coming, but he was the last to know.'

* * *

'If there's a devil in the wind let him slap me right now! I challenge you to slap me!' said Alfie, his hands raised to the sky, in front of his annoyed schoolmates who were tired of his never-ending buffoonery.

One by one they moved away to disassociate themselves from him and his arrogant taunting of the paranormal.

'What's wrong? Are you guys scared? Chicken shit!'

Some of them rode off in their bicycles, some walked through the gate, but everyone made a beeline out of Alfie's presence.

'Cowards! You sons of b—'

From the corner of his eye Alfie saw a large figure towering behind him and he knew it was going to be bad.

'Time to go home, Alfie.'

'Yes, sir, okay, sir.'

Alfie wheeled his bicycle out of the school compound and glanced back at the teacher who was still watching him. He didn't like school; he hated everyone in it. Out of boredom he pulled pranks that invariably landed him in unnecessary trouble. Between the beatings he got at home from his parents and punishments meted out by the disciplinary board, he was hoping to be suspended; but they preferred to keep him in school and prolong his misery by continuing with their torture during these, the best years of his teenage life.

Every now and then he tried his luck with the chair-pulling stunt, back-kneeing tricks, and shoelace-knotting gag, but they were quickly becoming dull. The one thing that he found exceptionally amusing was the exploitation of the paranormal. Everyone was afraid of things that slither, creep and crawl in the night and instances of 'who goes there in the dark?' That was when he started toying with all kinds of ideas that he had heard from older folk about taboos and superstitions. Since he could not play practical jokes or hurt anyone physically, he decided to frighten them instead.

Whenever he was in a crowd, he would summon the devil, demanding he show himself and this was a great way to clear the room. He tested it a few times by invoking the spirits or devil to slap him since it was said that if you shout at the wind, you will end up with a crooked jaw. But so far, he had yet to encounter anything paranormal to distort his face.

He was all set to go on a camping trip with the scouts in a week's time and he planned to do everything he could to wake the dead. He would have liked to bring along dog's tears, an apple, a handheld mirror, a long red string or a red ribbon, and a voodoo doll made of coconut husk but that would be taking things a bit too far. Not to mention, he could get sent home in disgrace for another good trouncing by his parents. For convenience, he brought only a bag of flour. That was good enough to scare his camping mates and best of all there was going to be a full moon that weekend.

When they arrived at Kem Maju, Alfie behaved himself for most of the day. He followed instructions, did his chores and was among the first to be ready for roll call and troop meeting. But when night overwhelmed the jungle and painted Kem Maju in complete darkness, he knew that he could now begin his real job.

He started with the usual 'monkey business' where he pulled out some of the other boys' belongings from their haversacks and tossed them around. He even sliced a kefir lime into two and sprinkled its juice everywhere. He left things thus in disarray and ran back to the HQ to rejoin the rest for roll call, from where he had snuck out a little earlier.

When they returned to their huts, his patrol mates were shocked, but they didn't think it was done by a monkey.

'Whoever did this is an asshole. That kefir lime is blessed by the gods and it's for protection,' Arosia said.

'Really? Against what?' Alfie asked.

'You guys are just terrible,' Arosia didn't answer but repacked his stuff with tears in his eyes.

'Look, whoever did this has to stop. Don't carry a prank too far,' Dani, their patrol leader, stepped in to console Arosia.

'What if it was Rokiah?'

Some of the boys laughed.

'Who's Rokiah?'

'The female orangutan that likes boys,' Alfie said.

Their hearty laughter travelled to the nearby shrubs and bushes and frightened the smaller animals into hiding.

Most of the boys were fast asleep by eleven that night. It was time for Alfie to bring out his bag of tricks and start his second antic. This time he sprinkled flour on some of his patrol member's faces and mud on their feet, shaped the top of his blanket into a head, tied a rope around the neck of this caricature and strung it up at the doorless opening into the A-frame hut. All he had to do now was wait.

The cold freezing night in Kem Maju was an experience to behold. In the pristine jungle teeming with wildlife, the temperatures dropped drastically in the night. For the faint of heart, camping in a natural environment was far from pleasant. Without the distraction of streetlights and man-made sounds, it was completely quiet but for the sounds of nocturnal creatures. And the cold could even rob one of sleep if one wasn't prepared to be seduced by its icy fingers that slipped under one's skin. To be in need of the toilet in the middle of the night was a cruel joke that Mother Nature could play on anyone. Number one could easily be done outside the hut but a number two would be a 'no-no'. Just thinking about the distance between the toilet and the hut was nerve-racking.

Everyone was fast asleep when one of the patrol members squealed in the wee hours of the morning. He cowered in terror, pointing to the person with a white face sleeping by his side. It set off a chain reaction of hysteria when, one by one, they screamed at each other's white faces and their own muddied feet. But the final straw was the hanged man. That was when they completely lost it and woke up the entire scout troop with shrieks and cachinnations.

At the HQ, as soon as the rest were sent back to their respective huts, the patrol responsible was detained to explain the ruckus.

Ironically, their group was named Hyena. The scoutmaster, furious to have been woken up prematurely, paced about to calm his nerves.

'This is too much,' Mr Jagarow said as he huffed and puffed through his beard. 'I should send the whole lot of you packing first thing in the morning and think about a suitable punishment when this camping trip is over.'

The patrol members bowed their heads as low as they would go to avoid eye contact with the infuriated Mr Jagarow. His beetling brows twitched in anger, and that meant severe repercussions would follow.

'You boys are on the threshold of adulthood. Pulling pranks like these will only set you back and keep you stuck in your teenage years. There's a time for everything and this is not it. What am I going to do with the whole lot of you?' Mr Jagarow's large bloodshot eyes looked piercingly at each and every one of them. 'I am disappointed with this patrol. If you want to behave like kids, then you will be treated as such. I want the Hyena Patrol to clean the toilets as a foretaste of the kind of trouble you can get yourself into if you don't use your head to think before you act.'

Alfie stifled his giggles as best as he could, but he was the only one in the patrol enjoying the reprimand. Mr Jagarow carried on for another twenty minutes or so, going off at a tangent about morality and bleak futures to add to their pathetic resumes. By the time he finished his harangue, it was almost three thirty in the morning. Everyone was nodding off and could hear nothing but the sound of their own dreams. The scoutmaster eventually let them go because the morning roll call was scheduled for seven in the morning.

On their way down the hill, the Hyena Patrol bitterly blamed Alfie for his idiocy that got them all in trouble.

'It's all your fault, Alfie.'

'We could get kicked out of the scout troop.'

'You and your stupid pranks!'

'When Mr Jagarow reports this to my parents, I'm as good as dead.'

'Why couldn't you have been in another patrol?'

'Hey guys, hey, hey. Stop,' the patrol leader, Dani, said. 'It's done. Let's go back to the hut and get some sleep. We have a long day ahead.'

'Yeah, cleaning those damn toilets because of Alfie.'

The patrol members strolled silently back but stayed close together because the path to their hut was demarcated by lallang and shrubs. With one torch in front of the group and another at the rear, they maintained a distance of an arm's length from one another.

Although Alfie felt that he had gone overboard, he wasn't going to admit it anytime soon. He may have been the cause, but it was their reaction that had made it worse. Who asked them to be so cowardly? He knew apologizing to them would improve his standing with them a little, but he didn't want to. It wasn't like it was the end of the world. In time, everyone would laugh about this silliness and even thank him for making the camping trip memorable. Mr Jagarow might even find this amusing when he retired in the years to come.

As soon as they reached the hut, the boys in front stopped abruptly and everyone craned their necks to see what was happening. The one nearest the door covered his mouth to keep from screaming. The others pointed in awe.

The blanket that looked like a hanged man was dangling from the other doorless exit. With the full moon shining in at the right angle and the breeze blowing through in precision, the hanged man swayed from side to side; simulating death in a gruesome manner.

'Damnit, Alfie! I almost died!'

'If I had screamed, we would be back at the HQ before we knew it, and it would be all because of you!'

Dani made his way to the front of the line to calm the rest down.

'Alfie, get that thing down. Now!'

Alfie dragged his feet to the back of the hut and tried to yank the blanket down. But the knot was too tight to come undone.

'It's stuck.'

'Well . . . we'll do it in the morning. Just . . . just cover that damn thing up.'

Alfie took another blanket and hung it on the nails on either end at the top of the doorway. When he stepped back the silhouette of the hanged man looked even more real than before.

All the other boys huddled close to the exit at the opposite end and yelled at Alfie to take the blanket down.

Alfie ran back to them after struggling for a moment and said, 'I think this is also stuck.'

'Can someone else go and take it down?' The patrol leader asked, but no one had the courage to even want to try. 'Okay, fine. Tomorrow, then. Now, get some sleep.'

The boys who were close to where the hanged man was, grabbed their sleeping bags and crowded together at the other end. They tucked themselves in haste to get out of the cold and rested their sleepy heads on their haversacks, facing away from the hanged man. Alfie pulled his sleeping bag towards the group, found a small available spot in between and snuggled in. It may have been funny before, but this time, he too was disturbed by the horrifying looking silhouette.

If it hadn't been for the crickets and the frogs, they would have heard each other's heartbeat getting derailed from the tracks of their hearts. A few snores here and there later, the ones who could not get back to sleep heard the rope squeak. The hanged man swung precariously as a howling wind made an entrance. The insomniacs inched closer and closer towards the rest, until they looked like the litter of a strange animal.

'I-I think it moved,' someone said in the dark.

'Don't be stupid. Of course, it did,' Alfie tried to calm Kevin's fears so that he himself would believe it. 'It's the wind.'

'Don't look at it. Get some sleep,' Dani said, and the others were surprised that he was still awake too.

'How are we going to sleep with that thing staring at us?' Arosia asked.

'You're scaring yourself for nothing,' Alfie said and turned to his side to face Arosia.

'Then why don't you go and take that thing down?'

'Easier said than done. The rope is stuck—'

'Yeah, yeah . . . you're just as scared as we are.'

'No, I'm not!'

'Hey, hey! Stop it guys. You want to wake Mr Jagarow? He may be at the HQ, but he's got ears like a bat.'

'So, what does that make him? A vampire?' Alfie asked.

The commotion woke the rest up; even the heavy sleepers.

'Shut up! Don't make things worse,' Arosia said.

'You shut up!'

'Hey—'

Something crashed to the ground while they were arguing, crushing the dry leaves and sandy floor. When they looked up the hanged man was gone.

'Where, where's th-that thing?' Arosia asked.

The piece of blanket that acted as a screen had no other silhouettes to indicate the presence of the hanged man.

'It's gone.'

'I told you guys not to fool around with my kefir lime. That was what the protection was for,' Arosia said.

'It fell. There's nothing to it.'

'But . . . but there's nothing on the ground.'

'Alfie, you're the one who made that thing. Why don't you go and check?'

'What for? It came loose . . . and fell. I'm going to sleep.'

The sound of cloth being dragged on the wet and sandy ground outside the hut silenced everyone.

'What was that?'

'Shhh.'

They listened intently and there it was again.

'It's . . . it's aliveee . . .' someone said and made everyone cringe.

'It's hunting us.'

'We're going to die.'

'Pretend to sleep and it will go away.'

Not wanting to make another unnecessary scene, the Hyena Patrol stifled their screams and fears and crouched under the covers. They huddled closer together, barricading themselves with haversacks, shoes, pots and pans, and their personal belongings. The barrier may not have been much, but it served as a false security for them to toy with the idea that everything was going to be all right; that whatever was creeping around outside the hut would be impeded from attacking them—but of course, no one actually believed that.

The Hyena Patrol was present at the morning roll call, but they looked like the undead. They had skipped breakfast because no one had any appetite and no one had wanted to cook. Mr Jagarow kept shaking his head in disapproval, but he did not bring up the issue of Alfie's prank. He only addressed everyone about the day's agenda, the lugubriousness in his voice expressing his disappointment at their behaviour. As soon as they were dismissed, the other patrols went away to take a short break before the Treasure Hunt began. As for the Hyenas, they went straight to toilet duty with continued antagonism towards Alfie.

By the time they had all their chores done, the Hyena Patrol was on the verge of punishing Alfie themselves. Had they not been distracted by the find, they would have probably done it. Dani was the first to find the dirty blanket which was grimy with sand, morning dew and red earth. The strange occurrence of the hanged man in the night was now accompanied by markings on the ground which indicated the blanket had been dragged around the hut.

'It's aliiiiive!'

'It was observing us.'

'Don't jump to conclusions. Someone did this,' Dani said. 'Alfie, if this is another one of your—'

'I swear I didn't do this. Look, I was in the hut with you guys. How could I even do this?'

The boys looked at the soiled blanket and the trail it left behind.

'Thank goodness this is a one-night camp.'

'If it were a two-night camp, I would've pretended to be sick and gone home.'

'You guys are really chicken shit,' Alfie said. 'It's just a blanket. It could be one of the other patrols come to frighten us.'

A dead silence creeped them all out until Dani said, 'I hope for your sake it's true,' pointing at Alfie to make sure the message got through.

In the evening, the rest of the troops parted with the soaring spirit of scouting, but the Hyena Patrol felt like scavengers skulking away with their tails between their legs.

* * *

Alfie was exhausted when he returned home and slept like the dead from that very evening right through to ten in the night. Disoriented and out of sync with time, he ate dinner alone and stared blankly into space without knowing what was real and what wasn't. The camping trip seemed so far away and his pranks hadn't been as satisfying as before. When he had started clowning around in school, everyone loved it when he made them laugh. But that novelty had died down to a few chuckles, a lot of grunts and some disgruntled harrumphs. He was losing his edge as an entertainer and he felt lonelier than ever—as he felt now at the dining table, all by himself, having a late dinner.

The hanged man was a joke. It wasn't meant to get anyone in trouble, especially not his entire patrol. He didn't know how long they would hold the grudge against him, but he was going to be on his own from now on.

'Alfie! Alfie! I can see it!'

Alfie's hair stood on end and he dropped the spoon into the ceramic plate when his sister barged in hysterically.

'What the f—,' he wanted to shout and cuss at his sister, but his parents were very strict about that. 'What the hell are you talking about?'

'I'm scared.'

'Of what?'

'The hanged man.'

Alfie stood up from the chair and accidentally knocked his knees against the leg of the table. 'Who put you up to this?'

'Don't you remember?' his sister wailed, 'You rubbed dog's tears into my eyes when I was asleep.' She tugged at his shirt to accentuate the repercussions of his prank.

'But that . . . that was so long ago. And you said, you said you didn't see anything.'

'I thought so too, but I can see it now. What am I going to do? It's in the house.'

'What?' Alfie scanned the room for signs of the hanged man. 'Where did you see it?'

'It was in front of your room. And then it jumped off and disappeared. It came back again into the hallway and—' his sister finished her sentence with a scream, pointing behind Alfie.

He spun around, expecting the hanged man to attack him but the only thing that frightened him was his own anticipation. There was nothing behind him. He was about to confront his sister, when he heard her laughing.

'You silly fool!'

'Huh?'

'Your friends told me about the stupid prank you pulled. This is me getting back at you for being such an asshole.'

'That's not funny.'

'It wasn't meant to be funny. Did I scare you?' she made a crying baby face at him.

'No.'

'Oh, yes I did!' Alfie's sister laughed in her squeaky voice.

'Stop bothering me.'

His sister flipped him the bird and walked away, 'Serves you right.'

Alfie's felt his insides doing a somersault and rearranged the position of his heart. Ever since that night, he felt fear as he had never done before. It may have only been a dirty old blanket strung up with rope, but at some point, the tomfoolery took on a life of its own and began to terrorize him. Now, any little sound made him jumpy.

He kept hearing the coarse material of blanket scraping on the tiled floor. Faint as it may have been, he could clearly discern the unnerving sound from amidst the many other distracting noises made by the creatures of the night. Every hidden nook and cranny seemed to be ominously harbouring an evil incarnate. Every shadow in his peripheral vision tempted him to do a double take to make sure he wasn't going insane. He sat in front of the telephone and reviewed the list of telephone numbers in his head but when he reached for the dial, he realized he had no friends. None who would even give him the time of day since he had pissed them all off with his shenanigans.

The only thing left to do was to lock himself in his bedroom, let the night dissolve into day and hope he wouldn't have the misfortune of bumping into the 'thing' he had created. He didn't dare fall asleep and he sat up all night long, nodding away with the lights on. To further protect himself from that evil thing, he dug out a triangular talisman from the drawer and wore it around his neck. He didn't believe in the hype that his mother had made when she had got it from the medium, but now, he felt he had nothing to lose.

When morning came, he prepared himself to leave as soon as there was light enough to leave the house. Perhaps being in a crowded place would help. How he was going to overcome this, was beyond him. His pranks had never gone this far.

They always ended with laughter and were quickly forgotten. Occasionally, some of the more sensitive people carried the torch of embarrassment with them for far too long, but that was their problem. Not his.

He had always been a loner. Perhaps not out of choice, because he did try to fit in, but, every time he did, he inadvertently offended someone. He had since given up trying. He chose to offend everyone instead. He didn't realize that fear exaggerated loneliness. He didn't want to stay at home, where no one knew he existed. For once, the thought of going to school was appealing.

When he arrived at the gates, he saw the tables had been turned. News had spread. The entire school played to the tune of the hanged man gag. Some of the boys pulled at their neckties up to simulate hanging, sticking their tongues out and following that with choking laughter. Others dragged rugs and their school bags around when they saw him. For the first time, he felt eyes on him wherever he turned. And it was not the good kind of popularity. It was a mistake going to school after having pulled that stunt, but he had nowhere else to go. Now that the shoe was on the other foot, he didn't like how it felt.

He was inattentive in class, although this was nothing new. He avoided as many people as he could and hurried to the school library the moment there was a break. It was empty as usual, except for the librarian.

'Mr Gregory, do you have any books on hauntings, superstitions and evil spirits?'

The grey-haired man with an upturned mouth that looked like a perpetual grin came over to the counter, patted him on the back and said, 'I heard what happened.'

'Looks like the whole school did.'

'The supernatural and paranormal section is at the end of the aisle on the left. But I doubt you will find any answers.'

'Huh? What do you mean?'

'You think the hanged man is after you, am I right?'

'Er . . . kind of,' he leaned forward to whisper. 'Do you believe in stuff like that?'

'I do believe in ghosts and stuff like that,' Mr Gregory replied. 'Like that jaga who roams around on the third floor, he is real. But this one is nothing like that at all.'

'Why? Is it worse?'

'No,' Mr Gregory shook his wise old head. 'I think this thing is from the power of suggestion. A manifestation of all of your fears that gave it life. The hanged man.'

'How?'

'You're better off reading the power of the human mind than all the myths and legends put together. It's more science than imagination,' Mr Gregory stepped down from the platform and was now face to face with Alfie.

'Are you sure, Mr Gregory?'

'Of course. I'm not very good at explaining it, but the human mind is capable of many things beyond our comprehension. We can communicate telepathically. We have the ability to move things with our minds. And we can also create something out of thin air. There are stories about people who can project images or visuals which may seem like ghosts or apparitions.'

Alfie couldn't comprehend anything the old man said. They were too fantastical. Besides, it was the ghost of the hanged man that he was trying to exorcise, not study the powers of the human mind. While Mr Gregory went on to explain about other cases, Alfie drifted further into his own world, feeling bored.

'There was a strange case of the girls in Maxwell Hill and then the one about the man who trapped birds. Are they real? Did it happen? Who knows?' Mr Gregory went on.

Alfie wanted to excuse himself, but he didn't know how to cut short Mr Gregory's unending monologue. Alfie saw something move behind Mr Gregory but the old man couldn't have cared less. Alfie shifted his focus and saw something sticking out of one of the shelves. He tilted his head to looked over Mr Gregory's shoulder and saw the hanged man. One end of the blanket tied up in a bundle to represent the head. Covered with sand and dirt and leaves. He jumped up, grabbed the table for support and accidentally knocked everything over. The fallen books, stationery and notebook were scattered all over the floor.

'I . . . I've got to go.'

'Don't you want the books?'

Alfie shook his head and ran off before Mr Gregory could get another word in.

He didn't know who he could turn to now. He walked past the busy canteen where the other students were having their meal. He tried to hide his face from them, but it was futile. Everyone recognized everyone in the school. Their gaits, idiosyncrasies and appearances. As he hurried past the crowd, he heard them whispering—that's him, hanged man, *pocong*, prankster. He quickened his pace and ran into the scout's den to gather his thoughts and salvage what was left of his pride.

There were a few scouts playing carroms, darts and learning to tie knots. They gazed at him with looks that could only mean disgust, annoyance and anger. He wanted to tell them about the hanged man, but everyone averted their eyes before he could say anything. He felt their cold shoulders shrugging him off and there was nothing else to do but leave.

He was at the corridor when he saw the hanged man coming at him like a ghost in a flying bed sheet. He ran and did not look back. He dashed out of the school's back gates and out on to the road. From the corner of his eye he could see the hanged man hopping as it were towards him. He did not see the oncoming car and he did not hear the screams that came from all sides of the road.

* * *

'From that day onwards, he was never the same again,' Ray said and ended the tale abruptly.

'What do you mean by that? "Not the same" in what sense?'

'Yeah, what happened to him?'

'He kind of . . . became paralysed I think.'

'What? How?'

'You mean he broke his spine in the accident?'

'No, the car didn't hit him. He fainted and was hospitalized.'

'Then how did he become paralysed?'

'No one knows. They say he just lies there like a paraplegic, but he seems fine otherwise,' Ray lowered his voice, leaned forward and said, 'but there's a rumour.'

'What rumour?'

'That it has something to do with the hanged man.'

'Really?'

'That's scary.'

'What actually is the hanged man? A ghost? A devil? A demon?'

'As I said earlier, what is unknown should remain unknown.'

* * *

'What's happening to him, doctor?' Mr Mung asked.

'As far as we can tell, he is fine. But he keeps drifting in and out of consciousness.'

'You mean he's in a coma?'

'No. He's as conscious as every normal person, except he seems to have very little control of his bodily functions.'

'Did the accident cause him to be like this?'

'No. The car stopped in time and he only sustained superficial injuries.'

'But . . . he isn't paralysed, is he? Will he be like this for the rest of his life?' Mrs Mung asked.

'It's inconclusive, at the moment. We've been observing him for the past week. Some days he wakes up with complete control of his body for a few seconds and then he slips back into this paraplegic state. It seems to be some form of catalepsy, but we can't be too sure. You need to send him to Penang or Ipoh for more tests,' the doctor glanced at Alfie and then at his parents and added, 'for now, you can take him home and monitor his condition.'

'Isn't it like sleep paralysis?'

'Mr Mung, it would be better if you could take him to a specialist.'

'Son, can you hear us?' Mrs Mung leaned over Alfie and said, 'He's awake. He just rolled his eyes to look at me.'

'He's a very strong boy. I'm sure he will get up in no time.'

'Did you hear that, Alfie? You'll be up and about soon,' Mr Mung said and pumped his son's hand to convey their hopes.

Alfie tried to speak but no sound came out of his gaping mouth. He pleaded for help from his parents and his friends who visited him, but only saliva dribbled down the sides of his lips. He could only manage a small cry that sounded like a breath escaping from the depths of his soul. His well-wishers kept assuring him that he would get better, but he knew it was a lie. The looks on their faces told another story. One that was tragic. He wanted to tell someone so badly about the hanged man who was sitting on his chest, making it difficult for him to breathe. Only when he was about to run out of air did the thing drag itself off his chest and wait by his side. As soon as he resumed his normal breathing and was about to scream for help, the hanged man hopped back on to his chest and lay there like a security blanket.

Although it had no form or face the shadows on the folds of the blanket anthropomorphized into a being that only Alfie could see. Something that had a wicked grin and eyes so dark that there was no end to the abyss from whence it came.

10

That Oily Thing

'I'm going to tell you guys about my mom's experience . . .'

'Not again. You told us that story last time.'

'We're supposed to tell new ghost stories each time we meet.'

'Yeah, but I like this story and I think it's really scary.'

'No, you can't use it.'

'It's not fair.'

'Wait, you guys. Hold on. Let him repeat the story one last time. But it *has* to be the last time, okay?'

'Okay,' Lai said in disappointment, but his eyes lit up again when he began, 'Back in the '60s there was an *or-eu-lang* or *orang minyak* scare. It was partly caused by P. Ramlee's movie *Sumpah Orang Minyak* and also by perpetrators who used this idea to commit crimes. Some people claimed to have seen this *or-eu-lang* running around at night, but no one could actually prove it. For a long time, everyone feared the dark and kept their activities confined to the day. Although no one was murdered by the *or-eu-lang*, a spate of unusual suicides among women rose without rhyme or reason. Yet everyone knew it had something to do with that oily thing.

'Mom was everything my grandparents hated. Poor. Uneducated. Cantonese. She had to live with my grandparents on Museum Road because dad could not hold down a job long enough to sustain us. My grandfather was a government servant and was about to retire soon. Once he did we would all have to move out of the government house. That was another worrying thought.

'Although I don't know what it was like since I wasn't even born then, mom told me this creepy and terrifying story that she said no one believed.

'She lived in the servant's quarters that was detached from the main house, linked only by a small cemented path. There was no way to contact anyone once the main house's doors were locked for the night. My mother had to endure being alone every night for about a year. Dad worked his fingers to the bone; returning home only late at night to sleep and then beginning his day again as early as six in the morning. He covered a wide range of activities in the construction line: from tiling floors to renovating homes, from driving lorries to delivering raw materials to the site.

'Although my mother was terrified of the surrounding darkness she braved herself in that little locked room that was their home, doing some simple sewing to get through the lonely nights. She grew used to the sounds of the nocturnal creatures that were her only company. It wasn't until one night, when the creatures fell completely silent, that she felt something was amiss. She peered out through the louvred window, but it was too dark to make out anything. She had an ominous gut-feeling that matters were going to take a turn for the worse but she brushed off the thought and soldiered on with her needlework.

'My siblings were very young then. Probably somewhere between three and five years old. Mom made sure they were safely tucked in and laid out beside her on the floor. It was one of those cold nights when my mother fell asleep before my father returned home. She must have been so very tired from her chores that she didn't even realize that dad was already asleep beside her. When she felt his presence, she turned to face him and see if he was awake, but she could not see anything in the dark.

'She reached for him, felt his arm and then froze. Something was not right. His arm was smooth. Hairless. My dad had hairy arms and legs, coarse weather-beaten skin. Whoever this was, his skin was slick. Like oil.

'My mom didn't dare do anything, but she turned away from him to watch over my siblings. She could not run out of the room and leave them there. She kept very quiet, very still, wondering what she could do to raise an alarm to alert someone about the strange man lying beside her. Whatever his intentions were, they couldn't be good. Tears started welling up in her eyes but she suppressed them to not show any signs that she knew about the intruder. He could easily hurt them if he wanted to.

'There was nothing within reach. No firewood. No tongs. No cutlery she could use as a weapon to defend herself and my siblings. The one thing she was prepared to do was to fight to her death to protect her children. She clenched her fists and gritted her teeth and waited. If the intruder laid even a finger on her or my siblings, she was going to scratch his eyes out.

'She was shocked when the light suddenly came on. Although it was only a low-wattage bulb, it was sufficient to light up that meagre little room and expose every corner of it. She swung about to confront the intruder when she saw my father locking the door.'

* * *

'Did you just come in?' she asked dad and looked around for the man with the slippery skin.

'Yes. Sorry I'm late. There was a lot of cleaning up to do.' Dad was getting ready for bed, when my mom got up and stood beside him. 'What's wrong?'

'There's someone in the room,' she murmured.

'What?' dad threw a quick glance around the room. There wasn't even a closet in which an intruder could hide. All their belongings were neatly stacked against a wall. There was not even enough room enough for a rat to hide in.

'I know it sounds crazy but . . . but I felt him.' She shuddered at the thought. 'He was lying next to me.'

'How can it be? I just came in. I didn't see anyone. Where could he have gone? The door was locked.'

They both fell silent for a while, staring at each other. My mother knew that the only explanation was the kind in which my father refused to believe.

'I'm really scared.'

'Could have been a nightmare.'

'No. I was awake,' she protested.

Dad held her arms to calm her down, 'From tomorrow onwards why don't you and the kids sleep in the hall of the main house until I return?'

'I wish your parents would give us the spare room up there.'

'You know them. They are angry enough as it is that we got married. That we are partially depending on their support now, doesn't make it any better.'

'But why would they treat us like this? I mean, these are their grandchildren.'

'We'll have a home someday and then, whatever they think of us won't matter one way or the other.'

Mom sighed and hugged dad, releasing all her pent-up sorrow.

'We'll get by somehow, but I need to go to sleep now. I've got a long day tomorrow.'

Mom nodded and saved her tears, again, for another day.

* * *

My mother was at the market, shopping for that day's meal. As always she only had very limited time for a social life when she could mingle with friends and acquaintances.

'Eh, they say there's an *or-eu-lang* in Taiping,' the fishmonger said and laughed raucously. 'So, you girls have to be careful. But not the aunties la,' he laughed again, squeezing out the explanation in between his giggles, 'he . . . only go for . . . virgins.'

Mom waited for his mirth to subside before asking the fish monger, 'Why do you say there's an *or-eu-lang* here?'

'Eh, some aunty said she saw him last night. Described him as described by P. Ramlee,' he guffawed heartily.

'I think she watched too many *pontianak* movies,' one of the aunties said.

'Not the same, aunty,' the fishmonger stated. 'One is a man. One is a woman. One rape virgin girls. One drink man's blood. No, not the same!'

My mother was feeling very disturbed by the conversation at this point. She was worried enough with the idea of an intruder, a supernatural one at that. She hadn't the luxury to hang around to glean more information because there was a load of chores to complete before lunch was served. She bought her *keng chai min* or the premade economical noodles for breakfast and some *nonya kueh*, the sweet gooey kind, for my grandparents as a teatime snack and stacked them in the rattan basket among the fish, meats, vegetables and other condiments.

She hurried back to the house to prepare lunch, musing over how best she could defend herself if the *or-eu-lang* was indeed real. She wished my father would do something about it, but she knew it was a vain hope. As it was he was dead tired by the time he got home and to burden him with yet another problem, one in which he did not even believe, was going to put a strain on their relationship.

One of the neighbours was a very kind, middle-aged lady who knew about my parents' situation. She would come over to the house to babysit my siblings whenever mom needed to go to the market or run some errands. She was just known as *Kak* Ida to my mom. She would ensure that my siblings, who were toddling around, stayed within the compound and out of harm's way, until mom returned. But of late *Kak* Ida's presence was not welcomed by my grandparents so she brought my siblings back to her home.

'*Kak* Ida,' my mom called out to her and parked the bicycle in the shade. My siblings ran to see if mom had bought any goodies for them.

The lady in the *kebaya* got off the mat on which she was sitting and returned my mother's call in a sing song response, 'Ooiii.'

'Thank you again, *kak*, for taking care of the kids.'

'Hai, no need to thank you-thank you at all. It's the neighbourly thing to do,' *Kak* Ida brought my siblings out to the porch. She then went to get me who was fast asleep in the sarong that doubled as a baby's cot.

'Have they been good?' mom asked, carrying the sleeping child in her arms.

'They were very well-behaved. Not a sound.'

My mother almost burst into tears at the stranger's kindness but, as always, there was no time for sentiment.

'I wish I had time to sit and chat, but I have to go and prepare lunch.'

'You go ahead. I know you're very busy. Call me if you need my help again. Just don't overwork yourself, okay?' *Kak* Ida said and mom smiled at her tiredly that was long overdue.

The two of them shared a moment of commiseration.

'*Kak* Ida, have you heard of any rumours recently?' My mother wasn't sure whether it was a good thing to share her fears, but she needed to speak to someone who was steadfast and had her feet firmly planted on the ground.

'Whatever you heard, Ah Nooi, they are only rumours.' By the way that's my mother's name. 'What is important is for you to know the difference and not give them any reason to be real. The more you dwell on them the more they will take over your life. Always remember that tomorrow is a new day with new beginnings.'

She didn't know what to make of the advice but nodded before she walked away.

* * *

After having fed my siblings, mom started to prepare the second meal of the day having her own breakfast as she cooked lunch.

As soon as lunch was ready, she cleaned up the kitchen and ascended the short flight of stairs to the main house to begin the daily menial tasks of sweeping, mopping and dusting the entire house as usual. It was an old wooden house on stilts. The dust and grime accumulated in the nooks and corners attracted insects, rodents, and even small birds. Her mind was still contemplating the rumour she heard at the market, when gramma, as I called my paternal grandmother, broke her reverie.

'Is lunch ready?'

My mother jerked out of her distraction about the supernatural being and answered immediately, 'Yes, *a-mak*.'

'We want to have an early lunch. Serve it by 11.30 a.m. *A-pa* and I have to go out after lunch.'

My gramma in her hand-printed batik sarong and baju *kebaya* with a *kerongsang* smelled of *bedak sejuk* and rose water. She was revered by many for having elongated Buddha's ears which signified longevity, and a broad face which symbolized prosperity.

'Yes, *a-mak*,' my mother said and checked the clock on the wall that gave her only ten minutes more to have everything warmed up to the right temperature.

She rushed back down to the kitchen. and heated everything up at one go. She fanned the slumbering embers in the clay stove to get the fire going. She placed the pot of spinach soup over the fire and picked up another piece of charcoal with the tongs to feed the flame. She woke up another clay stove from hibernation and placed a wok over it to fry *cheah-hu* or greenback mullet, a favourite among many since that fish was easily available and good to eat. To complete the meal, she also made prawns with green chilli in *assam ko* sauce, and fried pork marinated with spices. She was so efficient with it all that at the end she even had time to cut papayas and sprinkle the cubes with lime juice, and skin and slice some pears for dessert.

* * *

'Hold on, hold on Lai. You were not even born yet, how would you even know what your mother was cooking?'

'First of all, I love the prawn cooked with green chilli in *assam ko* sauce. My gramma loves it too. I think my whole family does. We have that quite often so it's a safe bet to say she must have cooked it that day.'

'Yeah, but how would you know all the details? You weren't there.'

'Mom told me. Besides, it's *my* story, okaayy?'

'Yeah, we know but no more food commentaries.'

'As I was saying . . .'

* * *

Mom managed to serve my grandparents in time and went back to tidy the kitchen. She was curious about where my grandparents were going, but it was not her place to ask. When my mother was done with her work, she sat down on a stool in the open-air kitchen to wait for the elderly folks to finish their lunch. My grandpa ate very slowly but gramma finished hers in half the time. My mother scanned around the perimeters of the government house, which was not barricaded by a fence, but naturally fenced-in haphazardly with shrubs and other small trees. In broad daylight, it didn't seem as frightening. And she had never been afraid of the darkness before the incident—life was hard and she had never had the time to worry about unnecessary fears.

This time, however, she had to find a way to protect herself. She didn't want to involve my father unless she had no other option. If it turned out to merely be a nightmare, she would have upset him needlessly and they would end up arguing for no good reason. What did that oily thing, if it was real in the first place, want from her? If it wasn't to claim her soul, why would it lie beside her and do nothing? She had to find someone with answers—perhaps a medium or a *bomoh*. But going to them would only open up a can

of worms. She had heard one too many horror stories about the
price of dabbling in black magic. Either way, something evil would
take control of her life and destroy her family if she did nothing.

She was startled by the sound of a car's engine and snapped out
of her reverie. Grandpa's old Morris Minor puttered away from the
porch to the driveway and exited onto the lonely road. Although
there were a few houses and schools around, it grew as quiet as a
library. She was watching my grandparents leave when she saw a
long dark shadow on the ground in front of the gateless entrance.
She didn't want to turn away or get paranoid so she observed it for
a little longer to see if she could identify it. The shadow stretched
into a slender-looking figure and my mother looked up to find the
source, but in the process caught the sun in her eye. The glare stung
her eyes and she was momentarily blinded.

When she could see clearly again the shadow disappeared. My
mother wasn't the kind to get easily distraught but this time she
was a nervous wreck. She made sure my siblings were accounted for
and brought them in the room, locked it and quickly fed them their
meals. As soon as this was done my mother fell asleep beside them
until the heat started baking the small confined space.

On days like these, when my grandparents were not home, she
would take my siblings to the main house, tuck them up in a corner
of the living room, choosing a place that was not too close to the
furniture or to the black-and-white television set. As my siblings
were fast asleep she had to carry them one at a time to the main
house and all the while she had an uneasy feeling that she was being
watched. As soon as everyone was in, she locked up every window
and door that had no business remaining ajar in the first place and
waited anxiously for my grandparents to return. It was almost two
in the afternoon and there was still no sign of them. If the terror
was this bad during the daytime, she dreaded sundown even more.

It got a little stuffy after a while, but she dared not switch
on the fan. As my parents weren't paying any bills, they were not
allowed to use the facilities. She used an old magazine to fan my

siblings so that they could get some respite from the heat. Every time she nodded off, one of my siblings would wake her up and remind her to fan them.

Mom was relieved when she heard the Morris Minor chug into the driveway at about three thirty in the afternoon. They would expect their tea to be ready soon, so my mother opened the door, ready to rush to the kitchen, but was confronted by gramma who started scolding her.

'Why is the house so dark? Why did you lock up all the doors and windows? Isn't it hot enough as it is?'

'No, *a-mak*. I was just, it was . . .'

'What? Are you hiding something?'

'No, no. I was just afraid to be alone.'

'What nonsense. We've never had any problems before. Why do you have to be afraid? Do you want to bring bad luck to the house?'

'I didn't mean to—'

'Didn't mean to? "Didn't mean to" what? Where is the *kueh*?'

'On the table.'

'And where is the tea?'

'I ha—have to boil the water.'

'Then go do it! Why are you wasting time standing here?'

My grandmother stormed off to her room, feeling quite ill-at-ease in her *kebaya* now, sweat patches appearing in her armpits. My grandpa strolled in with a pipe in his mouth and sat on the sofa to re-read the newspaper that he had already gone through in the morning.

My mother raced down to the kitchen to put the kettle on and my siblings inconveniently chose that precise moment to wake up, bawling. She stoked the fire beneath the stove, rested a kettle of water over it and ran back to the house. She picked me and half dragged the other two down to our room. I don't ever want to live like this again, mom reminded herself.

Before long, it was time to prepare dinner.

* * *

'Can you skip the food this time? It's not a foodie fable. It's supposed to be a ghost story.'

'Fine. But you guys don't know what you're missing out.'

'All this talk of food is making us hungry. So, yeah, it's okay to not talk about the food.'

'Okay, okay, already. I just love my mother's cooking, that's all.'

* * *

My mother lingered as long as she could in the main house. My grandparents went to sleep at about nine at night and they usually locked up the house just before they did. Mom had no choice but to move then, along with my siblings, back to the servant's quarters to wait for my father.

She switched on the night light at the far corner of the room. It was the one and only electrical outlet. My parents were not supposed to use any other light sources unnecessarily to avoid adding to the electricity bill. My mother could make out the silhouettes of my siblings and she tried to stay awake for as long as she could keeping a vigilant eye on them. But with the rising chill and the lullaby by nocturnal insects, she dozed off beside my siblings. She was deep in the sleep of exhaustion when she stirred as she accidentally brushed her arm on that velvety, oily skin again.

My mother knew what it was but was too afraid to open her eyes. She tried to move her arm away in the hope that it was just a nightmare, triggered by her imagination that had become hyperactive due to the rumour. But that disgusting feeling of something sticky smeared on her skin was inescapable. She thought that she could let it pass by ignoring its presence but when one of my siblings cried out briefly, mom turned to look at the child.

When she could not make out even the outline of the children who were just in front of her, she was seized with anxiety. Her heart started racing. All she could see was a massive dark figure blocking the night light. Something was lying between her and my siblings. She reached out in the darkness, pretending to shift her body in her sleep and again that greasy feeling brushed against her skin. She wanted to cry out but she worried for the safety of my siblings. If she screamed for help it could be too late by the time anyone responded. Although *Kak* Ida lived just in the next house, it would take a little while for her to come over. As for my grandparents . . . you could forget about them.

She lay there not knowing what she could do to make it all go away. She regretted not having kept a makeshift weapon at her side. It could have been a kitchen knife, a *tongkat*, a frying pan or even a pair of chopsticks, but there was nothing within her reach.

My mother was still wondering what to do when the door lock shuddered. Dad walked in unexpectedly and my mom sighed in relief. That oily thing vanished and my siblings could be seen again in the faint glow of the night light.

'You're back!' mom leapt up from the mattress and half-screamed, stifling her voice for fear of waking the children. She hugged my father with a deep desperation, but he held her back at arm's length. My mother nearly wept, but dad quickly explained, 'I hurt myself today.'

The room was still dark with the night light, so my mother walked around him and switched on the bulb and she saw the bandage around his arm.

'Is it bad?' my mother was trying to keep her cool, although her heart was begging for comfort from my father.

'No. It's just bruised. I can still do some amount of menial work.'

'How did this happen?'

'Someone dropped a bag of cement. I managed to protect my head by blocking it with my arm. That's why I'm late. I was at the hospital. They checked everything and I'm okay. No broken bones. It could have been worse.'

'Have you eaten?'

'Yeah, my boss bought a packet of chicken rice for me.'

'That's good. I'll help you clean up.'

'No need for that. They did quite a good job at the hospital. So, how was your day?'

My mom bit her tongue and said, 'The usual.'

She could not hold back the tears that night and cried silently when everyone else was fast asleep.

* * *

At first light, my mother opened her eyes and instantly plunged into a series of daily rituals. Prepare breakfast, handwash the laundry, clean the main house before heading out to the market. Although she was determined to get to the bottom of the terrifying haunting, she still had to make sure that the main house and the quarters were organized and running smoothly. Everything and everyone came first as far as their welfare was concerned. And that was how it had always been with her.

Mom expedited her visit to the market by avoiding small talk. There was no one she could confide in but one person—an estranged sister who had decided to pack up and leave everyone and everything behind to observe a celibate and quiet life in a temple. She had only three hours to spare after lunch to meet her sister.

My mother hurried home and prepared everything at lightning speed. She served lunch, cleaned up, prepared *kuehs* for tea and poured hot water into the flask. She was about to leave my siblings with *Kak* Ida again when she saw her neighbour going out in a hurry.

Sensing that my mother was coming over to ask her for a favour, *Kak* Ida called out as she loaded her bags into the boot of her car. 'I'm so sorry, Ah Nooi, I have an emergency in Kuala Kangsar. One of my old relatives is dying. I don't know when I will be back.'

'Oh, I'm sorry to hear that.'

Kak Ida grabbed my mother's hand and said, 'Life's too short to be unhappy about anything.'

Mom nodded and her eyes filled with tears but merely said, 'I'll keep an eye on your house.'

Kak Ida looked into my mom's eyes and continued, 'Whatever it is, you can and will get through it. You're stronger than you think.'

Mom nodded and replied, 'Thank you *Kak*. Have a safe journey.'

'You too.'

* * *

With no baby-sitter available my mom walked to the nearest school and found the trishaw man, Loh Ka, waiting under the tree. His name literally translated to long legs or a very tall person, which he was. He was too leggy for the trishaw, but when he rode it, it looked like the vehicle and the gangly man were made for each other.

'Loh Ka,' my mother waved to him, 'are you free to take me to Tupai Road?'

'Yes, of course.'

He had used the trishaw to ferry his daughter to and from school every day, but after she grew up, he rode it out of habit, occasionally transporting people to town or to the nearby housing area.

'Can you give me ten minutes to get the children ready.'

'I'll come over to your house.'

'Thank you.'

* * *

Mom and my siblings were soon on their way to my maternal grandmother's house on Tupai Road—my mom harbouring all the dread and concern in the world while my siblings were filled with the excitement of riding in the trishaw.

My mother invariably visited her mother (my grandmother) twice a week, sometimes buying her the round button candy that came in assorted colours. That was the most she could afford and that was also grandma's favourite sweet. Grandma would in turn give my mother eggs that she received from her neighbours for feeding their ducks and chickens.

My mother left my siblings with my maternal grandma and walked to the temple that was nearby where her sister resided. They hadn't spoken for years, ever since my aunt took a vow of silence and isolation. No one was to contact her unless it was necessary. This day, my mother thought it was.

The temple was always smoky with the joss sticks, incense and candles. It was visited everyday by devotees asking for favours, performing customary rituals, and hoping to get blessings and protection from all kinds of evil. During festival days, the entire temple would be packed to capacity and one had to wait for hours for one's turn just to get in to pay their respects to the gods.

But that day, being a normal day, my mother walked in without any trouble or hindrance. The temple was almost empty with the exception of the few regulars who were there practically every day. Mom acknowledged the presence of the gods with praying hands, trod gently into the sanctum sanctorum and found her sister sitting in the courtyard with beads in her hands.

'Ah Peng,' she whispered in the tranquil and rustic open space, shaded by a giant Bodhi tree. 'I know we are not supposed to bother you and you have taken a vow of silence, but I don't know what to do or where else to go.'

It took a while before my aunt came out of her deep trance and turned to look at my mother. She could sense the danger that was hovering over my mom and she chanted a few words of blessings.

When my aunt didn't initiate a conversation, mom voluntarily explained her conundrum. 'For the past few nights . . . I have been getting an unwanted visitor. He just lies there beside me, but I am afraid he might do something in time to come.' Mom lowered her voice as she said, 'I think it's an *or-eu-lang*. There's a rumour going around that it was spotted around town. I know it sounds silly and ridiculous, but I saw it. I felt it. I am concerned about my children's safety. Ah Peng, I don't know how, but can you help me?'

My aunt grasped my mother's hand and pumped it a few times. 'I am not that strong yet. You will have to find the old woman without sight in Aulong. She knows things. Although she has no sight, she sees more than any ordinary person can,' my aunt enunciated every word carefully and calmly as though each syllable was highly precious.

Mom sat down on the cold concrete stool beside my aunt and rested her elbows on the equally cold concrete table.

'Okay,' my mother said and hesitated to ask, but she needed to know the true reason for my aunt's eccentric decision. 'You never told us anything. You just left.'

My aunt took a long deep breath and gazed at the tree. 'In time,' she said. 'If there is a need to know. Why repeat something that is not necessary? I am at peace with myself now.' My aunt swept her gaze back to my mother and said, 'this darkness is strong. Go and keep your family safe.'

Mom checked the time and realized that if she wanted to meet the old woman today, she could still make it. The gangly trishaw man was waiting to take her back and she wondered whether he would mind making a detour to the other end of Taiping.

* * *

'Loh Ka, would you mind?'

'No, of course not. I'll even look after your kids when we get there,' the man in his fifties, deeply tanned and weather-beaten by the unforgiving sun and wrinkled by his punishing occupation, smiled a smile that was as youthful as a teenager's. 'I know how hard it is to find transport there. This is the least I can do.'

My mother was moved by his kindness, but she had to harden her heart for now and focus on finding a solution before nightfall.

'We'd better go now. The sky seems overcast. It could rain. Do you still want to go?'

My mother studied the heavy rain clouds full of portent but they were still some distance away. She was in a predicament as to whether to leave her children at my grandma's or take them with her. But then she thought that it would be ridiculous to come all the way back to pick them up, because it was well out of the way.

'Can we try and beat the rain?'

'In Taiping, that's a very slim "maybe",' Loh Ka laughed and made my mother smile. 'Get on. I'll cycle like the wind.'

* * *

Loh Ka was soaked to the skin with sweat from the severe humidity by the time they arrived. It was always hottest and stuffiest before a storm. My siblings were also feeling the discomfort but Loh Ka made every effort to entertain them with tasty titbits like haw flakes and lemon tablets. While they waited, Loh Ka even got them ice cream from the nearby sundry shop.

My mother approached the house at the address given by her sister and walked straight in through the front doors which were wide open. She was about to make her presence known when an old woman made a beeline towards her and took her hands.

'It wants you,' the old woman said with urgency.

Mom's skin crawled with goose pimples and she staggered back in shock.

The old woman led her to the hall and sat down on a rattan chair. Mom quickly sat down beside her and waited. The old woman's eye sockets were sucked in as though there were no eyeballs within.

'This thing is a lost being. A man who asked for favours from the demons and was covered in black oil as payment for his invocation.

He then sought out another medium who successfully removed the black oil from the man. But it took part of that man's life's essence with it. The man lost half of his lifespan and the black thing took the other half. Now it wants more. It wants to be complete.' The old woman touched my mother's arm with great gentleness. 'Do you consider yourself a strong woman?' she asked.

'I-I don't know.'

'This thing preys on the weakness of women. Like a man who wants to use his power to violate women, this thing wants to do the same. It will either drive you to suicide or it will push you to the breaking point of insanity. Whatever you do, you have to be strong. Stronger than you have ever been. It feeds on negative energy. Loneliness. Depression. Sadness. People who complain all the time about their tragic lives will attract entities and beings like these. You have to learn how to confront your fears.'

Mom thought for a moment and asked, 'Should I seek the help of a medium or a *bomoh*?'

'If you don't want to invite yet another unwanted being into your home, you had better stay away from them. A favour for a favour is what will be demanded. This thing can be caught and bottled up but if it falls into the wrong hands the consequences will be even worse. For now, it is still searching to absorb the kernel that makes us who we are. Once it gets enough substance it will become an independent entity without having to feed. I can sense strength in you, but you must nurture it more. Fight your fear. If at any time you give in, it will not hesitate to eat you alive.'

My mother was so shaken by the revelation she could only sit motionless, staring blankly at the old woman. She expected the old woman to give her some simple advice. Or a talisman. A charm. A potion. Something tangible to hang on to so she could use it to protect herself and her family. With this advice she felt cheated. It was so simple yet so unimaginably difficult. She was an ordinary woman with nothing to offer. Where would she find so much strength?

My mother was considering the best way to phrase her question, but the old woman beat her to it.

'No. There is no medicine for this. No short cuts to ward off all the evils in this world. Problems cannot be solved with pills or potions. You may be tempted to find someone to capture this thing but remember, there is always a price to pay. Now go and take charge of your own fate. Never expect anyone to save you. Save yourself.'

My mother reached into her handbag to hand the old woman an *ang pow* since it was a customary thing to do when seeking help from gods and their representatives.

'No. Keep it. You need it more than I do.'

My mother was at a loss for words. The old woman only had two empty eye sockets in her face. How did she know what she was about to do?

Loh Ka saw my mom emerge from the house in a daze. He bundled my siblings into the trishaw and waited for my mother to slowly walk out of the old woman's house. He knew better than to ask any questions, so he rode his trishaw as gently as he could. Mom remembered that she was going to be late and told Loh Ka to pick up his pace.

'Oh dear! I lost track of time. Can you take us back as fast as you can?'

'As fast as my legs can carry you,' he said and smiled, trying to lighten the mood that was beginning to anticipate the darkness of the sky.

To add to the dismal atmosphere, a few rain drops splattered down to warn them of the impending storm that was getting ready to unleash its fury. My mother didn't care even if a hurricane hit her at that moment; she was too concerned about what the night would bring and how it might change her life altogether.

Loh Ka pulled up the hood of the trishaw to protect my mom and my siblings from the rain and braved himself against it, pedalling twice as hard.

Halfway through their journey, the clouds burst. The torrential rains came down in a heavy downpour and got everyone wet. Loh Ka was soaked right through. My mother held my siblings close in her arms to protect them from the thunder and lightning. The journey seemed longer in the rain and by the time they reached home it was close to six in the evening. Needless to say, my grandparents were furious. They were expecting dinner in an hour.

My mother was transferring my siblings to the main house and had not yet settled the payment with Loh Ka when my grandmother stormed out to confront her in the porch.

'Where have you been? The water in the flask was not even hot. We couldn't make ourselves a proper drink at teatime. Why would you go gallivanting at a time like this when you have chores to do? It's bad enough that you are living at our expense! Behaving like an indecent woman will get the whole town talking. What are you still standing there for? Get our dinner ready in half an hour.'

When one of my siblings started crying, mom could no longer hold back her tears and she cried in the rain too. Perhaps she thought it wouldn't be so bad if no one could tell rain water from her tears. Perhaps everything at that moment was just right for shedding tears.

'I-I . . .'

'We'll settle the payment another time,' said the trishaw man, 'go do what you must. I'll take the children to the room.'

'No, you've done enough. I'll manage.'

* * *

Mom cleaned up my siblings, changed them and safely tucked them up in the servant's quarters while she speeded up her familiar cooking routines. She managed to serve dinner on time to everyone but herself. After she had got my siblings ready for bed, she sat down and ate by herself in the corner of the room in which she lived. Before the scare of the nocturnal visitor, she used to eat in the open kitchen, looking out into the darkness and feeling as empty as her uneventful life. Now, she preferred the loneliness to the fear. Although they were both consuming her, one was turning out to be more exhausting. Her life force was draining away and her world, that seemed to be shrinking, had now dwindled to the size of the room in which they lived. After a whole day of running around, looking for a solution in vain, it was now time to cry herself to sleep.

Mom stirred when she felt a shortness of breath in the middle of the night. The room had become stuffy and uncomfortably warm. A burning sensation rose from the pit of her stomach and gradually reached her throat. The nightmare became more intense when she struggled just to breathe. She reached for her neck to soothe away the pain and felt the glossy texture that had become too strikingly familiar and she forced her eyes open. The darkness she encountered was overwhelming. She could not see anything but the outline of that oily thing. This time it was attached to her. She felt it on her neck, legs and stomach. It felt like an immutable filthy slime had seeped into the very pores of her skin.

Mom tried hard to fight her fears, but she was pinned down by that oily thing. The only movement she could muster was to allow her tears to trickle down her face but she remembered the words of the old woman: 'Whatever you do, you have to be strong. Stronger than you have ever been.'

My mother lost all sensation in her body.

'It feeds on negative energy. Loneliness. Depression. Sadness.'

My mother closed her eyes and fell into the deepest darkest abyss she had ever known.

'If, at any time, you give in, it will not hesitate to eat you alive.'

My mother woke up to my father's voice and wondered if it was the beginning or the end.

'Ah Nooi! Ah Nooi!' Mom felt her body shake repeatedly in sync with the calling of her name. 'Wake up. It's already six o'clock.'

'What?' mom exclaimed sleepily. What is six o'clock?

'The kids are also up. I have to go soon.'

'Go? Go where?' Mom sat up and looked into dad's eyes.

'To work. I'm going to be late. Ah Cheong will be here in half an hour. But it's okay, I can get my breakfast outside. Just make it for the rest of the family.'

'Oh no. I've slept right through.'

'You must have been very tired last night.'

'I didn't hear you come in at all.'

'You were sleeping soundly. I didn't want to bother you until I saw you twitching as though you were having a nightmare. I called your name several times. You opened your eyes but stared straight at the ceiling, and then you went back to sleep. Do you remember what was bothering you?'

'No,' mom almost shouted out the reply to keep her worry to herself. 'I had better start breakfast. I'll whip up something really fast.'

* * *

That day my mother was not herself at all. Her energy was low and her spirit was down. People at the market said she looked worn-out and she told them she hadn't slept well the previous night to kill the conversation, but that didn't help. An endless stream of remedies and suggestions poured in. She grew even more depressed listening to them.

In the midst of all the chattering around her, she was lost in her own thoughts. How does one fight a losing battle? If she could not seek the help of *bomohs* and mediums, she didn't know what she could do. She was just a housewife. Uneducated. Powerless.

The rest of the day went by like a dream. She was dazed and disoriented most of the time, continuing her routine chores and duties as housewife and a daughter-in-law like an automaton. Before long, night fell again and everything turned feral for her. Every sound was menacing and every eye that gleamed was malevolent.

Things that could not be distinguished in the dark appeared to be terrifying things of all shapes and sizes and all my mother could do was wait for that oily thing to come and claim her again.

She no longer cared. She just made sure my siblings were comfortable when she lay down beside them leaving the door ajar. It was most unlike her to do this, but her mind was wandering farther and farther away from the reality she used to know. She was about to close her eyes when someone materialized in front of the door. She could barely make out the figure that was standing there, until she realized that it wasn't my dad, and that oily thing never appeared in this forthright manner. She got up to get a better focus and was shocked to see her sister.

'Ah Peng?' my mother exclaimed, hardly able to believe her eyes.

'You are not being fair to yourself,' her elder sister said. 'Why are you giving up without a fight?'

'How did you know? How did you get here? It's past ten at night.'

'I felt the disturbance.'

'You didn't have to come here at this time of the night.'

'I do what I have to do. You are in great danger. If you don't stand up to it now you will lose. But you're not the worst thing you can lose. Think of your children,' her sister moved closer, standing over them like the figurine of the Goddess of Mercy.

'It's too hard and I'm so tired.'

Her sister marched towards her and shook her by the shoulders.

'Listen. It will destroy you and your children.'

'But what can I do?'

'Something, anything that can make you happy.'

'Like what?'

'Sing.'

'Sing?'

'Don't you remember the song we used to sing when we were kids?'

'That was a long time ago.'

'Do it!'

'Now?'

'If you don't want to lose your family.'

'But . . .'

'It's coming. Learn to be happy or drown in your sorrows for the rest of your life.'

My mother wanted to ask her sister more but she woke up from her dream. She checked the room and saw no one else but my siblings lined up in a row. It felt too real to be her imagination. She could still smell the *bedak sejuk* her sister wore. Just as she was about to return to bed, she sensed that oily thing waiting for her in the darkest corner of the room. Her hair stood on end and she wanted to scream but she knew it wouldn't do any good. Screaming would only increase her desperation and trigger her vulnerability.

She took a deep breath and started singing one of her favourite songs '春風吻上我的臉' (Spring Breeze Kisses my Face) from the movie 那個不多情 (*That is not Sentimental*). The romanticism in the native language is, of course, lost in the translation.

Mom re-enacted the scene and sang it like a lullaby to my siblings who were already fast asleep. Her heart felt lighter and her mind gradually cleared from all the worries that had clogged her mind recently. As she fell into the rhythm of the cheerful song she saw that oily thing slithering all over the room, escaping through every gap, fissure and crevice that it could find. She stopped singing for a moment and the black ooze stopped escaping and quickly coagulated to gather at the foot of the mattress.

My mother continued singing and picked up the pace out of fear and determination, recalling the image of her sister in her head. That oily thing became sluggish with each melody that mom sang. She noticed the strange reaction it had toward the change in her temperament, so she took the song to a higher pitch and sang with yet more enthusiasm.

The slick-looking shadow fidgeted and shot out to the darker side of the room as it grew smaller in size; avoiding my mother who was now smiling, singing and swaying to 'Spring Breeze'. Mom recollected the times when she was younger, more spirited and carefree. The times when in her innocence she found the joys of life in little things. My mother kissed my siblings and then danced around the tiny room, making the song last as long as she could. Without any reservations she raised her hands up in the air and imagined the colours of spring blossoming in the dank and gloomy corners. She was so engrossed in the power of the melodic song that she did not realize dad had come back home. He stood observing her for a while, chuckling to himself. When my mom turned around and saw him, she stopped in the middle of her merriment.

'Don't stop on my account,' dad said.

'H-how long have you been back?' my mom panted breathlessly, as she tried to string the words together.

'Not long enough to appreciate this.'

Mom blushed and ran to embrace him.

'What's this all about?'

'I'm just happy.'

'Oh?'

'Happy that I have a wonderful husband and happy that I have three beautiful children.'

Dad sighed and wrapped his arms around her. 'I promise you this will get better. We will move to our own home someday and live a good life.'

'It may be hard now, but . . .' my mom cried, 'it's good enough for us to be happy.'

* * *

The next day my mother could not wait to see her sister and tell her about the whole ordeal. It was the dream that she had had of Peng that had given her the courage and motivation to reignite her youth and innocence to fight the darkness. As usual, her only window of opportunity for some time to herself was after lunch and before tea. She located Loh Ka under the tree at his usual spot and ran to him with excitement.

'Loh Ka, Loh Ka, can you take me to my mother's place, please?'

'Of course,' Loh Ka untangled his long legs and greeted her.

My mother bundled my siblings onto the trishaw and seated herself on the snug cushion.

'I will pay you today's fare plus what I owe you for yesterday,' my mother said and rummaged through her hand bag to get her purse out.

'When we arrive. No hurry.' Lok Ka climbed on to his trishaw and asked, 'I hope the rain didn't cause any problems.

'Nothing I can't handle. And thank you for ferrying me all the way to Aulong and back again in that heavy rain.'

'It's all right.' He stepped on the pedal and worked the first momentum to move forward. 'You seem happy today.'

'I am. I really am.'

They smiled at each other, my mother was still singing and dancing, but privately, in her mind.

* * *

The temple was always cool even when there was an event that filled it with devotees. The joss sticks, candles and burnt offerings could create extreme heat, but the rest of the temple always remained cool. My mother walked into the temple and made her way through the corridor into the courtyard. Just as before she found her sister sitting on one of the concrete stools, holding on to her prayer beads, and staring into space.

'Ah Peng, the strangest thing happened to me last night,' my mother said, sitting down beside my aunt, and looking straight at the space she was focusing on: an ancient raintree bonsai in a pot sculpted into the shape of a dragon. 'You were in my dream. It's as though you knew what was going on and you came to help. And . . . you actually did!'

Mom, who was not usually given to expressing her sentiments, waited for a response from her sister, but there wasn't any forthcoming to break the uncomfortable silence after her confession. My mother was reluctant to carry on the conversation and disrupt her sister's deep meditation, but she wanted to find a moment to show her gratitude. When she looked into her sister's eyes, she noticed that they were glazed over. She didn't know why, but it frightened her.

'Ah Peng,' she called and rested her hand on her sister's shoulder. 'Peng . . .'

'Your sister is not there,' a familiar voice wafted in like a draft and made her shudder.

The old woman without eyes stood behind my mother and acknowledged her as though she could see what was transpiring between the sisters.

'*Ah Phor*, what do you mean she is not there?' asked my mother, addressing the old woman as a venerable grandmother.

'This is what she wanted,' said the old woman.

'No, it's not. She went through a very traumatic experience and is just trying to recover from it.' My mother was upset by the old woman's assertion.

'There are things that are too strange for us to comprehend,' the old woman said, and reached for my mother's hand. 'Perhaps I did not phrase it properly. What I meant was that your sister is a selfless person. Her heart is pure and virtuous. She is always putting the needs of others above herself. That is why she chose this life. That is why she lives in this temple, praying constantly for the benefit of others. What she is experiencing now is her journey.' Once she was done speaking, she took her hand away as though some sort of transference had been completed.

Mom was still unable to accept my aunt's decision to choose a life this pitiable, but she didn't want to argue with the old woman. Even so, she had doubts about her own choices in life because marriage and having children were not as great as they were thought to be.

She held my aunt's hands and looked into her blank eyes and whispered, 'I don't know why you do what you do, but I'm always here for you.' She turned to the old woman to ask, 'Why won't she speak? She was all right the last time I visited.'

'She is in a deep, prayerful state. She can hear you, but she cannot break her concentration.'

'Will she be all right?'

'She is all right.'

'Can she function on her own?'

'She is still as normal as anyone of us. She will eat when she is hungry. She will clean herself when necessary. She will carry on her normal duties for as long as she is meant to be on this earth. She is in good hands.'

Mom broke down when she thought about the time they had spent apart, separated because of their individual life choices—each going their separate way and losing the sisterly kinship they had treasured as children. My mother didn't know what else she could do, so she sang the song again, the one that they sang together to usher in the springtime of their youth.

* * *

'That is such a sad and scary story.'

'I know. Every time I think about it, I get sentimental as well.'

'I can't believe your mother had to go through it all on her own.'

'What happened to your aunt?'

'No one knows,' Lai said.

'I wonder if your mother's dream affected her sister.'

'Mom has no idea. She said that my aunt always looked calm, like she was in a peaceful place . . . just that that place is not here.'

'Have you ever seen your aunt?'

'Yeah, once at the temple.'

'How old was she?'

'They say she was old, but she didn't look much older than her mid-thirties. And she died in her sleep. I have never seen anyone more serene than her. She must have had a good life,' Lai said. 'Good enough to smile on her death bed.'

* * *

The old woman without eyes did not like what she saw in Peng, but she could do nothing to discourage her. She could see her sitting in a lotus position in a zen state, chanting an invocation to keep that oily thing incarcerated. It struggled within the confines of the light source that served as an enclosure to free itself, screeching, braying and caterwauling. Changing its form repeatedly to penetrate the restraints. It tried to frighten Peng into abandoning the idea of using her body as a vessel to keep it immobilized, but she was unfazed. The old woman and Peng knew that by doing this no one would be bothered by that oily thing again. This was the only way to do it. When Peng's body disintegrated, that oily thing would cease to exist.

When Peng had told her about the plan, the old woman was completely against it. She didn't like the idea at all. The madness of luring that oily thing and trapping it inside the body for the good of others was unthinkable. But Peng wouldn't have it any other way.

No one knew that she had been gang-raped by four men who had then left her for dead. She had picked herself up from the back alley, went home to clean up and then turned to the divine for healing and never looked back since.

She sent an astral projection of herself to her sister to help her defeat that oily thing and it saw her past. It was angered with her interference, so it came to her that very night for vengeance.

But it didn't know that Peng was in total control of her life, her fate. She ensnared it, before it learnt that the power of her soul was unbreakable.

The recent spate of deaths of women from suicides suddenly stopped in Taiping. Those who were in a depression snapped out of it, feeling stronger than ever. The rumours of the *or-eu-lang* gradually died away and were replaced by new stories and new superstitions that came in the form of movies, sightings and gossip.

The old woman without eyes stayed with Peng for as long as she could. Backing her up whenever she faltered. Staying mindful and prayerful all the time and keeping a vigilant metaphorical eye out for the evil that one man had invoked and internalized, and safeguarding it from the reaches of others who sought it for its diabolical favours. Just as the four men who met their doom in a freak accident no one could explain. They were found dismembered and disembowelled in the car in the middle of nowhere as though they were marked by evil.

11

Hunt for the Were Tiger

'That date was 13 May. While chaos was sweeping across the whole country, somewhere in Air Kuning there was a different kind of threat besetting a small village. The village was made up of attap houses made from cheap salvaged planks, wood, zinc sheets, and other discarded construction materials. Many of them were farmers, some were rubber tappers and others did odd jobs in the village. They were like a self-contained world of their own. They had a school for their kids, a sundry shop, a wet market and even a Chinese physician who tended to their medical needs. If anything happened in Taiping town, they would be the last to know,' Cham narrated his story with a deep and resounding sonority in his voice.

'Strangely, the chaos of 13 May never arrived at the village. Although they were told by the authorities to stay within the school compound for the curfew, none of them experienced the kind of tragedy that changed the country.'

'Why stay in the school compound?'

'That was the only safe place in the village. No one knew why the school was built with concrete, fenced all around, under lock and key when not in use. Some said the school had been built a long time ago, even before the villagers had set foot on the land. They did not build the village from the ground up. They inherited it.

'Their isolation may have saved them from the unspeakable violence and killings that were swiftly approaching its perimeters, but there was something more sinister that was about to come.'

'What was it?'

'While they were all gathered in the school hall their suspicion of one another made it even more terrifying than the outbreak of the scourge that awaited them outside. To this day, no one knows what truly happened to the villagers. Were they murdered at the hands of humans or the monster?'

'Aren't they the same thing?'

Cham ignored that cynical remark and continued to say, 'Every last one of them!'

'If everyone died then how would anyone know what happened?'

'Because one survived. On her deathbed, a very old woman recounted the day that they were hunted by a weretiger.'

* * *

They call me *Siau* Sim.

Yes, *Siau* as in crazy. Mad. Out of her mind.

The village I come from is built upon rumours and secrets. I don't know if it is a fact, but I know that one could not exist without the other. According to rumours, three families tried to escape the authorities and started a village deep in the jungle where they would not be found. Their criminal activities were stacked so high that no punishment would fit the crime. That's what I heard, but it could be an exaggerated truth for all I know. And they were hidden deep in the jungle where no one dared to set foot to hunt them down. There was no visible dirt road, path or track. The families thrived and soon became a community where only like-minded outsiders were accepted to help create the numbers. It was located far beyond the reach of uninvited guests and that was how their secret was kept.

The village smelled like death to me. There were always skinned reptiles sunning in the open with hordes of flies congregating on the decay. I've seen flying foxes, monitor lizards, snakes, small crocodiles and other unidentified headless and limbless carcasses. There were always monkeys in cages or tethered by chains, pangolins in boxes, bullet-wounded boars, and there was even a sun bear once. As soon as these animals were brought to the village, they were destined to never see daylight again. They usually ended up on silver platters in exclusive and exotic restaurants or on some filthy rich man's dinner table. Growing up with these as the norm, I thought that was how it was with the rest of the world.

I started life like no other child. My mother was a prostitute and I was conceived out of ignorance. They said I killed my mother during childbirth because I was a cursed child. At a very tender age, I stepped into my mother's shoes and did everything that would destroy my childhood and distort my adulthood. It seemed like a tradition I needed to follow and since I was cursed there was nothing left for me to do but accept the fate that was given to me.

It was a near death experience that shocked me out of my misery. While I was deciding whether to live or die, on my deathbed, I was given a second chance to decide my fate. I was left to die of drug overdose in an old dingy room that also served as a pleasure room for the customers. Although it was tragic to know that no one cared whether I was dead or alive, it was also comforting to know that I was enjoying peace and quiet for the first time all by myself. No one came to bother me about entertaining a client. No one shouted at me for not performing well. No one mumbled in low voices to do things I never wanted to do. There were always noises in my head but now, at death's door, there was only silence.

I was ready to succumb to death when I saw my situation as an opportunity to become free. I wanted to become invisible, a person no one wanted to care about or have anything to do with. That was when I learned to be ugly—to lose my teeth, to decay, to retain the smell of death, and stain my skin with diseases; but most of all, to pretend I was losing my mind little by little, day by day. They thought I was gone for good when I walked around naked, wearing only sores on my body. That was when they threw me out. Left me in the middle of nowhere like a diseased dog. That was the day I found my freedom and also my family. Stray animals.

There were cats and dogs all over the village that were discarded like me. The animals showed me more affection than I had ever felt before.

Strays don't just appear out of nowhere. Humans have a hand in it.

Soon, the villagers started calling me *Siau Kau* Sim and laughed at me when they saw me among the strays. But they were beginning to be afraid of seeing me commanding as many as twenty to thirty dogs at any one time. The dogs protected me whenever they sensed the villagers' insolent behaviour towards me. I was their alpha.

I would go into town and the housing areas to gather up all the unwanted animals and bring them back to the village. To a safe place where they could live out their lives to the end. A vet was kind enough to help me spay and neuter the animals. She was the only one who understood the importance of the lives of animals. One day she took me aside and told me to leave the village. She said she could help me get started to get back on my feet so that I could have a better life. When I gazed deep into her eyes, I saw my own reflection and I wept. I never said anything that could contradict my pretence of being insane, but she saw right through me. The only thing she said after that was for me to think it over and then left me alone.

I just could not understand why people were so heartless. They could walk past a dying and diseased animal without batting an eye. And how they could allow their pets to reproduce unwanted litters that would be abandoned, was beyond me. When I was in town, I told off pet owners who mistreated their animals, but each time I was chased away. I argued with pet shop owners about the appalling conditions the animals had to endure until they were sold, or died. One awful man pushed me into the monsoon drain in front of his shop when he couldn't win the debate. Since I was considered crazy, no one helped me. They either stood around and stared, or jeered. When more and more people became too hostile, I decided not to go back into town but just live with the strays that I had in my village.

As my compassion for animals grew stronger, my hatred for humans increased. I was an object of desire and lust when I was young but now that I am older, I have become an animal activist and a misanthrope. Instead of hiding behind an invisible cloak like I used to, I stood in the front line to speak out for the animals. I highlighted their cruelty in murdering innocent animals for profit and gain. I even tried to use gods and religion, but it backfired. Someone started a rumour about a rabies scare, and the whole village decided to take it out on my dogs.

That day was the day of reckoning. I blame myself for what happened to my family of strays. I begged. I pleaded. I grovelled. But bullets flew and clubs struck at the defenceless animals. The bloody day left me more paralysed than ever. If I had been given a second chance to live and help the animals, why did this happen?

I was without a family that day. I embraced madness like an old forgotten friend, for real this time. I would have gladly given up my life then and there but two events changed my destiny.

The day they killed my family of strays was 13 May 1969. It was also the day the village was seized with the fear of a weretiger on the rampage.

They rushed to the school to take cover from both the unexpected emergencies that spooked everyone. None of the villagers even bothered to take me along. If I hadn't been curious, I wouldn't have known what was going on. In hushed voices the villagers spoke about a race riot and the supernatural being.

With the onset of the curfew, the children, the elderly and the sickly were gathered together to occupy the classrooms upstairs.

Beddings were prepared to make them as comfortable as possible and some stayed in the hall to act as sentries with makeshift weapons. But nothing would give them solace ever again. They already had blood on their hands. Now, it seemed like they would have to pay with every drop of their blood.

Within the confines of the school everyone was nervous and restless for having been taken out of their familiar environments. They didn't like the enforced proximity to each other and the subjugation, and they were aware that it was a false sense of security to say the least. If a band of armed fanatics broke through the gates, it would be the end of everyone, although there were chances that some might still have a chance to escape. However, if a weretiger was on the prowl, no one would even live to talk about it.

The incident started with Chong, a pot-bellied obnoxious man with a thirst for a game of chance, who was mauled and shredded at the fringe of the town. Since no one particularly liked him, they didn't make too much of a fuss or inform the authorities of the poor man's demise. By the time the villagers felt that they should at least have the decency to acknowledge his tragic end, the curfew had already reached them. So, he was left to rot and for the carrion birds to feast upon.

On the first night, we heard something loitering around the school compound. No one wanted to admit it, but they could catch the whiff of death. It was as though if they ignored it long enough, whatever that was stalking them would go away. It didn't and Lim was the second person to find that out.

He went outside the school hall to take a leak because the toilets were too far. He didn't think that the weretiger was something he needed to be afraid of, because they had fortified the school with walls and fences. According to some of the men, whatever got him did it when his legs were far apart and his fly open. He didn't have a chance to even shout for help, let alone ease himself. In an instant, he was dead. No one heard him and no one saw his body until first light, when he was found covered in urine and blood.

Everyone was obsessed with the terror of the weretiger, but I was sceptical. Not that I had ever seen a weretiger or knew how it killed its prey, but the dead man looked more like he had been murdered. The way he was mutilated looked more like he was slashed with a knife repeatedly. Living in brothels with damaged girls, I had seen how a knife could work on the flesh.

I decided to go back out to find the first victim to see if the killing pattern fitted. Looking and behaving the way I did, I was free to go in and out of the school as I pleased. I wasn't sure if it was wise to leave the safety of numbers, but then again, I was merely a statistic to them.

With the hot bright sun on my shoulders for company, I managed to find the body that had ripened quite badly. There was still a trace of the human body and it was definitely unrecognizable, but the gashes and tears were similar. There was no distinctive manner in which the bodies were mangled, although it did seem like an animal attack at first glance. The way the open wounds were cut could have only been made by an exasperated killer. Like a madman slashing at his victim. A weretiger would have had clearly defined claw marks. Moreover, would it kill for the sake of killing?

Not knowing what I should do, I kept to myself and merely hoped the killer would not strike again.

The villagers were scared to death with another murder that was too close to home for comfort, and all they could do was double the blockades and hide behind them. Even with the extra-precautions, Kuan became another victim on the second night. What was incredible was that they found him hanging from the ceiling fan in one of the second-floor classrooms. His family and relatives did not see or hear a single thing in the night. By morning, their horror awakened everyone who took shelter in the school.

Everyone was on edge and they had questions that would never get any answers. Even with the added security, the danger still loomed like an invisible phantom. How did it get in? How did it choose its victims? Why did it kill for no apparent reason? But since they believed in the weretiger, anything was possible.

With danger lurking in the school, all the villagers were moved down to the school hall to be together. Perhaps they thought they would be able to look out for each other, but I knew better. That was how they killed all my dogs. They prepared a corner for the weaker generation with walls of chairs and desks and blackboards. Even though no one believed it would make any difference, the flimsy refuge did buy them some time to get by another day.

No one in the village was innocent. Not a small child, not an elderly person. Not anyone in between. Everyone was rotten to the core. Whoever it was that was murdering the villagers one at a time must have a motive. And there must be clues.

One of the more outspoken villagers and a self-appointed leader, Soh, took matters into his hands when everyone was agitated by the gruesome killings. He was known for his loudness—he talked as though everyone was hard of hearing. Since he had the built-in amplifier in him, he commanded attention he did not deserve.

'I am going to say what we are all thinking. There is a weretiger among us.' Everyone gasped, although the whispers were getting louder each day. 'You have seen the evidence. Three of our villagers have been killed. Two of them in the school we thought would be a safe place to hide.'

The villagers cringed in the dimly-lighted hall that aroused chaos in their hearts; the way the beddings were haphazardly arranged only added to their trepidation. Their utterances and stifled breathing resonated with panic and fear.

Soh continued to demand the villagers' cooperation when he spoke again, 'We have to kill it before it kills us.'

Their anxiety flooded the empty spaces with susurrations of disbelief and anger.

'How would we know who among us is the weretiger?' one of the villagers asked.

'I have my suspicion.'

The statement inflamed the crowd even more, stirring them into a restless mob ready to kill the beast. I, too, had my suspicion, but should I tell everyone what I had found out?

'Who?' the villagers shouted in unison. 'Who is the beast?'

The villagers glanced around at each other, like wild animals trapped in a small cage.

'I gathered several pieces of evidence before we came to the hall. Strips of meat, bloodstains, paw prints and fur. All the clues led me to the south section of the village where there are only three houses.'

The villagers from that section were struck with dread and took offence at being singled out as harbouring the monster behind the killings.

'Are you sure? You have a reputation of accusing other people without any grounds in the past. That day, when you lost your money. That time, when you fought with one of the villagers. That situation, where you said someone's wife tried to seduce you. All those times when you twisted the tale, were also the times that you were yourself guilty on all counts,' Chuang, from one of the families who stood accused, came forward to reveal the truth about Soh.

The crowd murmured a low rumbling agreement, but they were more interested in the hunt for the weretiger.

Soh quickly turned the tables by pulling out a fuzzy chunk of evidence from his pocket. 'This is the weretiger's fur. With any luck, we'll find more of this in his belongings.'

'For all we know, that could be dog fur,' Chuang said.

Before the villagers lost interest, Soh reminded them with a terrifying shout, 'We're as good as dead if we do nothing! It will come for your children and then it will come for you!'

The villagers were seized with that frightful thought.

'We know that he is most powerful when the moon is full. He will still be powerful in the days that follow. Are we going to let him pick us off one by one?'

The crowd furiously chanted the words of justification—to kill before they get killed.

'You're talking nonsense,' Chow, the head of another one of the accused families, protested. 'It's bad enough that there are hostilities going on outside there. You're just making things worse for everyone inside here. And you're wrong, there won't be a full moon until the end of the month.'

'You say that because you are one of the three families who live on the south side. Are you hiding something? Are you hiding someone who is a beast in your family? Your sons perhaps? You?'

Everyone drew away from Chow and his family.

'Get them! We don't want the monsters running loose.'

As though of one mind and one heart in their judgment, the villagers surged forward and the three families were herded into the centre of the hall no matter how they resisted.

The Chows consisted of the parents and their three sons. The Chuangs had a daughter and two sons. And the old couple, Auyongs, lived with their speech-and-hearing impaired daughter.

'What right have you to detain us?' Chuang made a grab for Soh but the other villagers held him back. 'Other than the fur you found, there is no concrete evidence to make us suspects.'

'You want evidence? I'll do even better. I have a witness.' He called out to his wife, 'Ghim, come here and tell them what you told me.'

A short, stubby woman in her oversized T-shirt and shorts walked out to share her husband's limelight.

'As you know, I clean people's houses. I know the secrets of every household. Not because I'm a busybody or anything like that, but because people always think the cleaning woman can be ignored.' She shook her head is disgust. 'Sometimes I overhear them talking about things. Sometimes I accidentally find out for myself.' Ghim wobbled her head around to claim naivety, 'You think I want to know these things? Of course not. I'm a simple person but sometimes I hear things.' She sighed as though it was a burden to be in her shoes.

'Ghim, tell them already,' Soh grunted.

'Oh, oh, when Chong was attacked, my husband told me to inspect and gather evidence from all the houses. So, I did. I knew it was dangerous. I could have been killed. But my husband said it was necessary to find out what our neighbours were hiding, so—'

'Enough.' He pushed his wife back into the crowd. 'Let's not waste any more time. We'll give you until noon to come forward and confess. If none of you do, we'll have no choice but to use force.'

'What was your wife witness to?' Chuang asked.

'I saw the weretiger coming out from one of your houses,' she shouted from the crowd. 'But I didn't see which one . . .'

'Enough!' Soh shut her up by pointing a finger at her.

'And what are you going to do? Kill us?' Chuang stepped forward but was blocked by some of the villagers.

'If it comes to that, why not?'

The crowd went wild. The indicted families cowered, drawing closer to each other when they saw how the villagers had transformed into monsters themselves.

Soh raised his hands up like a messiah to bring order to the irascible villagers.

'Make sure the ropes are fastened. Tight. And watch them closely. If any of them change . . . even a bit . . . you know what to do.'

'With what?' someone shouted in morning light. 'We don't have any weapons.'

'Make them.'

The weaker ones in the three accused families began to tear up and sob despairingly, knowing that their fate was hanging by a thread.

'This is a school. Grab anything you can to make wooden stakes, daggers with any kind of metal and gather sharp objects to fashion them into killing tools. We have to protect ourselves.' When no one took the initiative to move, Soh shouted to incite more fear, 'Now! While there's still light. Get ropes, chains, and anything to tie them down.'

The moment he finished his speech, the villagers scattered haphazardly to beat the moonrise, although it was still morning. Those who were standing close to the families formed a human barricade to lock them down. The others gathered as many items as they could to fabricate into weapons. Soh watched them going about in a frenzy and he liked what he saw.

When the first group returned with ropes and binding materials, Soh instructed them to restrain the families.

'Make sure it's tight. Double or triple it if need be. A weretiger can snap such ropes like they were raffia strings.'

'Please spare the women and children,' Chow begged.

'How would I know that they are not the weretigers?' Soh shouted and ordered the villagers to treat them like animals. 'Don't go soft on women and children. There could be more than one weretiger. They are not who they appear to be. If we let our guards down, they will kill us when they get the chance. Tie the ropes as taut as you can make them. Draw a little blood if you must. These are bloodthirsty creatures.'

'Stop this! You are making a mistake. We are innocent,' Chuang struggled with two of the deranged minions who were caught up in the hysteria.

'If you are innocent you have nothing to worry about. Gag him.'

'Leave them alone!' I could not stand their stupidity any more than I could bear their senseless aggression.

'Who said that?'

'I did.' I came forward and everyone froze when they saw me looking as normal as they were.

They chanted my name *Siau* Sim, *Siau* Sim, *Siau* Sim, as though it were an incantation to ward off evil.

'*Siau* Sim?' Soh looked dumbfounded.

'The killings, or murders, were not done by a weretiger. They were done by a man.'

The horde went into a delirium of mutters.

'What? And we are supposed to believe a mad woman like you?'

'If you check the wounds, they are inconsistent. A weretiger, or any wild animal for that matter, could not have done that.'

'I thought she was a mute.'

'No, she's crazy.'

'Why was she pretending to be dumb or insane?'

'She has never spoken like this before.'

Instead of listening to what I had just said, the villagers continued to be bewildered by the label I was given many years ago so that they could dismiss my very existence.

'She should be locked up!' Soh stated and pointed his twisted finger at me. 'Go stay with your dogs and leave human affairs to humans.'

'I have no more dogs. You killed them!' I made sure everyone heard that and were reminded of their cruelty. 'All of you killed my dogs.'

A few giggled and some snickered in the enormous hall and they all had the same look on their faces—coldness.

'If you want the truth, then hear me out,' I tried one last time.

'Wait a minute. Since you were always hanging out with the dogs, maybe you're a werewolf,' Soh managed to pull another distraction out of his hat. 'Perhaps we should tie you up with the weretigers!'

The throng of people went berserk. They closed in on me with bloodshot eyes and a monstrous disposition. I backed away and ran out of the crowd before they could capture me.

After I was outside, I heard cheering and applause before Soh's final announcement, 'Let her go and don't let her in again.'

I must have run right to the very edge of the village before I stopped to catch my breath. I was angry, exhausted and on the verge of admitting defeat. No one would believe me even if I had the evidence in my hand. I now wanted to leave the village for good as the veterinarian had advised, and make an entirely new life for myself if I wanted. But two things held me back. This was not the right time for me to take my chances out there and my gut instinct said I needed to do some snooping before I left.

The most obvious place to go to was Soh's house. Since he had triggered the panic of the weretiger, he was probably more desperate than I thought. I wouldn't be surprised if he turned out to be the murderer. He was known for his short fuse and fistfights wherever he went. Although the villagers didn't like him, they tolerated him because of his lineage that could be traced to one of the founding families.

The stench of death was everywhere in the village, but it was almost unbearable at Soh's house. While everyone plundered the wildlife to make a living, his house was the centre of hell itself. It was filled with animal skins, bottled organs, dried collectible bones, jars full of powdered substances made from animals parts, and unidentifiable pieces of gristle rotting away in the backyard. I could hear the screams of the dead animals in my head. They were heinous crimes, but no one shared my sentiment.

I was enraged afresh, grieving and in tears as I opened up every cage and unhooked every chain to free the animals whether they were dead or alive. Some crawled away, but others stayed where they were, shuddering in their death throes. I felt the emptiness of being human, a vacuum that rendered me distraught.

I wished I hadn't stepped into this house of horrors, but I was sure I would find something to incriminate Soh, although it might not make any difference.

Cages, chains, ropes, sacks, knives, and an assortment of torture instruments were all over the house. I didn't know why death hadn't claimed him for his crimes against nature. But it has always been that way in this world. I was revolted and disheartened at the sights, but I forced myself to search diligently in the foul-smelling slaughterhouse.

While rummaging through the layers of abomination, I heard a small and weak cry under the canvas sheets. I stopped moving and tuned in to the sound to locate the source. In a very dark room that stank of doom, I trudged over the grimy floor caked with desiccated blood and glutinous fluid. I reached for the switch beside the open door and a low-watt bulb shone on the carcass of a tiger. It was disembowelled and what was left of the legs were stumps where the paws were supposed to be. Soh must have left his trophy when news of the curfew reached us.

The soft cry that sounded like a cat's mew shook me out of the trance. Something was still alive. I searched around the room and saw the cage under a table. A tiger's cub lay dying in a cage that was too small for it to even move.

I drew out the cage gently, unlatched it and lifted the cub out of that awful confinement. I placed it on my heart and cuddled it for a while, feeling the limp body and the shortness of its breath. A piece of my heart broke every time the cub drew in a shaky breath. This was no place to be if I wanted the cub to survive. I tucked it into my blouse and left Soh's house as fast as I could to look for sustenance for the cub.

I walked into a pleasant looking house that belonged to a bachelor and set the cub down on some fluffy towels. I then found some milk in the fridge which had been, thankfully, left switched on. I fed the cub by first dabbing its mouth with milk. After a while, it opened its bright yellow eyes and started licking and wanting more. When it could hold its head up, I poured a bowl of milk to let it lap up the milk and watched it closely. I wondered whether tigers had nine lives like the common house cat.

The cub went back to sleep and I poured more milk into the bowl in case it woke up hungry. By this time, the sun was low over the horizon. I recalled the time when I was on my death bed and saw the Taiping hills that gave me a sense of hope. I loved looking out of the window to see the varying hues of the hills that were coloured by the sun. Their magnificence was pure magic.

I slept beside the cub which was now breathing calmly and quietly. I could feel its will to survive. Perhaps in a few days it would be back on its feet again. Out of all the horrific twists of fate I had faced recently, this was a turn for the better.

I must have fallen asleep while watching the cub and recuperating from the exhaustion of my earlier predicament. It was dark by the time I woke up and the cub was gone. I went around looking for it, but there was no sign of its presence at all. I didn't know how it managed to get out because all the doors were locked. And it was too small to jump out through the window.

I sat on the sofa and thought about it for a moment, when I heard a very intimidating roar. They say a tiger's roar can be heard from far away, but this sounded like it was coming from the school. I ran towards the screams and heard thundering bellows that could only mean one thing.

I was at the school gates in no time, but they were chained and padlocked. Obviously to keep me out. And there, as I stood watching, a shadow that was swift as the wind leapt from person to person, making them fall like dominoes. It happened so quickly that I didn't know what to do, but stand there and silently witness the entire thing until the last cry was silenced.

Moments later, I saw the weretiger as she staggered out of the hall. I recognized those bright golden eyes and I thought that would be the end of me.

* * *

'So, there was a weretiger after all?'

'Yes.'

'How did it kill all those people in the beginning? I thought it was caged then.'

'It didn't. The first three people were killed by Soh. He took the opportunity to make up a story to get away with murder.'

'What happened to *Siau* Sim?'

'Did the weretiger kill her?'

'Obviously not. How else could we have heard this story?'

'Everyone died?'

'Yes. But it was covered up because the authorities thought it was due to a race riot. They felt it would do no good to report the massacre.'

'So, can tigers transform into human beings?'

'I think so.'

'If all animals can do that, we don't need Doctor Moreau anymore.'

The boys laughed and someone roared like a tiger in the cold dark night.

* * *

But she stood there. Regal. Poised. Elegant. Even in the faint light I could see the colours of dying leaves on her fur. She was unlike the stories I had heard. She was not a killing machine. She was not a bloodthirsty monster. If she were, we would have all been dead a long time ago. The weretiger vanished into the night before I could admire it for a moment longer. There it was right in front of me. A tiger, albeit in a human form—no other description would do it justice. The strangest thing of all was seeing Soh crawling out of the hall on his knees. He was covered in blood and the slivers of the flesh of some of the villagers and crying like a baby. He mumbled something to me, but before I walked away I told him something he never wanted to hear.

'Do you know why it let you live? It's like a house cat. It will play with you until it is satisfied. Everywhere you go, a pair of eyes will be observing you day or night. You will always be gripped with fear when the sky turns dark or the road turns too quiet. You can expect the weretiger to attack you and tear you to pieces, but it will wait.

'You will know when she is there. Always watching with her keen eyes and elongated fangs and claws. The small scratches you hear in the walls and the unusual tapping noises that could not be located will keep you awake every night. The smell of dead flesh will always be suspended in the air, teasing you with its sweet and pungent scent. And at the most awkward moments you will catch glimpses of the weretiger from the corner of your eyes.

'You will stir between sleep and wakefulness. You will see a fleeting shadow outside your window. It will be gone by the time you take a second look. You will cry out for it to kill you already. But you are the game. You will not know whether you will live another day or be mauled to death in that very instant. You can rest assured that you will die someday, but you won't know when. The only certainty is that you will die horribly.'

I never saw him again. I only heard he had transformed from a tenacious young man into a bedraggled derelict, losing his mind over the existence of the weretiger. No one dared go near him for fear of contagion. Soon, he wasted away into a skeletal frame, but he was too weak to kill himself.

The only tell-tale sign of how he died was the terror on his face as though he had been to hell and back.

People say you can hear the tiger's roar from the zoo as far as Air Kuning. But sometimes, deep in your heart you know it's not. The roar could be closer than you think.

12

The Old Man who Wouldn't Die

'I heard another version where the whole cowboy town disappeared,' Ashkraf said.

'I didn't say the whole town disappeared in my story. All its inhabitants were murdered. And it was a village.'

'I know. I'm saying in mine it did. It was a small town deep in an abandoned rubber estate.'

'What? Another were-tiger?'

'No, this is the story of the old man who wouldn't die.'

'You mean he did not die?'

'No, he did.'

'Then he would be the old man who died and came back to life.'

'No, no, no. Let me rephrase that. I mean he was the old man who wouldn't stay dead.'

'Like an undead.'

'Huh?'

'An undead person is a zombie.'

'Vampires are undead too.'

'So, which is it, Ashkraf? A zombie or a vampire?'

'You guys are not giving me a chance to tell my story!'

'Shush! All of you! I want to hear this.'

Ashkraf waited for silence before he began. 'The funeral lasted for seven days. No one knows how he died. He was eighty-one; not very likable; he repeatedly told everyone that he wasn't ready to die. But then one day, he just never woke up. The doctors, mediums and even a fortune-teller came and confirmed his death.'

'What?'

'Yeah, the old man was afraid of dying so he told his family to be very, very sure before they buried him. But in those seven days, although the old man was pronounced dead his body parts continued to grow.'

'Did he come back from the dead?'

'No.'

'He's one of the living dead.'

'But he hasn't resurrected yet.'

'Guys, guys! Stop arguing. The rest of us want to hear the story. Carry on, Ashkraf.'

'No one was at the funeral except his immediate family. He was a stingy, mean and difficult old tycoon. On top of that he had very disgusting habits like loudly expectorating in public and spitting anywhere he wanted. His death was secretly celebrated by everyone in that small town, even by his own family. But the old man wasn't ready to call it quits.

'When he was alive, he made it hard for everyone who worked for and served under him. He was always demanding. Everyone who had dealt with him knew about his obnoxious ways. He would not pay for his food at the *kopitiam* if it came a little too late or if its temperature was not to his liking. He would not pay for parking, but he would tell everyone to keep an eye on his car in case the meter man came. He would join others for breakfast and leech off their tea and *seow bak* to avoid paying a single cent.

'It was even worse when it came to his own family. Since he always suspected that his wife and children were only eyeing his wealth, he never was a loving husband and father to them. He had wanted his funeral to last longer but his family decided that seven days were long enough for the wake of a cruel and heartless man.

'Strangely, he did indulge in philanthropy although the sordid truth was, he used it as a front for his philandering. It turned out that, even after his death, he did not make it easy for anyone—it was just the beginning of very bad days to come.'

* * *

Day 1

One of the first signs they noticed was his hair. The old tycoon was mostly bald, but during the wake they noticed that his hair had started to grow back. There were just a few stubbles at first but later in the evening his head was almost fully covered with short spiky hair. Everyone was bewildered by this strange occurrence but they took it as a blessing, a forgiveness from the divine since the old tycoon did do some charity for the poor and needy. His family decided not to mention his womanizing in the same breath as his charitable acts to show some respect for the dead.

Day 2

By now, the old tycoon's head was filled with hair as white as snow and still growing, albeit at a slower rate. The hired mourners now noticed that his fingernails and toenails were growing longer. By the time they informed the family, the talon-like nails had grown pointier than normal. Again, the family took this as a good omen and felt blessed to witness such a wonderful event. Speaking ill of the dead could incur the wrath of the deceased.

Day 3

By this time, more and more curious cowboy towners came by in the guise of mourners; some managed to get themselves hired while others volunteered for free. Everyone wanted to see the old tycoon's body for themselves. They had heard about the miracles that were taking place in his enormous mansion. Since it was a funeral, and because it was always better to have a large crowd, the family allowed people to come and witness the strange phenomena. For a while all the cowboy towners let the bad memories of the old tycoon slide since they were fed with rich and scrumptious foods and entertained with mahjong sessions.

As if the bodily growths were not peculiar enough, on the third day the scent of mildew and earth rose from the old tycoon's dry and wrinkly skin, although some claimed he exuded a damp-wood-and-rancid-blood stench. With lots of food and a reason to gamble, no one minded the off-putting smell. News travelled farther and brought even more people flocking in to witness the old tycoon's bizarre funeral.

Day 4

On the fourth day everyone waited eagerly for another miracle to amuse them. Other than a deep raspy sound emanating from all over the mansion, there was nothing else spectacular to see. They didn't bother to find out the source of that sound because it didn't really bother them. They carried on with their celebrations and the funeral, which had gotten merrier by the day. The old tycoon's family was getting a little worried about being able to provide for the numbers that were growing larger by the hour. Their only consolation was that the funeral had only three more days to go.

Day 5

Speculations about the old tycoon's condition got out of hand. Everyone had a version of how it would end on the seventh day. Some said he would ascend straight to heaven. Some said the gods would come down to escort him to the heaven. Some said the old man would revert to his youth and never to be reincarnated again.

Everyone wanted to peek into the coffin, wanting to be the first to see a new change and announce it to the visitors. Nothing extraordinary happened the entire day. It was not until the sun went below the horizon that a very loud scream arrested everyone. It was not a scream of joy but a scream of terror.

The crowd flocked to the old tycoon's side and were mortified by what they saw. His eyes had protruded so much that they forced his eyelids apart and were bulging out like bloody marbles.

The tycoon's hair was now shoulder-length and had turned completely black. His nails were bestial to behold and the earthen smell was replaced by a ripe and sweet stench of rotting flesh. People were beginning to fear the worst. It finally dawned on them that it was probably not a blessing in disguise after all.

The tycoon's family immediately hired another group of priests to perform extra prayers in case things took a turn for the worse. Now, people started to get suspicious of the old tycoon and his never-ending insistence to live forever. His family urged the priests to chant harder and longer to ensure that the old tycoon did not come back from the dead. Even the people who bore no relation to the old tycoon, joined in to chant the mantra to strengthen the power of the prayer.

Although people had arrived in droves to satisfy their curiosity, gorge on the exquisite food and make a quick buck, most of them decided to stay despite the impending doom. They could not take their eyes off the freak show. The people were now losing respect for the old tycoon and whispered among themselves about his nasty habits and a probable pact with the devil. The darkness of the situation raised concerns and disquietude, but the seduction of the unusual events was too delectable to resist.

Day 6

The exhausted priests took turns to continue reciting their prayers and verses. The entire mansion was filled with the smell of burnt joss paper, hell money, candles and incense. The cacophony of drums, cymbals, flutes and *suonas* were deafening. It became more of an event to keep the old tycoon from reanimating than to send him off to the underworld.

At this point, everyone was frazzled and appalled by the thing into which the old tycoon was metamorphosing. At dawn, someone noticed his teeth stretching out of his mouth. They were ragged, razor-sharp and savage looking. The family did not know if they should allow the old tycoon to transmogrify into some creature of the night or stake and decapitate him before it got any worse.

No one wanted to do the dirty job for fear of inadvertently incurring a curse upon themselves for generations to come. So, they left the old tycoon alone but became wary of shadows and things that bumped in the night.

Finally, the family agreed to execute the old tycoon at the end of the seventh day, if the need arose. This would mark it as the final stage of the ceremony and if the old tycoon were to indeed turn into a bloodsucking monster, they would have had a very good reason to do so.

Day 7

No one could sleep a wink on the last night. The gambling sessions were disrupted by the constant fear and having to look over their shoulders every so often. Conversations became whispers so as to not wake the dead. Everyone waited to see what the seventh day would bring.

The whole day was a quiet ordeal. Some people, including relatives, disappeared on the sixth day, citing lame excuses for their precipitate departure. The family had no choice but to continue with their incessant prayers and vigils, although they prepared the stakes and machetes for an ultimate confrontation, if it came to that.

It was close to midnight when everyone heard firecracker kind of noises at a distance. The bursts seemed to be too loud and strange; besides, there weren't any celebrations being held in the vicinity. Those who were awake exchanged blank looks. They had a peculiar feeling that something was badly amiss. The booming fanfare ceased abruptly and a deathly silence fell over the house. A bloodcurdling scream reached their ears just as a black cat jumped over the old tycoon's coffin, knocking over a candleholder.

Before anyone could consider a stake through the heart or decapitation, a group of uniformed gunmen stormed in.

* * *

'Who would want to crash a funeral?'

'Japanese soldiers.'

'Japanese soldiers?'

'World War II. No one knew they were coming. They stealthily took control of the whole country within days. That suburb was the first area in the outskirts that they had to pass to get to Taiping town.'

'And the old tycoon?'

'By the time they noticed, he was gone.'

'So, he did become a vampire.'

'I guess.'

'What happened after he escaped?'

'No one knows. Everyone in that cowboy town died. The Japanese soldiers who invaded it also died. There were ashes everywhere.'

'What's a cowboy town?'

'A very small town. Smaller than Port Weld.'

'What about the story? Is that it?'

'That's it, but rumour has it that if the Japanese soldiers hadn't managed to infiltrate this cowboy town, Taiping would never be what it is today.'

'What about the details?'

'No one survived. So, there are no details to tell you.'

'If only someone did. I would love to know what exactly happened to the vampire. How did they die? Who killed them? Must have been some kind of a superhero.'

'I guess we'll never know.'

* * *

Xin did not want to leave the wake.

He was curious to see the old tycoon's transformation into a creature of the night—he didn't know why, but the way people were freaking out about it had piqued his curiosity. Although he was uneasy with the grisly anticipation, he wasn't swayed by their panic. His close encounter with the old tycoon in the past made him extra vigilant. Extra cautious.

He overheard people talking about the best way to kill the vampire, a bloodsucking monster that had no right to live off other people's life forces causing them to turn into monsters themselves. He found a cubbyhole in the tycoon's house where he could hide and observe the goings-on without being noticed. It was already the last day and he had to know if the old tycoon would return from the dead. He didn't like the idea of encountering it, but was mentally prepared for the worst. He would rather know now, than later, what he might have to deal with in the future.

He saw a black cat walking towards the coffin as if it were enchanted. It hopped on to it and peered at the old dead tycoon. Suddenly it was yanked into the coffin, bringing down a candleholder that was standing precariously by the side. Some witnesses could have sworn they saw a hand reaching out and grabbing the cat, but before they could do anything, the soldiers barged into the house. From the way the soldiers handled everyone roughly, Xin understood that violence was the order of the day and withdrew deeper into his hiding place to wait out the frightening confusion.

While struggles and screams were exchanged between the family members and the intruders, Xin saw the old tycoon creep out of the open coffin. His long, curving nails hooked on to the sides of the wood, making long deep grooves on the wood where his nails scratched the surface, as if a cat had sharpened her claws at precisely those places. He had finally become a creature of the night, but everyone was too busy to notice that. Xin wanted to alert them, but he felt that their tug-o-war for control would make his efforts futile.

The old tycoon ascended from the coffin and flexed his unhinged jaws to expose rows of shark-like teeth. His hungry eyes analysed the situation. The awful smell that emanated from his body was nauseating. Any sign of the old tycoon before was gone. It was now a monstrous thing that had the jerky agitation of a housefly and an anatomy of a carnivorous predator. When it stood fully erect, it drew everyone's attention to it.

In a terrifying moment of silence, everything froze. No one moved as much as an inch while they gazed at the creature that was observing them with tilted head.

Xin foresaw what was about to transpire so he closed his eyes and covered his ears, but he could not block out the high-pitched squealing and screaming of the kind he had only heard in abattoirs. Gunshots went off and agitated feet scuffled to get to safety. Warm splotches of blood landed on him and forced him to open his eyes and see the massacre up close.

Soldiers and townspeople alike turned to bring the creature down but they were collectively as helpless as a child defending itself from a feral animal. Bits and pieces of people were splattered everywhere. Xin winced. He stifled his fear and waited for a break to dash out of the bloodbath. When a gang of soldiers charged at the creature Xin ran out of hiding and never looked back.

He knew the ins and outs of the town in his mind's eye. While everyone thought he was just an unkempt seven-year-old urchin, neglected by his mother, he went around mapping the entire place out of curiosity. He could move around the village like a rat to scavenge for food. The townspeople either didn't know that he had no family, or they preferred to forget that there were children who were conceived out of wedlock and abandoned. What they also forgot was that some of these children survived. The society just didn't have the time or patience to nurture waifs like him.

The first thing Xin did was to find shelter. He had a few hideouts he could go to in times of trouble. Some were up on treetops that no one could reach. Some were deep in the earth that no one knew existed. To get a better view of the ground situation he climbed one of the taller trees to maximize his vantage point.

Camouflaged in the foliage, he watched the chaos down below. The funeral went beyond anyone's expectation. Cries from the injured and the maimed were deafening. The creature brought down everyone who was in his way and escaped into the darkness while the men with guns shot at it.

When the terror was over, the surviving people were marched by the soldiers into the community hall, which was some kind of a rendezvous point. Some sobbed. Others bled. The dead were dragged and dumped on to a pile. Even if there was no creature on the loose now, Xin knew it was unsafe for him to venture down since the uniformed men were not there to make friends or protect them. They were doing whatever was needed to take whatever it was that they wanted by force.

He curled his tiny body to fit into the hollow of the tree while he cowered from the cold and terrifying experience. It was unlike anything he had ever seen before. He gazed at the night sky for comfort. It was something he did whenever he felt out of place or disconnected with reality. He was afraid to close his eyes but sleep soon caught up with him and lulled him into a dreamless world.

* * *

He felt the first light creep up on him even though his eyes were shut. His body ached from sleeping on the tree although he had forged a makeshift bed from the foliage. It wasn't the first time he had to do this to escape human hands. There were times when some of the people of the town had tried to touch or grab him, but he had been lucky to escape their advances. He had no idea what people wanted of him, but he disliked proximity with strangers. All this time he had survived on his wits. He found other people's wastage to be his gain. From putting food on the table to clothes on his back there was always an abundance. Although he could do with a thorough scrub, he was best off surviving on his own.

He plucked a few *rambutans* from the tree he was perched on and devoured them before facing the new day. He observed that the soldiers and locals were both confused about their respective roles caused by the unexpected turn of events.

The bodies, two men and a woman from the village, and three soldiers, were laid out in the sun, weighed down with rocks and tethered with ropes to grounded pegs. The family members were crying and begging for their loved ones to be released. Some victims had bite marks and some, open wounds, while some had both, like they had been mauled by a wild animal. And those were the only ones he could see.

There were a lot of discussions and arguments and they no longer behaved like prisoners and captors anymore—they had a common enemy; one that could not be killed with bullets. An interpreter bridged the gap and made it easier for them to converse. From what he could gather, Xin understood that they were hatching a plan to trap the creature, knowing that it would inevitably return for more blood when darkness fell.

Even from that distance, Xin could see the corpses twitching although it was very clear that they were dead. When he had a closer look, he saw something that did not make any sense. The dead bodies were contorted, and their fingers had hooks sticking out at the tips. They too had turned into beasts albeit of a lower pedigree than the old tycoon. One of them shot up from the ground, trying to break free of the ropes and rocks that held it down. It snarled and snapped at the people around, sniffing and extending its elongated tongue and exposing its fangs.

A soldier raised his gun and fired at the beast. It fell back, but lashed out, almost immediately. The solider pointed his gun at the beast again but a senior officer held the barrel of the gun and shook his head, conveying the futility of the action. A crowd had already gathered in a circle to watch the creatures wake up one by one, struggling to break free of the restraints. The families of the deceased had long given up hope for their dearly departed especially when they started looking the way they did. Although the axes and machetes were at hand, no one made the first move. They stood by and looked on helplessly.

Before anyone could do anything, the sun seared the beasts in the cool morning air. The heat ate into their skin and created boils and blisters that looked ready to pop. The beasts let out long hideous ululations that echoed through the town as they convulsed uncontrollably. The families who mourned their loved ones, watched in horror as the agonizing cries led to popping sounds from the bursting of their flesh. At the end of their suffering, the beasts finally combusted, silencing the last screech to announce their agonizing end.

When the fires burnt themselves out, all that remained were charred bodies in tortuous forms that lasted only seconds before disintegrating into dust. It was a cautionary sign for the witnesses; a foretaste of what was to come. Xin imagined the worst when he remembered that the old tycoon was still alive, hiding from plain sight, and probably watching and waiting to hunt again at nightfall. Seeing how crucial the situation was, Xin decided he had to do something to help the village and himself. He heard them referring to the old tycoon by another name, whispering to each other about what it was capable of. They called it Vampyr and they claimed that it could destroy the entire town within days.

Xin had never trusted anyone before but now his distrust deepened. Although the victims who were contaminated by the Vampyr were obviously destroyed, he didn't want to wait around to find out who else had already been infected. It could already be too late. He rested his head on a branch and slumped on the tree, wondering how much worse this situation could get. He could hide in the trees until everything played out completely, but that hardly meant that he was safe. Life had never been easy for him, but he always knew what he had to do to survive. Just like now; he knew he had to find the Vampyr's lair.

The town was open to anyone who wanted to access it, but it only had one route. The dirt road leading into it was a maze without landmarks. The road was surrounded by rubber trees and every rubber tree looked the same in repetitive rows in all directions. The east side was demarcated by a mangrove forest so nothing could get through the thick and gnarly root system. But one could still trudge through the swamp to get to the river provided there was sufficient motivation.

The only way to stay out of the sun was to take shelter in one of the many abandoned buildings. Of all the damaged structures, one that resembled a castle came to mind. If Xin guessed right, the Vampyr would want to live in a place like that in his afterlife.

Xin stole some rice from someone's kitchen and downed it quickly to strengthen himself for the expedition. He could have run off to another town and forgotten everything that had happened here, but he knew that it would haunt him wherever he went. If not the Vampyr, then the memory of the bloodbath. As much as he hated some of the people in that small town, there were still some good and innocent people among the evil ones; those who had been generous and kind to him were worth his time.

The mangrove swamp was a ten-to-twenty-minute walk from the town centre depending on who was doing the walking. Xin managed to reach the network of gnarly roots in less than the minimum time. Located at the edge of the swamp was a mansion known as the Ang Mo Lau; most of its interiors hadn't seen the light of day since it was abandoned.

Rooms without doors, halls without decorations and a void without the warmth of human touch was all that remained of this once magnificent edifice. Every child and every adult had visited it although they were warned against trespassing. The barbed wire fence and padlocks did not stop them. Teenagers rendezvoused at the mansion to live out the expectations of their wasted youth.

Lovers wanted to stake a claim on the romantic nostalgia upon which the mansion was built. It was also the occasional sanctuary for dipsomaniacs and addicts as a respite from the world.

The only thing that stopped everyone from loitering at the mansion for too long were the sightings of malevolent spirits. A few people claimed they were attacked. Two boys said they were enchanted into doing things they would have never done of their own free will. A girl claimed she was impregnated by a ghost after sneaking into the mansion at night. The uncanny and fascinating stories that were attached to the mansion read like Entertaining Comics or more commonly known as EC comics. Xin must have been the only person who did not encounter any spirits when he had temporarily made it his home. It was as good a shelter as any, especially during the storms, until he freed some flying foxes locked in room. It was the best time of his life watching the large fruit bats take flight into the great expanse of the night sky. He angered a lot of people because he hadn't realized that the citizens had stashed the creatures in the mansion, to be turned into delicacies on a later date.

He loved the way the mansion had assimilated with the mangrove trees through the years. The biodiversity of the swamp embraced it as though it were, in fact, a part of the swamp. Wild animals took shelter in the mansion, hiding in nooks and corners while others nested in places where the roof had caved in. He was familiar with the mud-skippers and fiddler crabs occupying the ground floor as they ran helter-skelter to take cover whenever they were disturbed. A couple of buffy fish owls were permanent residents and a few brahminy kites circled the building like they were watching over it.

The top floor was exposed to the sun by day and the stars by night. However, the ground floor had always been cloaked in shadows. No one remembered whether the building of the roof had ever been completed or if thieves had had a field day removing the tiles and fittings to resell them or if someone had vandalized it to vent their frustrations. Xin had surveyed the entire mansion from top to bottom, both in light and in the dark—he hardly knew what fear was. It felt cold and miserable on nights when he couldn't find any food, but it was always better when it was not frequented by people with bad intentions. He had seen kids torture a stray dog. He had seen a man ravaging a young girl. He had seen an unwed mother abandoning her newborn baby. All these made it conducive for the Vampyr to live here because it personified a similar kind of evil.

Xin re-surveyed the abandoned building meticulously, observing where the sun's rays touched the ground. Vegetation thrived in these areas. He found a piece of mangrove root and clutched it tightly in his hand to use as a stake if the need arose. He trod quietly between dry leaves and twigs with his tiny bare feet, keeping a lookout for things that did not belong. The ground floor, strewn with broken tiles, abounded with creepers, undergrowth and the stench of neglect. He stood motionless, inhaling the smell of rotten eggs and waited for his eyes to get used to the pitch blackness. Silhouettes gradually morphed into shattered parts of the building, ramshackle furniture and other stuff discarded by trespassers.

It was rumoured that the mansion had over twenty rooms. Some claimed there were more, but no one knew for certain. The top floor was ruined by the ravages of time and there was nothing left but awkward looking partitions that stood without reason. The ground floor was the darkest area in the entire building. Although the sun had claimed the entire top floor it could only peek into the rooms below through cracks and crevices.

Xin tentatively set a foot in the shadows and something tried to grab him. He withdrew it just before the Vampyr could seize hold of him. It lay still again, but the dust, dry leaves and trash spun around in a small whirlwind. He adjusted his eyes to the dark, trying to find the creature of the night. There was something huge suspended from the ceiling. It flung open its massive wings to reveal the old tycoon just before it swooped down and stood before Xin. They were separated by a narrow beam of light. If the Vampyr had reached out, it could easily grab hold of Xin.

'What are you doing here, little boy?' the Vampyr flexed its clawed hand in front of Xin's face. 'Did you come here to die?'

Xin didn't want to show his fear although he wanted to run away and forget this crazy idea of saving the town.

'Aah, you are that boy they call Xin. Such a beautiful boy with such fine features.'

Xin was petrified with dread. He hadn't thought it through carefully. Death was inevitable now.

'I know you understand me, so understand this well. Do you think you can kill me with that root?'

Xin fought back his tears and moved his hand behind his back.

'I can crush it in one hand.'

Xin dropped it on the ground and moved further away from the darkness.

'Come. No need to be afraid. I can heal you. I can give you the hearing of a bat. The sight of an owl. And the agility of a cat.'

The Vampyr extended his open palm to Xin but stopped just before its nails could touch the sunlight.

'There will be wonders. There will be . . . perfection. You will live forever. You are special. You have the wisdom of an old forgotten tree. And the courage of an alpha male. All you have to do is step into the darkness.'

Xin was tempted to claim the prize, but he saw how desperate the Vampyr was, trapped as it were, in the darkness. He took a deep breath, gathered his thoughts and stepped back.

'If you are not with me . . . then you are against me!' The winged creature took off and fluttered out of the room with anger and contempt. 'Beware, Xin. I will come in the night like death. And once I have fed on every living person in this town, I will come and get you. You can't hide. I can smell you like a succulent piece of meat. You have until then to decide.'

The Vampyr screeched through the empty hallways and shook the foundation of the abandoned mansion.

'Don't ever come back here again!'

Xin ran from the building and stayed in the sunlight as much as he could, avoiding the slightest shade as well as the deepest shadow, both of which were plentiful.

* * *

Xin stayed hidden when the sun went down and ventured out to forage for food as soon as it came back up. Each night he heard the death screams that echoed throughout the town. Soldiers with guns and the support of the inhabitants could do nothing to stop the savage massacre. There was not a single safe sanctuary. It was futile to try and hide from the creature that could smell the blood flowing through their veins and hear their hearts thumping in fear from afar.

Within a matter of days, the number of townspeople and soldiers dwindled to half. He witnessed a few incidents of bloodshed that were quick and death almost instantaneous. When the common folk and the Japanese soldiers wised up enough to want to leave town, it was already too late. Those who had been turned by the Vampyr were stationed at the borders and exits. They hid in the tunnels they had dug around the perimeters and like antlions, they waited for the slightest movement above ground to yank escapees down for food.

Those who did not turn were mangled and strewn all over the town and left to rot. Those who did, transmogrified into horrible versions of themselves—malformed, wretched, and perverted. Xin could not save the place and the people any more than he could save himself. The shrieking and screaming gradually turned to growls and bellows and Xin knew his time was almost up.

His ultimate stronghold was the mangrove swamp where he had hidden from predators before. There was a part of the swamp where the mangrove trees were cut down by some mercenary local businessmen. What was left were mutilated trunks that poked out of the bog. While the Vampyr was busy annihilating everyone in town, Xin spent his time honing the ends of the trunks into dagger-like sabres and made his sanctuary deep in the heart of the swamp. There he stayed for days with his bare minimum supply of food and water, waiting to meet his end. Although the booby trap could impale any of the demonic intruders coming to get him, he knew they weren't enough.

Eventually, as he waited on the prop roots of a mangrove tree, he heard them approaching in the dark. The crawlers sniffed out his location and stormed into the swamp without any awareness of the lurking danger. They charged to their deaths, staking themselves upon the bayonets fashioned from the trunks. The unending squeals of the bloodthirsty beasts did not stop until Xin was captured.

He passed out from fear, hunger and exhaustion and woke up in the abandoned mansion.

'You knew it was inevitable,' the Vampyr said and took the boy's hands in his. Xin yanked his hands away and locked them under his knees. 'We have all eternity to play this game.'

The chirping of morning birds distracted the Vampyr for a moment and he frowned at the sign that the sun was about to make its presence felt.

'Too soon,' he said and rose in all his glory like a fantastic bat out of hell. 'I shall turn you before we go to sleep. That way we will wake up to a brand-new night and we shall hunt together in the next town.'

Xin kicked the approaching creature, but he was pinioned by the Vampyr's elongated fingers.

'My adorable little fighter,' the Vampyr's unnerving laughter drowned out other sounds in the abandoned building and sent the animals and insects scampering away. The crawlers slid over each other's bodies like a blob of worms, twisting and writhing in a mass of confusion at the sound of their master's voice.

The Vampyr brought its face close to Xin's as though it was about to give him the kiss of the afterlife. Xin tried to resist but he was mesmerized by its demonic gaze.

'Now open up,' it whispered and forced Xin's jaws apart. The Vampyr coughed up a dark substance that flowed into Xin's mouth to inherit the hunger and immortality of the Vampyr. The pungent and foul-smelling goo made him shudder with disgust and at the same time he felt electrical charges bursting within his body.

His vocal cords started loosening and his eardrums vibrated to the sound of his own gushing blood. He felt cold and numb as if his life essences had been drained and fire had been pumped to replace it. The callouses on his feet flaked away and scabs on his arms smoothed over. His heart pulsated one last time and then began to freeze, slowing down its rhythm to the beat of a dirge and then the pulsations ceased completely. His world collapsed into itself and turned black. He knew he was dead.

It was a menagerie of nightmares going down the rabbit hole. Xin felt the ultimate pain and pleasure meant for bad trips and he was drowning in a cesspool of the Vampyr's rancid blood. He would have seen the last of the brilliant daylight by the time he awoke. It would soon be a forlorn memory and he would have to come to terms with that and eventually forget what sunshine looked like. Although he was wise beyond his years, he would grow old too quickly in a child's body.

The sweet smell of nocturnal flowers was fading. Xin would no longer have the pleasure of appreciating them since his sense of smell was going to be totally overridden by a lust for blood. He opened his eyes not to the world he knew but one in the Vampyr's embrace. He unhooked his arms, pushed them aside and fell straight to the ground below. He managed to right himself with his heightened reflexes even before he hit the floor.

The Vampyr only stirred a little to reposition himself on his perch amongst the rafters. Xin stood among the crawlers that were piled haphazardly all over the ground like victims of a holocaust. He heard more chirping and the singsong tunes of birds at sunrise. He ran out of the darkness to see the glow in the morning sky still thick with mist, hoping to get immolated by its power.

He continued running aimlessly because he didn't want to have anything to do with the creature of the night and its beasts. When he saw the sun's rays streaking out from beyond the hills he dropped to his knees and wept. The mist had finally dispersed. Instinct told him to find cover like any other nocturnal animal, but his innocence kept him rooted to the ground. He felt the temperature in his body rise and he waited to combust with the heat of the day. When first light stretched its finger out to touch the world a flock of flying foxes, or pteropus vampyrus, swarmed overhead like a storm cloud. They flocked in from all corners of the village and grew into an enormous blanket to prevent the sun from scorching Xin. He got up and moved away from their shadow, but the flying foxes followed him, shielding him from sunburn.

'What are you doing? Go away!' Xin's melodic voice emerged from his throat for the first time. 'I can speak,' he exclaimed and looked around for someone to share this moment of joy, but there was nobody around—just a wide-open space, dead leaves and debris of broken concrete.

He watched the flying foxes swirl in the sky and looked down on the ground to see a custodial shade all around him. The sun had lighted up everything else outside the perimeter. He made another attempt to leave the umbrageous refuge, but the flying foxes continued to protect him. He then recalled the time he released the flying foxes that had been caught and caged for sale to the Chinese restaurants as exotic delicacies. To him, it had been a small and necessary gesture, but to the flying foxes it must have meant something much more.

Although he was safe from the scorching sun his eyes could not adjust to the dazzling brightness which was too overwhelming. He raised his hands to the flying foxes and said, 'In that case, we have work to do.' As though they understood what he said, a group of flying foxes flew down and lifted him up while the rest maintained the airborne canopy over him, taking him back to the abandoned mansion.

The beasts were exactly where he had left them, splayed or curled up on top of each other in clusters. He crept back in and stood among them, feeling sad and horrified for what they had denatured into. To live this way was not only an abomination but sheer cruelty. He screeched and wailed with the sadness he felt for them. This had to end here and now. Sensing danger at the high-pitched cries, the crawlers scattered in the dark, rolling off one another. The flying foxes swooped down and attacked the crawlers, scattering them haphazardly but wherever they ran they invariably kept to the shadows. Some of the rooms were already bright with sunlight, leaving only the lounge, the hallway and the parlour.

The cacophony woke the Vampyr and it was furious when it saw sunlight streaking into some of the rooms. The entire ground floor that used to be in total darkness had been compromised. He raced to the source of the trouble and saw flying foxes whirling around like a maddening storm, lashing out at the crawlers. The Vampyr snapped the flying foxes that lunged at him like dry twigs.

'How dare you defy me and my minions!' the Vampyr screamed at the flying foxes.

'Because they are with me,' Xin stepped up to him.

'Little boy . . .!'

'I am not your little boy!'

'I gave you life.'

'Which I never wanted.'

'Ingrate. You are no threat to me.'

'Maybe not, but we are.'

Xin let out an animalistic ululation and the flying foxes flew away from the ceiling that was directly above the crawlers. Layer after layer the flying foxes took off to reveal the hole that had been widened and punched through the floor above. The sun breached through the opening and ignited the crawlers that had clumped together to escape the flying foxes. The Vampyr realized that it had underestimated Xin, but it was too late. Before it could hurl itself at him and snap him in two, Xin ran into its arms and held the Vampyr down, but he was no match for the monster. The Vampyr shook him off and took to the air before they could get too close to the light.

Xin hung on to his legs and the flying foxes came back to surround them, clutching and grabbing at the Vampyr's hair, clothes and skin. The flying foxes dragged both of them into the sunshine and the Vampyr shrieked like a wild animal, killing some of the flying foxes in its attempt to break free. Xin let go of the Vampyr's legs and fell back into the shadows.

The brilliance of the morning sun cauterized the Vampyr's face and wings. It tried to battle with the forces of nature to retain its mortality, but it was no match for the sun. The flying foxes took turns to replace the wounded or exhausted, keeping the Vampyr locked in place. They were chewing away at its wings, gnawing at its legs, and stripping the creature apart faster than it could regenerate itself. By this time, the sun managed to incinerate most of the Vampyr and its death throes shook the very foundations of the old mansion. After a long and extended combustion, it exploded in a puff of smoke, its ashes spreading across the town to envelope everything in a film of grey.

The flying foxes tended to their wounds and injuries before flying off into the trees where they roosted. In the middle of the darkness of the abandoned mansion Xin waved to his guardians with gratitude. He sighed with relief as well as dread. Not because he was all alone but because he didn't know how strong he could be when it came to controlling his lust for blood.

* * *

'Oh, I heard that one of the vampires survived and is still wandering around in Taiping town,' Ashkraf said between his giggles.

'Oh yeah, and we believe you.'

'Hey, it could be possible.'

'You watched too many Christopher Lee movies.'

'I prefer Peter Cushing.'

'It's true.'

Everyone turned to the voice that didn't seem to blend in.

'What's true?'

'That one of the vampires is still around. Although he tries very hard, sometimes he can't help himself.'

'Tries what?'

'Not to drink human blood.'

'How do you know?'

'Because he is watching us right now.'

A very long and uncomfortable silence gripped the campsite. For a moment, they didn't even hear the sounds of the nocturnal animals. It was only when someone burst out into hysterical and raucous laughter that the disquietude broke and had the rest imitating him.

* * *

On many occasions Xin denied his hunger by avoiding human contact and staying with the flying foxes to feed on nectars and flowers.

But sometimes he could not help himself, especially on nights when his prey are alone. He watches them through the gaps between windows, doors, and roofs. In this part of the world a vampire needs no invitation. When all is still and dark, he creeps in to drink only as much as he needs, affecting his victims only with bad dreams and night terrors, but not turning them into bloodthirsty creatures of the night.

13

The Thirteenth Ghost

'Do you sometimes feel like we're in a black-and-white horror movie?'

'Yeah, I feel it.'

'Me, too.'

'Well, this story is about the boy who can see ghosts.'

Wen King started his storytelling by leading the others into a realm he created. He expected questions, but everyone just gazed blankly at him, their laughter from the previous tale dying down.

'It started when he was very young,' Wen King continued to drain the humour from them to inject life into his narration, reintroducing the caliginous atmosphere. The others began to feel uneasy about the way Wen King glared at them.

'He would tell everyone he sees his dead *ah mah* or *ah kong*, grandma and grandpa, walking past or sitting in the corner or looking angry.'

Soon, everyone's attention was drawn towards Wen King. It was quite late by now, after having heard so many other stories from the rest but they didn't look tired or distracted.

* * *

Everyone thought it was cute when he was five. But as he grew older no one thought that anymore. No one wanted to hear that sort of thing.

Once he went to a relative's house for Chinese New Year and told everyone that there was a man walking up and down with a meat cleaver in his hand. It freaked everyone out because, a long time ago, a man had killed his whole family before slitting his own throat in that very house. From then on, the boy was no longer welcome in anyone's house. No one wanted to know the dark pasts of their homes or of the lonely roads they frequently travelled on. No one wanted to know if there was an angry spirit in the building or if someone was murdered in cold blood.

Everyone avoided the boy. They were afraid to even look at him because they didn't want to know what his eyes were focusing on. Sometimes he looked over people's shoulders, behind them when he was talking to them. At the beginning they thought he was just being peculiar or cross-eyed. One day someone asked him why he kept staring behind him and he said there was a ghost attached to this person's back. That person fell sick for weeks—with high fever and delirium. He almost did not survive until they sought the help of a medium to exorcise the ghost. Word got out and the boy was ostracized. They treated him like he had the plague.

What made it worse was the fact that he was abducted by the school bullies who took him to a haunted house. That old abandoned house was known for all kinds of strange phenomena. What the bullies didn't know was that the boy was not afraid. He was used to seeing ghosts and demons and monsters. So when they tied him to a chair and asked him to tell them what he saw he said to the bullies, 'If you want to know I will open your third eye and you will be able to see everything yourself.'

The bullies didn't believe that the boy had the power to open other people's 'third eye'. The leader said, 'You can't bluff your way out. We're leaving you here for the night.'

'What are you afraid of?' asked the boy.

The bully did not want to be challenged in front of his toadies and he replied, 'Why don't you try?'

The boy closed his eyes and went into a deep meditative state and the three bullies who were there backed away from him, sensing trouble.

'What if he's telling the truth?' the youngest bully said.

'He's bluffing,' the ringleader replied and whacked the boy's head to show his dominance.

'Don't do that,' the heaviest of the boys caught at the leader's hand and added, 'don't make him angry.'

'There are various types of ghosts,' the boy said, ignoring the bullies' argument. 'There's the corner-of-the-eye ghost. If you roll your eyes to the corner, you will see a shadow always moving away before you can see them.'

The boy opened his eyes to look at them. The two younger bullies could not resist the power of suggestion and did what the boy said.

'I . . . I see something . . .' the young bully said.

'He's tricking us into doing this. Don't listen to him,' the leader shouted to snap them out of the stupor.

'And if you blink fast enough you will see a ghost approaching. That is the eye-blinking ghost. So, if you can, try not to blink.'

The bullies started to see what the boy had conjured up in their minds' eyes and they grew agitated with the darkness.

'Stop listening to him!'

'Not forgetting the look-behind-you ghost. You can feel it breathing down the back of your neck, but don't ever look back because it is always there, just waiting for you to turn around. Waiting for you to acknowledge its presence. Then of course there's the behind-the-door ghost, under-the-bed ghost, in-the-window ghost . . .'

'Let's get out of here. I'm scared,' the youngest one pleaded.

'Yeah, let's just leave him and go home,' the heavyset bully said. 'I don't like this game anymore.'

'Cowards! He's playing you,' the leader said, but was feeling anxious himself. 'But we might as well go home. We're done here. We'll leave this freak alone in this haunted house.'

'There's also the mistaken-for-a-ghost ghost. Sometimes you think you see a figure or a form but, on second look, it's just a mop or a garbage bin or a shirt hanging from the hook. But they are actually ghosts that disguise themselves as these things. They are always waiting for you to notice them. Once they know you know, they will never leave you alone. They may want you to do something for them. They may find your energy attractive and want to latch on to it. Or they may just want to play with you, like a toy. Like it or not, your third eye is now open.'

The two younger bullies ran off bawling for their gods and mothers to protect them. The leader remained behind, infuriated by the fact that the boy had frightened them with his tricks.

'You don't fool me for one second,' the leader sneered.

'I'm not. Look around,' the boy said and smiled.

The leader could not help turning around to quickly scan the room. He thought he saw a very tall man in a dark suit, but it turned out to be a dark patch on the wall. He thought he smelled something bad and decaying and that something was trying to get his attention from the corner of his eye. He didn't want to give in, but he was defeated by the cold sweat and buckling knees. Something touched his shoulder and he froze. He closed his eyes, but a nagging feeling forced him to open them again to see a woman charging at him. He shut his eyes immediately, but he couldn't help but flip them open again to see the woman within inches from his face. He caved and ran screaming like a blind man in a maze into the night.

* * *

Wen King smiled and looked around at the faces that were looking at him expectantly.

'Wh-what happened to the bullies?'

'Oh, the bullies went crazy with fear. One of them fell so ill, he never quite recovered from it. One died mysteriously and the other went insane.'

The rest of the boys did not know what to make of the story. It felt empty and unrewarding. They were aware that something was not right. It wasn't this way when they told ghost stories. At the end of the story, it usually felt complete but now, it felt like it was out of place and underwhelming.

'Something's not right.'

'I agree.'

'Yeah, yeah.'

'It's the story.'

'No, it's the way the story is told.'

'What about it?'

'Do you guys realize our group seems a little tighter? Like, like we are not as spread out as we used to be.'

'Yeah, it feels a little tight.'

The boys glanced at each other but the night obscured many details for them to make out any anomaly.

'Let's do a head count.'

'Why?'

'Because . . . we'll go clockwise. I am one . . .'

'Two.'

'Three.'

'Four.'

'Five.'

'Six?'

'Seven.'

'Eight.'

'. . . Nine.'

'T-ten.'

'Eleven.'

'Twelve.'

'Thir-teen . . .' Wen King ended the count and the silence that followed was ear-splitting.

'But there were only twelve of us,' Lot said but no one responded. They could feel their hearts racing in the darkness. 'This time, we will go anti-clockwise,' he paused and then said, 'One.'

'Two.'

'Three.'

'Four.'

'Five.'

'Six.'

'Seven.'

'Eight.'

'Nine.'

'Ten.'

'Eleven.'

'Twelve.'

'Thirteen.' It ended with Wen King again.

'According to superstition every time you tell ghost stories a thirteenth ghost will appear.'

'So, one of us is a ghost?'

Everyone grew a little panicky. Edgy. Terrified.

'That's just an old wives' tale.'

'Nonsense.'

'That's not even true.'

'But there are thirteen of us.'

'We must have miscounted.'

'Let's do another head count. This time I won't start. Jackson you start counting.'

'Okay, one . . .'

'Two.'

'Three.'

'Four.'

'Five.'

'Six.'

'Seven.'

'Eight.'

'Nine.'

'Ten.'

'Eleven.'

'Twelve.'

'Thirteen,' Wen King said for the third time, not knowing how it ended with him again.

'It's you!'

Everyone backed away from him.

'Hey, hey! Let's not jump to conclusions. Calm down. Why don't we state our names instead of numbers this time? I am Lot Ser Ling.'

'Rao Dhal.'

'Ser Lee Ee, Jackson.'

'Alan Poh.'

'Darshan.'

'Jun Jee Toh.'

'Mah Teh Son.'

'Ta Ba Liew, Jacob.'

'Ray Beh Lee.'

'Lai Bak Ker.'

'Cham Hoo Bert.'

'Aspi Ashkraf.'

When it came to the last person Ser Ling asked, 'Who are you?'

'I am Wen King.'

'What's your full name?'

'Tee Wen King.'

The silence that ensued was deafening. All the boys sat bolt upright and glanced at each other although the darkness only revealed part of their faces and expressions.

'But . . .'

'We don't know anyone by that name.'

'It's you.'

'You are the thirteenth ghost!'

Before he could say anything else, the group of boys screamed and ran hysterically into the night, leaving everything behind. Including Wen King.

Epilogue

'I am the thirteenth ghost. I am the thirteenth ghost,' Wen King chanted to himself and watched as the fire died out and ushered in the darkness.

'Wennn . . .' a girl's voice drifted past him.

'Guys . . . I'm not a ghost,' Wen King stood up and wrapped his arms himself around to ward off the cold.

'Wennn . . .' the voice grew louder and drew closer.

'OMG! It's the . . . the . . . *siloban*. But *siloban* can't talk. Or is it the Maxwell ghost? The Chifa ghost?'

'Wennn . . .'

'Guys, don't leave me alone!'

Wen King didn't know in which direction to run. There were no landmarks or signposts, only terrifying shadows and angry silhouettes.

'Wennn!!!'

This time he felt the thing screaming in his ear. He tried to run but something kept him from moving. His legs were thrashing about, but they took him nowhere.

'Hellppp meee . . .' he screamed one last time and felt the stinging blow across his face.

'Wennn! Wennn! Stop it!' Sally slapped Wen King across the face and woke him up. 'Wake up, you idiot.'

'Owww, why do you have to slap me?'

'Because you were kicking me, and we've been calling you, like, forever. Who asked you to go missing like that? You know you scared us shitless? Mom and dad went ballistic. They blamed me for not taking proper care of you and that it was all my fault that you disappeared. Did they stop to consider who it was who wandered off by himself, although he knew better? No-oo!'

'Wait. Where am I?'

'Urgh! Don't you even know where you are? This is somewhere in between Kem Maju and Burmese Pool. Or what used to be Kem Maju. You got lost, you fool! I told you not to go wandering around, but did you listen? I thought you died or something. It would have been great if you had, but mom and dad would have never let me live that down. Lucky for you the search-and-rescue team found you before the wild animals did. We've been looking for you all night. And you made me cry my eyes out.'

'You cried for me?'

'You wish! I cried because it was late, and I didn't get enough sleep.'

'What about the rest?'

'The rest of what?'

'The boys.'

'What boys?'

'The ones who were sitting around the campfire telling ghost stories.'

'Are you kidding me? You wanna go there now?'

'It's true.'

'Yeah, right.

A member of the rescue team squatted down beside Wen King to check his condition.

'Are you hurt?' the medic asked.

'No.'

'Did you fall?'

'No.'

The medic felt his joints to see if anything was broken.

'How do you feel? Are you feeling all right?'

'Yes, I'm just cold.'

The medic wrapped a blanket around him.

'I tell you, sis, I saw them! They were here with me. All twelve of them,' Wen King said to his sister who was standing aside to give some space for the medic to do his job.

An elderly member from the search-and-rescue team overheard Wen King and walked towards the siblings to join their conversation.

'Did you say twelve of them?' the man asked.

'Yeah, we were sitting around a campfire and . . . and . . . telling ghost stories.'

'Wen, stop that nonsense. You had a nightmare. You were hallucinating.'

'He may have experienced something more than that.'

'What do you mean?' Sally asked.

'A long time ago, twelve teenage boys were killed in a flash flood. Rumour has it they come back to tell ghost stories every night because they don't know that they are dead. Some say they come back to relive that moment because they died too young. Some say they are caught in a time-warp because they were at the wrong place at the wrong time.' After dropping the bomb, the elderly man walked away before they could get their heads around what he had just said.

'See, I told you, sis.'

'You and your creepy friends. Just stay away from me from now on.'

Sally noticed that Wen King was carrying on a conversation by himself.

'Who are you talking to? Another one of your "ghost" friends?'

Wen King merely smiled. Sally shrugged and walked away, muttering, 'You and your ghosts!'

'I know you're looking at me right now and I know you're just as curious. Perhaps I should open your third eye so you can better understand what I am talking about. What do you think?'